POST
NO BONDS

ALSO BY THE SAME AUTHOR

The Makeover

POST
NO BONDS

Marcia Biederman

CHARLES SCRIBNER'S SONS

NEW YORK

Charles Scribner's Sons
Macmillan Publishing Company
866 Third Avenue, New York, NY 10022
Collier Macmillan Canada, Inc.

Library of Congress Cataloging-in-Publication Data
Biederman, Marcia, 1949–
    Post no bonds / Marcia Biederman.
    p. cm.
    ISBN 0-684-18952-6
    I. Title.
PS3552.I344P6 1988   87-37578
813'.54—dc19   CIP

10 9 8 7 6 5 4 3 2 1

For my mother
and in remembrance
of my father

POST
NO BONDS

One

It was a full hour before court would convene, but Phil Stark was already making his rounds. He left a package in the public defender's empty office. He gave his all-purpose, pocket-sized cop gifts to the first two cops he saw hanging around in the hall. Then he walked up the stairs to arraignment court.

"Here he comes again. Santa Claus in September," Inez, the court clerk, called out. Her assistants looked up from their coffee cups.

It was true, Phil thought. They all wear nail polish. Maybe he should have listened to his wife Grace's advice about the gifts. She had plenty of advice to give.

Inez snatched the box from him and tossed it into her "In" basket. Then she changed her mind, pulled it out, and shook it.

"No booze," she announced to one and all. "How come you only buy booze for the men?"

Phil touched his glasses, fingered the business cards in his pocket, said something inaudible.

"Silver wrapping paper," said Inez, very audibly indeed. "This your anniversary, Mr. Stark? You been writing bonds twenty-five years today, maybe?"

Later, Phil would see Inez's gift, a pair of gloves, splattered with coffee in the wastebasket. But now he was down the hall, near the pay phones.

One of them rang as he walked past. These days it was never for him, but Phil picked it up, out of habit.

A mumbling, long-distance voice had something "real important to say to Mr. Isaacs, my bondsman." And, as usual when these people had something important to say, there was bar music blaring in the background.

Phil got the caller's name. "Hold it a minute." He walked back up to arraignment court, checked something, came downstairs. At the end of the hall he saw Isaacs, the caller's bondsman, joking with a cop.

Isaacs and his cop pal were near the front door. That meant the side exit for Phil. He made for it, passing the pay phones again. The one he had answered was still dangling from its cord. As he walked by, he could hear music playing softly out of the receiver.

There was nothing here for Phil until two, and he had no more mealymouthed smiles left for Isaacs. He crossed the intersection and headed back to his office.

The call meant that Isaacs had a no-show for a plea. Long distance; the guy had panicked. Eventually, though, he'd get his ass down to court and Isaacs wouldn't have to forfeit the bond—not that any well-connected bondsman actually ever did that. Besides, the fee, the 10 percent, was already in his pocket.

Robbery One, a $5,000 bail. Phil, in his tight new white loafers, had gone all the way upstairs to check it on the docket. Another five hundred bucks for Isaacs.

In the late afternoon, Phil got in his car and swung by the courthouses in two adjacent counties. He wondered why he bothered. They were affluent areas, the kind of places where people didn't lock their doors. If you were lucky, you'd find a drunk driver in the holding pen. But more often than not, the driver would have been sprung already on his own promise to appear.

Phil's main business was back in Huddersfield, a city of several hundred thousand, a fairly big deal for New England. But if you mentioned it on a vacation in Vegas, you'd find that five out of ten people thought it was in Illinois. Two would ask about Filene's Basement, which was way the hell over in Boston, on the other side of the state. And the rest would be busy watching the floor show.

Phil had grown up in Huddersfield. He owned a house here, rented an office on the ground floor of a building catercorner to Huddersfield District Court. This city had plenty of high-bail felonies and was a nice place to live. Not downtown, which had gone completely to pot, but in Orchard Grove, which used to be a separate little town until the city annexed it. That was one hundred, maybe two hundred, years before Phil moved in.

It was a historical neighborhood. Phil lived in a split ranch with a sloping front yard and a long driveway. There were lots of big shade trees, because cutting them down would have cost a fortune, and a sidewalk hedge that never grew as big as the nursery said it would. But complain as you will, you can't return plants to a nursery.

The exterior of the house was white, and the aluminum siding would keep it that way. Inside, though, there was enough peeling paint to rival those antique houses, like the one Phil's son owned two towns away, in the sticks.

Peeling paint or not, Phil was glad to be home until the Carson monologue was over. Then his wife, Grace, started in again about the gifts.

"Nail polish would have been a cheap gift," he told her. "This Inez would have spit in my eye."

"Not if you got ten bottles. They have these sets. Rainbow Tips. Buy them in any drugstore."

She was still reading upholstery swatches in bed, Phil

noticed. And paint chips. "Business stinks," he said. "Forget about redecorating." He got out of bed, crossed over to the telephone on the dresser, where he'd dragged it by its long cord, and turned up the ringer.

"If it stinks," she said, "why can't we have the phone on a night table, like normal people?" Grace was a morning weather-spotter for WHLD radio, and she liked to phone the station from bed after checking the thermometer through the window. She reported the Accu-Weather from Orchard Grove, in both Fahrenheit and Celsius.

"Because I'm gonna get a call tonight. I can feel it," he told her as he climbed back into bed. "And walking over there wakes me up. My feet hit the cold floor, and my blood starts rushing."

"What cold floor? We've got wall-to-wall carpeting in here. Everyone else has a dhurrie rug."

There was no call that night, but Phil was up anyway. He chewed a heartburn tablet, got dressed, took dimes from one of the dime bowls, looked over at Grace.

One breast had almost worked its way out of the elastic on her nightgown. Not a bad-looking woman for fifty-two, thought Phil. The new blond hair helped. But in his line of work, you could do better than fifty-two. There was always a girl junkie who couldn't pay the bond fee. And the occasional sanitary hooker, the kind who cleaned under her nails.

A woman could figure out a marketing plan for a bondsman, Grace kept telling him. Then maybe she could afford new curtains and slipcovers.

A lot she knew, thought Phil, fumbling in the drawer she never cleaned for his strange new gun. He didn't want to live this way.

"Who's there?" yelled Grace, bolt upright in bed.

He stopped looking for the gun and closed the drawer. "Nobody. It's nobody."

This is going backward, Phil said to himself as he emptied his bladder in the police station parking lot. This is how I used to operate when Ted was a baby.

Except that back then it was worth it. That was before Isaacs started recruiting ex-cops into his stable. It used to be One Guy, Isaacs, versus One Guy, Stark. And Marchetti, of course, for the organized crime cases.

Fall. It was getting cold out. Phil was almost glad when he reached the door of the police station. Hello, hello, hello, everybody said, as if they still steered business his way.

Phil knew the desk sergeant. But those police academy grads working for Isaacs probably knew him a hell of a lot better.

The desk sergeant was circling some ads in the "personals" section of the *Crusader*—Huddersfield's Alternative Newspaper, as it said on the cardboard displays around town. The regular paper didn't have ads for swinger parties and didn't make fun of the mayor. Phil waited until the circling stopped, then he approached.

"How's the two daughters?" he asked. Some of the young ones hated that, the way he memorized details. Years ago it was always an icebreaker.

The desk sergeant grunted. He slid the blotter over to Phil, stuffing his paper into a drawer at the same time. Evidently the guy was not a family man. You never could tell.

It wasn't exactly what you'd call a jackpot night at the station. An Assault Two and a Breaking and Entering. Both were first-time offenders, and both had been hauled in just an hour or so earlier. That was probably why no one had phoned Isaacs. Anyway, with the size of their operation, Isaacs and Company didn't need to lose sleep over penny-ante stuff like this. The morning was soon enough for them.

Not for Phil. He was over at the phones with his dimes and address book, dialing for dollars in the middle of the night.

He looked up the number of Nat Barkan, owner of a dry cleaning place and friend of one of Phil's poker buddies. For some cockamamy reason, Barkan had become a justice of the peace. And in this state, that made him a Person Authorized to Set Bail. Otherwise, it didn't get set at night by anyone. Funds for night court had dried up long ago.

Barkan's wife answered the phone. "I thought it was one of the kids—"

Almost bit Phil's head off until she remembered. Phil and Barkan had made the deal a while back, but this was the first connection.

"It's money, honey," Phil heard her say. Probably another case of worn slipcovers.

Barkan took his time getting down to the station, and when he came, he didn't listen.

"I know the rates. I've made a study of this," the dry cleaner informed Phil.

"I've made a career of this," Phil answered.

Barkan set bail at a measly $2,000 for the Breaking and Entering, $2,500 for the Assault Two. Then he trundled home to bed. Phil, it was agreed, would bring Barkan's half of the take to the dry cleaning place later.

"Maybe drop off your dirty pants while you're at it," Barkan suggested.

By the time Phil rounded up the relatives of the accused, ran a verbal credit check on them, and had them sign collateral, day was breaking. A weekday.

The Assault Two's mother counted out cash for Phil's fee. She had said she had the $250, but it only came out to $195.

"C'mon, man. Take it," urged her teenaged son, brother of the accused. He had brought his fifty-pound radio down to the station with him. Nothing like a little night music.

"Ten percent or forget it," Phil told them. It killed him, but if he came down on the fee, word would get around. Maybe if Barkan had stuck around, he would have reduced the bail. But Barkan was getting his beauty rest.

The Breaking and Entering's family was less of a problem. Phil scooped up their $200, and the desk sergeant sprang to life, barking out orders for the kid's release. When he was brought in, the family went crazy, hugging and screaming at him at the same time.

It was lost on the desk sergeant—not a family man. As for Phil, he took a good look at the kid. He'll appear, he decided.

A light rain fell on Phil's glasses as he shuffled across the parking lot. He tried to remember why he had parked so far from the station. Oh, yeah. To pee. Wouldn't be a bad idea now, except that it was daylight.

He was tired, but not so tired that he couldn't spin around when he heard someone running behind him. His hand went for the gun that wasn't there, and the fifty-pound radio landed full in his face.

He took that pee after all, leaning over the hood of his car, pulling pieces of eyeglass frame off the bridge of his bleeding nose.

He wondered what Barkan would charge him to clean his pants.

Grace was getting on his nerves, hovering over him like that. He told her to go play mah-jongg.

"I told them I wasn't coming."

"You didn't say why, I hope."

"I'm not stupid." One of Grace's mah-jongg partners was Marion Buchsbaum, wife of Richard Buchsbaum, the *attorney* (Marion never said *lawyer,* a dirty word, apparently).

Grace took the tray away. Black eyes, a broken nose, but Phil still chewed up the lemon slice from the tea instead of leaving it alone like a civilized person.

"So if Richard doesn't tell everyone, the cops will," Grace said. There had been plenty of cop cars at the other end of the parking lot, and one of them had carted Phil to the emergency room.

"The cops don't want to know me," Phil said. "If they hadn't called you, I woulda sworn they lost my phone number."

Grace was tired of his self-pity, especially since he wouldn't consider alternative plans. If he had taken her into his business as a marketing consultant, this whole thing wouldn't have happened. She told him that.

"I need an employee on the payroll like I need another broken nose," he said, touching his bandage. "There's no way to get a bigger piece of the action anymore. All the action goes to Isaacs. I've tried the gifts, everything."

"Try me," she said.

After his pain pill, Phil felt sleepy. Grace told him she had called the girls to tell them she could come after all. Actually, she had never canceled in the first place.

Go, he told her, and act natural. She put on fresh makeup, buttoned up her mouton coat, and went out to do just that.

The snacks were skimpy and the house was cold, but that was no surprise. Susie Kantor didn't know how to be a hostess.

"How's the redecorating coming?" asked Marion Buchsbaum, wife of the attorney.

"It's not coming at all," answered Grace, very natural indeed tonight. "Financial problems."

8

"One crack, two bam." Some tiles were thrown on the table by the stranger who'd been called to be a Fourth. One of the regulars couldn't make it at the last minute.

"It's not worth it anyway without a decorator," said Susie Kantor of the chilly but professionally decorated house.

Grace didn't agree. "With Eli the decorator, I'd end up with the same Austrian curtains he gave everyone, including you. And I don't want Austrian curtains."

Everyone was silent for a moment. Such things weren't mentioned.

"A woman who doesn't need a decorator also doesn't need a career counselor," said Marion Buchsbaum finally. Personally, she didn't have Austrian curtains. But she was the only one here who could come to the rescue once Grace Stark got started.

"Two soap," said the last-minute Fourth.

"That career counselor has opened up my eyes for me," Grace said.

"In the old days," continued Marion, "a person looked through the want ads, drove downtown, and got herself a job."

"Tell me how the counselor helped. I'm interested," said Susie Kantor, who didn't know how to turn up a thermostat when guests were coming. She knew one thing about hosting mah-jongg, however: keep everything nice.

"He gave me tests. He's a specialist. Practice limited to reentering women."

"Reentering?" asked Marion, finding it a little hard to keep the hostilities going. She was just a few tiles away from making mah-jongg.

"Reentering the paid labor force. When I worked for my father as a young girl, that's when I entered. When I raised Ted, that was the unpaid labor force. Now I'm reentering."

"Isn't that something?" marveled Susie Kantor, who did

9

the books for her husband's plumbing supply business but drew no salary. She wondered where she fit in.

"What I want to know is whether all this entering gets you a job," said Marion, just a hair away from making mah-jongg.

"One flower," said the strange Fourth.

"It's wonderful nowadays to see all these professional women," remarked Susie, who had never in her life stopped working.

"Oh, no," said Grace. "I'm not going to be one of those. Not like my dear daughter-in-law who dials a phone with a pencil. My career counselor tells me I should be in a helping profession."

"How nice," said the Fourth. Nobody paid attention.

"That's why I want to help Phil in bail bonds. Marketing and promotion." They had all heard it before.

"It's a corrupt system," said Marion Buchsbaum, borrowing the opinions of Richard the attorney. "It preys on poor people. Only those who can pay get out of jail. Checkbook justice."

"And I suppose Richard doesn't mind if his clients can't find their checkbook?"

"If you had grandchildren, you'd already have a helping profession," said Marion, grandmother of four.

"You're behind the times," Grace told her.

"Mah-jongg!" yelled Marion.

Everyone screamed with excitement and envy. But when Marion counted out her tiles, it was found that she'd been going by the previous year's rules. The National Mah-jongg League had just published its new list of winning hands.

"Your rule card is right in front of you. Why didn't you look at it?" the strange Fourth rebuked Marion.

It was the nastiest remark that had been said all evening.

Two

Pity worked better for Phil than the gifts had. Once he showed up at court with his bandaged nose and shiners, the calls started. People were trying to throw him some business—the criminal court clerk, the public defender, even Inez. Everyone except the boys in blue.

"They're going to stop authorizing j.p.s to set bail," the public defender told Phil. He had heard how Phil got beaten up, and he could fill in the rest. "There's talk around the capital about letting cops set night bail instead."

"Terrific," said Phil. "Up until then, maybe I can meet my mortgage payments."

He'd been called in by the public defender to write bond for a prostitute. That's the kind of crumbs he got. The serious felonies still went to Isaacs and his fleet. Every arresting cop knew the formula: a ten-cent call to get 50 percent.

"Sure, I'd do it, too, if I could," Phil told Grace. It was better in the old days when she hadn't been interested. "But I can't swing something like that, and neither could you. They only trust their own. You know how IBM goes to Harvard to recruit the graduating class? That's Isaacs. He's down at the police academy on Commencement Day."

"I'd develop more business from the clerk side," said Grace, who'd been talking funny ever since she started with that career counselor. "A woman's touch."

"They call whoever's around. You don't know nothing." She still hadn't found the gun, or she would have asked about it. Some housekeeper.

Barkan was interested in doing more night business. He told Phil that at his dry cleaning place, right in front of an employee who was steaming a shirt on a machine.

"I know a guy in the roofing business. A justice of the peace, like me. He could use some extra cash, too."

"What! Are you broadcasting this to the whole world?" Phil asked. "Fee splitting is not kosher." The shirt machine, shaped like a big inflatable man, flung out its arms with a hissing noise.

This is the end of the line, Phil told himself on the drive down to court. That jerk is going to get my license revoked.

In arraignment court, he gave out dozens of his cards, just as he did every day. He gave them to relatives, bystanders, people looking for the place to pay parking tickets.

I look like shit, he told himself, as he passed out the cards with his usual smile and quip: "You'll never know when you'll need it." The bandage and bruises on his face bothered him; he was a man who used a sunlamp year-round.

The card said:

PHILIP A. STARK
Professional Bondsman
Anytime—Anywhere

After that came the office address and phone number and

"Call Anytime" next to the number of the home business phone.

The flip side of the card had the usual, "You Must Appear at" with blanks for the particulars. Just like dentists use. Below that was a warning: "Notify Our Office Immediately Upon Change of Address."

Isaacs had the same card. Only for him, "Our Office" meant a secretary, a bookkeeper, and a platoon of bondsmen—ex-cops included—buzzing around a suite in one of those reflective-glass office towers. For Phil, "Our Office" was a linoleum-tiled hole in the wall with a desk, a phone, and a file cabinet. As for the phone at home, it made a good paperweight. Phil didn't even kick anymore when Grace used it for personal calls. It hardly ever rang anyway.

When the big bandage on Phil's nose became a little one with wing tips, he knew it was time to do the night rounds again. But the beating had knocked the cotton out of him. He couldn't get motivated.

Grace was happy. "If you get called, I'll go out and warm up the car for you, get the heater going. But wait till the phone rings. Why go out looking for trouble?"

"If I go out on my own or if I wait for a call, my head can get bashed in the same," Phil countered. Why couldn't she worry, like other women?

"A person has to make a living," Grace said. "Especially if his wife isn't working."

Phil knew how to make a living. He had to work the night shift, going from jail to jail, courthouse to courthouse, finding the business before it found Isaacs. And he had to take a bail-setter along with him to clinch the deal on the spot. And he had to pay the guy half, because that's how you got people out of bed.

But he couldn't get himself to do that again. Not that he didn't keep busy. There were still those courthouse pay phones to dial, calling the deadbeats who didn't show for pleas or sentencing. A lot of appearance dates were left over from previous months, before the pipeline dried up.

"You got a no-show" is how Inez granted him one fine afternoon.

"Give him some time," said Phil, checking the docket. John Thigpen. A $5,000 bond. "He's only fifteen minutes late. Relax."

Very relaxed himself, Phil was out at the pay phones an hour later. No answer at John Thigpen's. No answer at his mother's, who had put up her belongings for collateral.

Thigpen's mother, Phil knew, was on welfare. He had written bond for her son before, and he'd always showed. Her collateral was worthless.

"They're no jet-setters, living over there on Up Street. They're in town," Phil told Grace later at home. He was dialing the phone in the bedroom every three minutes.

"There are these new phones you can get," she told him. "Automatic redial."

"I'm not getting new phones," Phil barked. "And put those goddamn paint chips away. You'll drive me to the poorhouse with this decorating."

"Dreams cost nothing," Grace informed him. "I haven't lifted a brush."

She was fed up with all the misery. She went downstairs to call her son, Ted, on the other phone.

"I'm coming over for a brief visit," she said to Ted. "*Very* brief, you can tell Barbara."

"Don't be silly. How's Dad?"

"I'm coming alone. Just Mother this time," said Grace, who'd never been called Mother in her life. "Your father is driving me crazy."

Invite yourself or you'll never be invited, she told herself as she drove two towns over to where Ted lived in a Dutch Colonial.

As usual, there were papers and books spread from here

14

to there. Ted and his wife, Ms. Barbara Lubin, looked ill at ease as they sat Grace down in the living room.

Barbara began with the usual apologies about the house being a mess.

"Without built-ins, it's hard," said Grace, genuinely sympathetic. But that's the way they liked to live, in a house that had to be checked for dry rot before they bought it.

"Track lighting would help," she added, when they dragged over a lamp so she could read Ted's latest annual report.

"Isn't that something?" Grace said, flipping fast through the glossy pages. She could barely see the damn thing.

"Now he's working on a really neat brochure," announced Barbara.

"Who's in p.r., you or him?" Grace asked. Barbara's own career accomplishments were seldom mentioned, being much greater than her husband's. Barbara was an investment banker. Her annual bonus alone could have redecorated Grace's house from the den to the laundry room and back.

Grace had promised a very brief visit, and she always tried to keep her promises. Barbara and Ted were treated to a brief rundown of the trouble with Phil.

"Your career counselor sounds like a nice guy, but Dad doesn't need a promotion person," Ted said. "It's not like his business is expanding. Isaacs seems to have the whole thing locked up."

"I'd change that."

"I mean it's wonderful about your wanting to work and all, but this is—such a strange business," said Barbara, whose own father was a doctor. "The competitor is using illegal means. Look at the way Phil got beat up."

"That's from working at night," Grace told her. "I'd fix it so he'd have enough day action."

"How about something at the radio station?" Barbara suggested. "I hear them thanking you for phoning in the weather when I drive to work. It's really fabulous how you and those other people volunteer to do that."

"You bet it's fabulous," said Grace. "But my counselor and I have decided. No volunteer work, not for WHLD and not for Phil Stark. Paid labor force only. "Women," she began slowly, trying to remember the counselor's words, "are not on this earth purely to serve others.""

Ted could believe that. He had been the only kid in his fifth-grade class to pack his own peanut butter sandwiches.

"Anyhow, there are no jobs in radio for me. It's one big clique, and you can't break in, no matter how much talent you have," said Grace, in the voice that made Directory Assistance operators call her Mister.

They continued arguing, with Grace very insistent on her bail bonds marketing scheme. Barbara came close to saying something about how exploitive the bonding system was, but Ted stopped her with a single glance. He was very good with meaningful glances. It wasn't for nothing that his company had put Ted on TV during their recent product-safety crisis.

"Use the media," he finally told his mother, sensing that she wasn't going to give up. "Tell the papers what Isaacs is up to. If it works, it'll free business up for Dad. Then he can think about putting you on the payroll."

Grace was interested. Ted described to her just how to do it.

It wasn't very brief after all. Barbara fell asleep. How can she get comfortable on that crazy old chair, Grace wondered.

Finally it was all settled. "So am I going to see you on the evening news anymore?" she asked Ted, giving him a rare hug at the door. She even called him Teddy Bear.

"Not anymore. Russett cribs have been totally rede-signed. The railings no longer strangle babies."

"Too bad," said Grace. Ted on TV had impressed the hell out of the mah-jongg group. It sure beat being a radio weather-spotter.

When she got home, Phil didn't want to hear about it. "It's late," he said, "and I've got a fugitive on my hands. If Thigpen doesn't show, I'm out five thousand bucks."

"That never happens. You told me yourself. This guy will materialize, and if he doesn't, you'll arrange things."

"That was when I could pull strings," said Phil. "Now I'm Mr. Nobody from Nowheresville."

Mr. Nobody, Grace noticed, was staring at her chest. She still wore tight sweaters to show off her best assets. In high school they used to call her the Sweater Girl. That was back in the days of Orlon.

"Tell me what you've got to tell me in bed," Phil suggested.

Grace yawned.

She made him hold his horses until she got into a nightgown. As he fiddled with the drawstring, she asked him what he was going to do about Thigpen.

"I don't know," he said, less nervous now and murmur-ing into her ear. "I'm probably worrying for nothing. Things may be screwy, but nobody's going to ask a bondsman for all that dough. The whole system would fall apart. Worst comes to worst, they'll hit me for twenty percent."

"Worst comes to worst, you can hire a bounty hunter," said Grace, vamping for time.

"That's movie stuff. Fairy tales."

"Fairy tales can come true sometimes," she said.

Phil's voice was hoarse. He was murmuring, "Hey, baby," and the other things that always made him seem like a stranger.

She couldn't wait to tell her career counselor about Ted's idea. Reentering, she thought, as Phil pushed inside her.

Phil was coming out of the bail commissioner's office the next day, congratulating himself on straightening out the potential Thigpen mess, when he thought of it. What had Grace said last night? Something about Ted and newspapers?

He chewed a heartburn tablet and dialed Ted at work. They put him on hold. What else was new?

The other pay phone was ringing. "Call for you," said the court employee who had picked it up.

Phil hung up on the hold music and took it. It was Jacqueline Woods, a prostitute and junkie.

"I'm all messed up, Mr. Stark. I was going to make my appearance, really I was."

Phil had a chat with a clerk. The judge issued a warrant for Woods' rearrest and raised the bail by $1,000.

Your honor, I love you, thought Phil as he rushed down the courthouse steps to his car. Another $100 for him, and Jacqueline Woods was good for it. Cash only, this time. If she didn't have it, he could wait in his car until she did.

One hour—no, forty-five minutes—with a sponge and an electric broom, and Grace Stark could have had the *Crusader*'s newsroom sparkling. Grace couldn't look at those crumbs on the carpet. You didn't even need a vacuum, just an electric broom—$39.95, tops. Evidently, this paper had no cleaning lady.

Cigarettes were something they did have. The managing editor was on his third already. Eric, his name was—no last name, or else he thought he was so famous he didn't need to say what it was. And he was also so famous that he didn't have to get off the phone when a nicely dressed woman came to see him.

Kooks were something else the *Crusader* had plenty of. Even if Grace had to sweat in her coat for the next hour, listening to Eric say, "Yeah? Yeah? Yeah?" into the phone, it beat the reception area. Every sickie in town was out there, lining up at the desk to write out personal ads. They didn't even whisper when they asked for the form. And everyone in Huddersfield knew what filth those ads were.

That's why Grace still couldn't believe she was here. This was the kind of newspaper she wouldn't even stuff shoes with. She had begged Ted to let her go to the *Courier-Inquirer,* like a normal person. But he said the *Crusader* would give the story better play. Whatever that was.

Someone knocked on the office door.

"I'm busy," snapped Eric Editor. He went back to his phone conversation.

The door opened anyway, just a crack. Grace couldn't see anyone, but she could smell the perfume. Tons of it.

A woman's hand appeared, waving a message. Eric looked disgusted. It kept waving. Grace got sick of the whole thing. She got up, pushed the door all the way open, and stepped outside.

So who was wearing a whole bottle of expensive-smelling perfume in this filthy newspaper office? A very expensive-looking young lady. Beautiful, too, with dark hair and violet blue eyes, like Elizabeth Taylor.

Grace was all set to give her a lecture, but the girl spoke first. "Isn't it *horrible* how Eric makes you sit while he yaks on the phone? And he never offers to take your coat. Can't you just *die,* sitting there and sweltering?"

If this girl died from that, then at least she'd die happy. Unless Grace was wrong, she was wearing a genuine mink.

And she was still waving that note. She asked Grace to give it to Eric.

"Okay," said Grace, trying to look uninterested. But she must not have done it right, because the girl shot her a sly look and folded the note in half. Pulled her hand away, too, as if she wasn't going to fork it over after all.

"Are you Eric's mother?"

Her? The mother of an editor of this paper? Grace stretched up to her full five feet four inches. "Guess again, honey." What was that word Ted used? "I'm a source. What's the matter? You nervous about meeting the mother?"

The girl made a face, like a pill just went down the wrong way. "I'm a source, too, as a matter of fact. You didn't think I was *involved* with Eric?" Grace liked her again.

She handed over the message, unfolded. "Please just tell him that Darcy was here. I've got to run."

And she twirled around in her mink and walked away. Very classy. Grace felt better about being here. "It'll be strictly confidential," she called out after her.

Sure enough, the note had nothing romantic in it.

"Two more friends of Heywood's got busted last night," it said. "I'm sure he's next. What to do? Please call, but not the work number. Darcy."

Grace was disappointed. News about arrests was no news for the wife of a bondsman.

Once Eric Editor finally got off the phone, he didn't seem very interested in Darcy's note either. He just opened his middle desk drawer and stuffed it in. Never-never land, it looked like to Grace.

She could see that her son and daughter-in-law were right. There must not be any hippies anymore, because the editor of this hippie newspaper didn't dress like a hippie. He wore a suit that didn't fit and a crap-colored tie. Twenty-five years old, maybe, and already looking like someone who comes for dinner and announces he's on a gallbladder diet. Definitely not someone for that Darcy. Too flabby.

But he listened hard. When Grace told him who she was—wife of Philip A. Stark, the bondsman—he sucked on his cigarette and said, "Yeah? Yeah? Yeah?" *much* more interested than he had been on the phone. She could get used to treatment like this, very easily.

He cut her off in mid-sentence and talked into his intercom. "Jason, get over here. We got a crime story. Bondsmen. *Hard news.*"

A very short young man appeared. Sat on a corner of the editor's desk after pushing an ashtray out of the way. He had mustard stains on his shirt, Grace noticed. But a nice sports jacket, you had to grant him that.

"Listen to this," Eric told this Jason. "Isaacs is pulling his shit again."

"No kidding," marveled Jason. Then, after a second, "Who's Isaacs?"

Eric was annoyed. "The bondsman." He turned to Grace. "We don't have anyone covering the court beat right now. Well, not very closely. Everyone does a little of everything. But we've done stories on Isaacs in the past, believe me. I remember, because I've been here for three years."

He reached for the intercom. "Jennifer. Get me a story about bail bondsmen from three years back. August, I think. Or July."

A crackling voice came out of the box. "The archives don't go back that far. There isn't enough room in the closet."

The editor looked back at Grace, ran a shaky hand through his hair, grabbed for a cigarette. "Yeah. Well. Anyhow, it's all on microfilm at the public library. And your husband, Phil Stark, he's mentioned in that story, too."

"With a picture?" Grace hoped.

"Uh, I'm not sure. I didn't really work on that piece—not directly. I was more the film reviewer at the time. But I remember that it ran."

Jason was doodling in a little notebook he had brought with him. "So what's this hard news crime story?"

"It's Isaacs, the biggest bondsman in town. He's got this whole army working for him. And he's pulling his shit again."

"Oh, I know. It's that bail forfeiture scam. The way they never have to pay the bail, even when their suspects skip. That stuff you were talking about—"

"Cool it a minute."

"What?"

"We're going to let Mrs. Stark do the talking. The situation is, the little guy, Phil Stark, is getting squeezed out. Listen, Mrs. Stark, I know this is a drag, but could you go through the whole thing again for Jason? This is going to be his assignment."

Grace wasn't sure she liked the idea of Phil being the little guy. A *real* little guy is this reporter Jason, she thought. Five-foot-five, maximum.

No one so much as offered a cup of coffee, but she went through the spiel again.

"Fee splitting with the cops. Terrific!" Jason jabbed his pencil into the notebook, and the tip went flying. Then he and Eric shook hands like black people do in the movies.

"Now, your husband is going to go on the record with this, right?" Jason was feeling around Eric's desk for another pencil.

"My husband has no idea I'm here."

Both boys were about to say something, but a girl holding a newspaper beat them to it. Barged right into the middle of the conversation.

"It was in the archives after all," she announced. "I found it on the floor, behind the bicycles."

It did have a photo of Phil. He looked good, what you could see of him. A picture of someone sitting down and looking away from the camera was not Grace's idea of the greatest snapshot.

Another thing. Phil was pictured very small, because there were a lot of other people in the photo, all sitting at a table. The mayor was there, and so was Isaacs. Isaacs, the fat pig, had a forkful of food going into his mouth.

"His honor shares a moment with the purveyors of checkbook justice," said the caption. "Clockwise from left, Phil Stark . . ."

She skipped down to the headline, which was very long. Really there were two of them. "Lunch With the Bail Bonding Bunch" came first. The rest was underlined: "They give the keys to freedom only to those who can pay. They exploit the city's poor black population. And the mayor invites them to lunch."

"We've changed a lot since then," said Eric, who had been reading upside down. "We were really naive back then. You wouldn't believe how different we are now."

"Wait a minute," said Grace. "I want to keep the picture."

"A lot of people left over from the sixties were on the staff then. Basically, they were deadwood. They're all gone now, completely. The guy who wrote that story is working on an astronomy journal. Way, way up in Maine."

Jason joined in. "We've got a new professionalism around here. Our format has changed totally—have you noticed? We've got TV listings now, and we're the only paper in the area that doesn't put the cable listings separate. We mix them right in with everything else."

"And we've got a home and garden section, because a lot of our readers are young professionals buying homes for the first time." This contribution came from the girl who had barged in carrying the paper. "And we have a fashion section. We just ran a terrific feature on wearable art."

"We have sports now. And a table of contents."

"Actually, the sportswriter just quit," Eric said.

"You're kidding!"

"Something about delays with the free-lance checks. But it's a totally new *Crusader,* Mrs. Stark. We're not into knee-jerk radicalism at all, like the old staff used to be. Basically, it's a newspaper *for* baby boomers *by* baby boomers."

"There's something I don't like here," said Grace, looking at the photo again.

Eric coughed, a phlegmy smoker's cough. "I understand what you're saying. But, see, nowadays—"

"You call him Phil Stark through the whole thing. In about five places. The name is Philip A. Keep that in mind this time."

"Sure. Of course. Sure." Everyone's head was bobbing up and down. The editor started asking questions again. When Grace repeated that Phil knew nothing about this, the party was over.

"But Mrs. Stark, we need him on the record," protested the girl who had brought the newspaper. She seemed to have barged in for good.

"You don't need anyone on the record. You're not going to mention my name or Phil's name. You're not writing about us. You're writing about Isaacs and the fee-splitting." Ted had prepared her for everything.

"What you need is names of cops—the ones that aren't getting dealt in by Isaacs." She opened up her pocketbook and took out a list. Not for nothing had she been pumping Phil these last few nights. "Talk to them."

"Can we get pics for this?" Eric was excited again. "Do we have a file photo of Isaacs?"

"Use this one here." Grace thumped the paper she was holding. "Look at him, stuffing his face."

"Terrific!" yelped Jason. "We'll blow it up."

Ideas bounced back and forth over the coffee-stained desk. They'd get photos of a cop car, the courthouse steps, a set-up shot of money changing hands. Phone numbers were exchanged.

"Don't tell the *Courier-Inquirer* about this, okay?" Eric said as Grace got up. "It's exclusive, okay? We'll do a bang-up job, but it takes us a little longer because we're a weekly. We can't compete with the dailies."

"I could see that right away," said Grace, brushing her coat off with her hand. "When my girlfriend's grandsons came to visit last month, she took them on one of those tours at the Courier-Inquirer Building. I bet there aren't too many tours coming through here."

Before she left, just to clinch things, she suggested a headline: Bail Wars.

"Bingo," she shouted later, alone in her car, waiting for the automatic garage door to lift. They all loved the headline. Ted was a genius.

Three

The next day was Saturday. Along with coffee and grapefruit, Grace got a lot of yelling and screaming for breakfast.

Phil didn't want to get involved with the paper. Not as Phil, not as Philip A., and not as the Husband of a Person Requesting Anonymity. He didn't like the *Crusader,* and he didn't like brassy broads who didn't consult their husbands but just went ahead and connived with their smart-ass sons. And he didn't like the job that filth-mongering newspaper had done on him some time back. The thing about lunch with the mayor.

"They're totally different now," Grace informed him. "Table of contents and everything. It's a whole different ball game."

"They're a sex sheet like they always were."

"How would you happen to know?" She turned on the radio to make sure they credited her for calling in the Accu-Weather. Once they forgot.

Phil called Ted at home. This time he wasn't put on hold.

His son walked him through it step-by-step. "Relax. It'll work," Ted said. Phil didn't know what to think. It wasn't every kid who could help his employer tiptoe through a big scandal. The railings on those cribs had killed a couple of babies, but there was Ted on the six o'clock news, saying that white is black and black is white.

Maybe he really could fix Isaacs' wagon.

"What if they get the whole thing screwed up and write it all ass-backwards?" Phil couldn't think of a way to tell Ted about his fears.

"They're okay. Really. They're all right at the *Crusader*. They're small but they check their facts."

Phil was sweating. He hoped the *Crusader* wouldn't check their facts so much that they'd dig up his deal with Barkan. On the off chance that he'd find Barkan in, Phil drove over to the dry cleaning place. There he was, the jerk, waiting on customers at his own establishment.

"You can't find some kid to work the counter on Saturday?" Phil asked when there was a break between customers.

"I put a help-wanted sign on the door," Barkan said. Phil had seen it, hanging next to the justice-of-the-peace notice. Just in case anyone wanted to get married at the cleaner's.

They were behind the counter, near the mechanical conveyor belt that brought the cleaned clothes down from overhead. Barkan's foot was on the pedal, making the rack whir around. Phil had insisted on this. It helped mask the conversation. The employees in the back might be interested; you never knew.

"They're all plugged into their little stereos," Barkan protested. "Or on drugs."

"How do I know that one of them isn't a reporter?" Phil explained about the *Crusader*. No one, but no one, he stressed, was to talk to anyone about the deal. Not Barkan, not his wife, not that other j.p. in the roofing business that Phil didn't want to meet.

"Phillie. Trust me. Don't worry so much," said Barkan,

27

patting Phil's cheek with a hand that smelled of dry cleaning chemicals. "I got no problem with secrets. My problem is that you haven't been calling me. Isn't tonight a big time for arrests, Phillie boy? Saturday night. Let's get with it and do the rounds again. Call me. I don't need much sleep. I take vitamin C."

Phil said okay. His face was more or less healed now. He still felt spooked when he thought about being attacked with the radio, but he'd have to get over it. There was money to be made on the night rounds.

"Attaway, Phillie. I could use a little extra. I'm socking it away to buy an Airstream, the Cadillac of recreational trailers. The wife and I are going to go traveling next summer. Hey, you only go around once, right?"

Speak for yourself, Phil was about to say, when he realized how stupid that would sound.

"Heads up," Barkan was yelling.

Something caught Phil on the shoulder, nearly knocking him over.

"You were standing too close to the rack," said Barkan. "I tried to stop it, but the damn pedal sticks. Phil, I love you, but you shouldn't stand here, back of the counter. I'm not covered for it."

Phil rubbed his shoulder. "Get it fixed." He couldn't believe he had to see this jerk later on. Twice in one day.

The *Crusader* hit the streets early Tuesday morning. By 9:30 there were none left in the corrugated-cardboard display in the courthouse. Usually they sat there all week.

"Someone called up the newspaper office and said to bring more papers over here," a court employee told Phil. "Everybody's asking me for the *Crusader*."

"Why not? They're free, and they've got those dirty personal ads." Phil was trying to act blasé. He had already stuffed four copies into his raincoat inner pocket.

Phil walked over to his office, jogged the piles of papers on his desk, checked the answering machine (no messages), raised his swivel chair. Then he dug out the reading matter.

Thirty inches into it, Phil knew he was a ruined man. It wasn't so much the main story. Headlined "Bail Wars," with some other stuff about "The Kickback Cops," that part was about Isaacs, Isaacs, and more Isaacs. There were quotes from Officer X and Patrolman Y, lots of photos of Huddersfield P.D. cars, and some strange shots of cops with their heads cropped off (later, Grace would tell him that these were *Crusader* reporters, dressed up in costumes). About a dozen of Huddersfield's finest "who spoke only on condition that they not be identified" were bellyaching in print. They hadn't been dealt in on Isaacs' fee-splitting deal.

It was the second page that had Phil crouching on the chickenwire tile in his office bathroom, wishing that something would come up besides the dry heaves. "Nobody Wants to Play Forfeit," they called it. It was a much shorter story, with a line drawn around it. It didn't have any pictures, but it had Philip A. Stark's name and Carmine Marchetti's name, and the title of the insurance firm that underwrote Isaacs.

No colorful quotes from cops in that piece, but there was plenty of data. Ted was right; the *Crusader* checked its facts. And the facts showed that bondsmen didn't forfeit bail, even when bailees didn't show up for court dates.

They'd really done their homework. There was a neat little list of fugitives, with the dates they were supposed to appear, the bail amount, and the bondsman.

Claude Gauthier (*Philip A. Stark*), Robbery One, $10,000.

That led Phil's list. Good old Claude. Phil hadn't thought about him for years. Hadn't given much thought to the other six people in front of his name either, the ones whose bails added up to about fifty thousand bucks.

Just like the newspaper said, the bondsmen had paid portions of the forfeitures. Just like it also said, "collusion with court employees and officials" had taken care of the rest.

When all you wanted was cold water, it didn't matter so much that the sink had separate taps. Phil threw some on his face and sat down with the paper again, reading the main story over.

There was some bad stuff even there, he thought, stopping to buy two rolls of heartburn tabs on his way back to court. It didn't take a genius to figure out who was "the source close to a smaller, competing bondsman." There were only two smaller, competing bondsmen in town, and Marchetti—whose sole business came from the Mob—wasn't about to hang around reporters. Grace might as well have hired the Goodyear blimp to drag a banner saying, "Stark Screws Isaacs."

Of course, the real screwing was the no-forfeitures information. That was the kind of thing politicians liked to sink their teeth into. They didn't want to mess around with the cops.

Phil's legs somehow took him up the courthouse steps. Isaacs shouldn't really mind, he reasoned. If they came after him for old forfeitures, his insurance company would pay. As for a bondsman like Stark, operating out of his own assets—well, that story had a black border around it for a reason.

Isaacs did mind, though. Phil could see that as soon as he walked into the lobby. Isaacs, Phil remembered from the days when he used to talk to him, was not big on reading. But he'd been using the old bifocals today.

"Stark, you s.o.b.!" The acoustics were terrific in the old marble building; you could hear it loud and clear from the other end of the hall. "Stay out of my way. You better stay the hell out of my way."

That wasn't going to be easy, because he was charging into the lobby like a warthog. Everyone turned to look. It wasn't every day you saw two middle-aged men in porkpie hats and raincoats, with one wrapping his hands around the other's throat.

"Sit, sit, sit on it," said Isaacs, pulling Phil by the neck over to the *Crusader* display. "That's your throne. Take a crap on those papers."

There still weren't any papers, to read or crap on, and Isaacs lost his hold by pushing Phil down so low.

By the time Phil worked his behind out of the display, Isaacs had vanished. That would be the end of it, Phil knew, except for maybe a lunger or two. Isaacs had gone through bypass surgery two years before, and he was very careful of his heart.

It was a different story with the ex-cops working for Isaacs, and the cops who were on his kickback roster—two of whom were on the courthouse steps, muttering "scumbag" at Phil as he scurried back to his office. They were born with heart bypasses.

That *Crusader* newspaper had somehow found its way to every single girl in the mah-jongg group. They began by remarking on the ads. But Grace knew it wouldn't be long before Marion would start dishing up dirt.

Susie Kantor was squealing about some kind of Oriental mattress she'd seen in an ad. She wanted to buy it for her daughter. "Maybe this is what the young people are buying. I understand that this newspaper is for young people."

"I have a question," said the regular Fourth, who had showed up this time. "What's SWM?"

Everybody paused for a minute, thinking of attractive single white males. Nobody answered.

Marion Buchsbaum rearranged her tiles. She had that smug I'm-going-to-win look on her face.

"I got a kick out of one of the things in that paper," she said. "You know that article about bail?" As if anyone didn't. "I thought that was very clever."

"I suppose it's bad news for Phil," Susie Kantor said kindly. She was wearing some way-out earrings tonight—big Lucite wedges with geometric designs. She'd seen them advertised in the *Crusader*.

"Not really," Grace answered, with everyone's eyes on her. "By the way, we can't play at my house next week. I'm finally getting it redone."

It was true, in a way, about the house. Workmen were going to wire every windowsill and door jamb with a burglar system. Phil had told her that much, but he wouldn't tell her what day they were coming. No sooner had she phoned in the Accu-Weather one brisk eighteen-degree-Celsius morning than the doorbell rang, and there they were. With her still in her nightgown.

Phil didn't want to hear about it when he came home. She didn't have the right to complain anymore.

"Look at this. Look at what you've done to *me*," he said, tugging at the waistband on his brand-new pants. He had gone out and bought three pairs, all of them one inch too large, so he could fit a gun holster inside.

"If you'd asked me first, I could have gotten you three or four pairs from the attic. From the time we went to the country and you put on ten pounds. One's a nice glen plaid, too."

"I'm carrying a Colt Commander in my pants because of you and that stinking paper, and you talk to me about glen plaid. Tell me, how many cop cars did you see cruising outside the house today? Ten? Twelve? A hundred?"

"A number of them."

"You bet, a number of them. Thanks to you and your mouth, they're looking for Phil Stark."

The *Crusader* story had put the lid on Isaacs' kickbacks to the police, and the cops were none too happy about it. But aside from their anger, which Phil worried about plenty, things were actually going better. Nowadays, if a guy got arrested, he'd figure out for himself what bondsman to call; the cops weren't making friendly referrals anymore. Phil was in the Yellow Pages same as Isaacs, and the clerks liked him okay. Phil was getting a better share of the market.

"Why go out at night risking your neck when your day business is so good," Grace said. And, "Don't you dare drip paint on that bureau scarf."

He had ended up buying Rainbow Tips nail polish after all, but not to give to the court clerks as gifts. He was painting the sight of his autoloading pistol with nail polish. The icy blue shade.

"See here?" he said to Grace, waving the gun in her face. "I'm going to put some right here, in the notch of the rear sight. You'd be surprised how much that helps a shooter at night."

How many times could she say I'm sorry? And the night work still didn't make sense.

"Even the Price Chopper doesn't stay open twenty-four hours," she pointed out. "Not every single night. If I was you, I wouldn't worry about cops being after me. I'd worry about a coronary."

"No, no. You wouldn't worry about anything. Not you. You didn't worry before you waltzed down to that newspaper. Let me tell you something, Mrs. Anonymous Source. They're going to come after me for those forfeitures any day now. Already there are noises about a Superior Court panel to investigate the forfeitures—thanks to you and those snotty-nosed kid reporters."

He put the brush back in the bottle. "And when they come after me, I'm going to offer them whatever dough I can make in a hurry. Plus this house, plus my car and your car. They can clean me out like a chicken, but Phil Stark is going to stay in business."

"And Grace Stark could help out."

Phil answered that by shoving his Colt into his holster. And the nail polish wasn't even dry yet.

Barkan was supposed to meet him at the Church Street jail, which was the real reason why Phil was still working at night. He was afraid that once a probe started, Barkan would talk. Let him earn enough to buy what he wanted. Then he might keep his mouth shut.

He was waiting for Phil outside his little Japanese car, the one he wanted to hitch an Airstream trailer to. Phil pulled up in his Buick and rolled the window down.

"I'm not going to tell you again," he hissed. "Wait inside your car. With the doors locked."

"Phil, baby. Worrying isn't good for the system. So, ready to make hay while the sun shines?"

It was about one in the morning.

Barkan didn't know the heat was on, even though the regular newspaper had got hold of the story by now. Dry cleaners don't read the papers, Phil guessed. But he'd find out soon enough.

The warden told them that one guy had been brought in. Phil recognized the name—a bad risk. He didn't want to write a bond.

"Let's do it," Barkan coaxed. "We're here already."

"I should have checked it out before I got you down here. I called first, but they got the first name screwed up on the phone. Sorry. That's all I can say."

"C'mon, Phil. You said yourself, if the guys jump you can fix it up."

The warden, who did read the papers, gave them a sly look. Phil decided it was time to have a heart-to-heart with the cleaner. He informed him that they were going out to the Dunkin' Donuts for some coffee and a chat.

It was about a mile from the jail. Barkan, who wasn't a coffee drinker, said he'd follow Phil. And Phil could see through his rearview mirror that someone was following Barkan. Very, very closely.

It was a nice big American car with a big, grinning grille. Barkan's tin can of a Jap model wouldn't have a prayer.

Phil's steering wheel was squeaky with sweat. The three of them—Phil, then Barkan, then the other car right up Barkan's ass—were on School Street. By day it was a main thoroughfare, but now it was a ghost town. Not that the driver behind that big grille gave a damn whether anyone saw or not. Off-duty cops didn't have to fret about things like that.

If Phil pulled over, Barkan might pull up right behind him. Then they'd be two sitting ducks in a row. Not that the Jap car could make much of a dent in Phil's sedan, but why double your trouble?

They were approaching Putnam Avenue, the turnoff for the Dunkin' Donuts. Not that Barkan knew that. If the jerk had only known the way, Phil thought, then he'd sense that something was funny when Phil didn't hang a right. But he'd said he didn't know the way.

That's why Phil couldn't believe what happened next. Quick as a wink, Barkan's foreign shitbox executed a U-turn, made a neat little circle around the guy behind him and zipped down Putnam, honking his horn the whole time.

Phil couldn't match that. If the pursuer had moved up behind him, he would have been dead. But instead, the guy took off after Barkan, heaving his big car around. It screamed onto Putnam on two wheels.

A minute later, Phil was out of his car and jogging the six blocks to the Dunkin'. He stuck close to the buildings, practically scraping up against them, in case any vehicles felt like taking a ride on the sidewalk.

The doughnut shop was all windows, lit up like a Christmas tree. Phil stuffed his gun back in the holster, caught some of his breath and walked in.

Barkan was washing down a cinnamon cruller with decaf. "Right after we passed that corner, it dawned on me," he told Phil between sips. "Ten, maybe fifteen years back, I had a contract cleaning uniforms for this place. I used to come over here every few weeks, making deliveries."

He had a couple of things to say about crazy hopped-up teenagers who ought to have their driver's licenses revoked. And Phil had a couple of things to tell him.

It took him three cups of coffee, but he finally got the situation through Barkan's head. Sort of.

The dry cleaner mulled it over. "Okay. So nobody said it would be easy. Hey, I'm no dope. I felt terrible about the time you took that radio on your head. So we're dealing with the scum of the earth. I knew that."

He was playing with the sugar container—one of those glass types with the sliding spout. "You see this stainless steel?" He was getting fingerprints all over the handle. "That's the same color as the Airstream. Reflects the sun so it doesn't get too hot in the summer. And it's the prettiest thing on the highway."

When the tab came, Barkan dived for it: $3.08. "Hey, that was some fancy driving I must have done. Better than a cop. Can you beat that?" Phil was sure the countergirl was listening. "That's from the old days, when I used to deliver. It isn't easy, driving clothes around in traffic."

He gave Phil a lift back to the Buick. It was parked at a crazy slant on School, about two feet from the curb. Seeing it brought all the night's horror back to Phil in a rush.

"Stay off the caffeine," Barkan advised. "I hope you

don't mind me saying that lately you look like hell. And, hey, if they're really about to shut you down, let's do this more often."

Damned if he didn't say it again: "You only go around once."

Nat Barkan was working the counter on a Saturday when a nuisance customer came in. He wanted his coat and suit, but he didn't have his ticket. Didn't remember the month they'd been dropped off either.

"I see them up there." He pointed to a distant point on the overhead rack. But his eyes didn't follow his index finger. They were fixed on Barkan. Hard.

Barkan looked up from the ticket pad. He had been doodling on the cover—little ovals like Airstream trailers inside a ring of palm trees. He saw where the guy was pointing, but he didn't see the look on the guy's face. Not at first.

"You got good eyes. Like Superman. To see your clothes all the way up there through plastic bags."

The customer was still looking at him. This time Barkan noticed his eyes. They were nothing like Superman's at all. They were small, and mean.

Barkan coughed. "Listen, it's possible they're up there. But all that stuff is from months ago. See those spindles every couple feet on the side of the rack? There's a blue tag stuck on the one over there. August."

"I don't know when my wife brought it in. That's the suit, though. Bring it down."

Barkan was going to say something, but instead he walked over to the foot pedal. The customer pushed through the gap in the counter and joined him. Barkan pressed the pedal lightly; it still had that sticking problem. The clothes began moving, swishing against each other in their plastic bags.

"Employees only on this side. Insurance company rules."

Barkan took vitamin C and didn't drink coffee. He was the kind of guy who could stay up all night, and the kind of guy who needed three blows on the head before he passed out.

He was still half on his feet, slumped against the rack, when the spindle with the August tag passed by. It speared through the back collar of Barkan's jacket, the one he'd just taken off the pressing machine that morning.

He was three feet off the ground when the rack finally ground to a halt with a groaning noise, loud enough for the employees in back to hear through their personal stereo headphones.

He only went around once.

Grace couldn't believe it when she saw it on the six o'clock news.

"A terrible thing. People will be scared now to bring their clothes to the cleaners."

Phil, for one, was scared stiff, but he didn't let it show. He had never mentioned Barkan's name—Grace didn't know anything.

The cops were saying it was some kind of combination heart attack and industrial accident. No indication of foul play. But the cops knew a lot better than that.

Homicide, that much was an accident, Phil figured. They probably only meant to give Barkan a good fright. The jerk should have gotten the rack fixed. Snapped his goddamn neck.

Phil patted the Colt Commander, which he'd taken to wearing around the house. Security system or no security system, you couldn't be too careful. The .45 ruled out the kind of rude treatment you could give an unarmed dry cleaner. Maybe Phil wore his pistol inside his pants, but everyone knew he was carrying.

On Monday there was more news. A three-man Superior Court panel had been set up. It was going to look into a little matter called bail forfeitures.

Phil wasn't too worried when they called him in. Not that he was worth fifty thousand. But the way he figured, even the phone company made deals with late payers before they pulled the plug. He'd suggest a second mortgage on the house, and offer his cash on hand. Business had been good lately, very good. Calls were coming in from federal court. The Drug Enforcement Agency was cracking down on cocaine users in the area. These cokeheads were mostly professional types, with plenty of cash and solid collateral. And the bails were high, because the judges with political noses could smell antidrug public sentiment.

The day before the hearing, Phil called Mishkin, his accountant, and Cashman, his lawyer. They put the whole repayment schedule into writing, so beautiful you could have framed it. The hardest part was getting Mishkin and Cashman to stop screaming at each other.

"They should have put in there that you're going to buy a beeper," Grace told him as he left for court. "That'll develop business. You know what you should say? That you're using modern marketing methods to run an up-to-date, promising enterprise."

Phil had no reply for that. But he had something to tell Grace when he came back.

"I'm declaring bankruptcy. You're taking over the business."

Four

Red's Newsstand had given Darcy her coffee in a leaky cup again. She thought of pitching it down the watercooler drain, then reconsidered. There was a copy of the *Crusader* on the corner of her desk. She slid it under her cup.

It was a slow leak and a useless newspaper. Eric still hadn't covered the drug bust story. Darcy hoped he'd gotten the note from that woman who was supposed to pass it on. It wouldn't hurt to check—she could call the newsroom and make a lunch date with him.

Later. There were other things to think about now.

Darcy Kohler knew what her boss meant when he complimented her shoes, her jewelry; when he said, "Hey, who are you today? Madame Butterfly?" because of the chopstick-thing stuck through her French braid. It was never like this in the old days; he wouldn't have mentioned something about Tinkerbell when her bracelets jangled during a meeting. The message was, I want you out. You're wrong for this organization.

It had happened even more often a few months ago, when she went through her Japanese period, her pre-Raphaelite period, her fin de siècle period. That was also when she had her summer cold, for just about the whole summer. A couple of toots off a mirror every lunchtime and break, and your nose would run all day. That was also when Heywood was buying some of her clothes. He never cared for the Japanese numbers, though he did like open kimonos.

She was completely off coke now. Did it by herself, like she did everything else. That's why it never felt right to accept things from Heywood. Of course, all the big things she'd bought herself: the condo, the fur coat, the car, the cappuccino maker from the restaurant supply store. Heywood had been very good to her, but the stock market had been even better.

Darcy was a self-taught analyst, a natural. In college, she had studied liberal arts, investing a little money that her grandmother left her. That grew into enough to buy a small art gallery, but redevelopment mowed it down. So, at the age of twenty-three, Darcy marched in here, looking for a job. Personnel was all set to send her to the newsletter art room until she whipped out the stock portfolio she'd created out of tips, study, and news reports.

They didn't like the velvet cloche she was wearing, but they liked her returns on investment. She was hired—that was five years back.

She never found the time to get an M.B.A., like the preppy-looking girls up the corridor, the ones who followed minicomputers and mainframe makers for The Garrison Group, corporate gossipmongers. The product here was rumors about high-tech companies. The customers were competitors, investors, banks—whoever would shell out for it. A brokerage house might have paid better, but Darcy had done well here. She was the hotshot analyst, tracking A.I.—artificial intelligence.

Her boss wanted her out, though. You had to be part detective to succeed as a market analyst, and her boss was a major success. He put Darcy's flash together with the summer cold and came up with coke.

She couldn't tell him she was off it, because that meant she'd been on. Lately she'd been toning down—still wore perfume and maybe too much jewelry, because she agreed with that Sammy Davis song, "I Got To Be Me"—but she'd bought a half dozen suits. With flounced miniskirts, just to add a little flair.

Funny thing. Just about the time she started to dress straight, the preppies started snorting. Darcy could hear it in the stalls of the ladies' room, and she could smell it in that phony friendliness they turned on. Everybody knew who her boyfriend was. Any day now, someone was going to ask for a connection.

That's why Darcy was acting like a royal bitch these days, turning down lunch invitations and keeping the office door closed. It came naturally, after losing all that sleep worrying about the arrests. Maybe she shouldn't bother, she thought. Maybe Heywood should supply the business-school wonks. At least none of them were likely to be informers.

But all they wanted was a couple of lines, and Heywood only bothered with big money. He was selling to a smaller and smaller circle these days. Half the people he and Darcy knew had been busted—turned in by the other half.

It was only a matter of time before Heywood's number came up, Darcy figured. It would be in the papers, and she'd get canned. Had she imagined things at the planning meeting this morning? Had her boss really scratched his nose while he was talking to her?

The phone rang. It was Dave, one of Darcy's spies, calling from the New Jersey listening post near SynthIntellect, Inc. She got a pencil and pad out, ready to write down the figures. But Dave was balking. He didn't have them.

"I can't believe you're taking this product seriously," he said. "TallStory is a total bomb. The dealers stopped accepting it months ago. No one can move this turkey."

He was supposed to be watching the trucks at night, on her orders. He hadn't. Darcy began raking her nails through her hair, then stopped. If you did that with hair gel, it made ridges.

"Darcy, are you crazy?" Dave said. She let that one go. She needed him. He said, "What's all this interest in a defunct machine?" TallStory was a flop, he said, hadn't Darcy seen SynthIntellect's second-quarter losses? Darcy let that one go, too, even though it wasn't easy.

She gave Dave a little time, and he got to the heart of the matter. He was not going to freeze his ass watching for fictitious shipments. "You know I hate doing that, anyway. The factory guards can get nasty."

So could Darcy. But instead, she turned on the charm. She asked Dave how his Saab was running (turned out it was a Volvo) and inquired about his vacation. Then the clincher: a hint about the regional meeting coming up in December.

She even managed to work in a reference to a previous regional meeting, when she and Dave had been assigned to the same hotel floor. "You know, I never did find my earrings under the bed," she said very softly. "But it was worth it."

"Yeah?" This was followed by a chuckle and a pause. "Hey, by the way, I'm divorced now." So much the better. Actually, there hadn't been any earrings, but it had been a good time. Except for the fact that he did calisthenics in the morning.

They chitchatted a bit more. "Get me the number of ships," Darcy said. "By tomorrow."

She hung up and pulled out the Dictaphone, putting her mouth so close to it that she left lipstick stains on the gray metal.

TallStory, SynthIntellect's artificial intelligence story-telling device, has been modified and repackaged and will be sold as a novelty item. Originally positioned for the academic and computer hobbyist market, the product was plagued by flaws. Cued by the user, it created gibberish instead of the coherent text promised by the manufacturer. Frank Tarasuk, SynthIntellect's new marketing head, has decided to reintroduce the product as a game, parlaying its defects into an advantage.

She hit the pause button. Frank Tarasuk. She knew him from his previous position at a company that made cheap telephones. He was a gold bracelet kind of guy, dopily knocking back rye and water when everyone else was ordering Stingers. Knew his business, though.

She hit the button again and the machine resumed its whirring.

Our information shows that deals with three mass-discounters have been closed, and two more are in the works. A major New York advertising agency has devised a campaign. Early reports indicate that the product will be ready for Christmas. First shipments began this week, number of units to be determined soon, and other specifics to follow.

This would go over the wires to clients who were interested in SynthIntellect. She was sticking her neck out, she knew. But her hunches were usually right, and a victory would come in handy. Darcy knew she was the best there was. Her boss, however, needed a reminder.

Once the memo hit Wall Street, it would move markets. Darcy picked up the phone and dialed her new broker. The discount one, who never asked questions.

The next day was a good one for having lunch with Eric, in the greasy spoon across from the *Crusader's* offices. Darcy was antsy all day, waiting for the TallStory news to hit.

She couldn't concentrate on much. But that was just right for a meal like this, when the hamburger had a carbon coat of mail around a slimy center, and the coffee should have been labeled Made of Recycled Materials.

There was a little French bistro not far from here. Heywood had taken her there one evening to test the piano bar. The piano wasn't great. The food had been fairly decent, though.

A clean, well-lit place like that wasn't Eric's style. Darcy wasn't sure what was. For weeks, she had been pounding him with a story idea that just might save Heywood's neck. Eric wasn't interested.

The *Courier-Inquirer* had come out with a piece about a woman who did a fair amount of drug dealing until she got collared some months ago. Darcy and Heywood knew her slightly, but they didn't know about the collar. That's because the D.E.A. had made a deal with her. She became an informant.

Following instructions, the woman gave up drugs and dealing. Heywood hadn't run into her recently. Good thing, because these days when she talked to friends, she was wearing a federal wire.

Maybe she hadn't picked up much sound footage that the feds could use. At any rate, they apparently soured on her for some reason—because the next thing that happened, an old pal of hers begged her to score an eighth of an ounce for him.

She had closed up shop, she said, at first. But then she caved in. Okay, just that little bit, just for you.

Turned out the pal was a federal informant, too, sent to tantalize her. This time she was busted for good.

The establishment paper hadn't printed the whole story. They just reported the bust, complete with name and address, provided courtesy of the D.A.

Darcy had heard the rest of the story through the paranoia grapevine. She wanted the *Crusader* to run it.

Eric didn't like it. "The girl was stupid. She went back to dealing."

"Once, as a favor," countered Darcy. "There's a message there for everyone involved, stupid or not. The D.E.A. will use you and throw you aside. It doesn't pay to turn government's witness."

Eric began to sneeze, then covered it. Darcy looked away. His handkerchief needed a trip to the laundry.

"It must pay, Darce. Because everyone's doing it. Maybe the real message is, get a new set of friends."

Heywood had already done that, thought Darcy. Anyone from their old druggy circle could be poison ivy. So could anyone else.

"What are we supposed to do? Hide out like hermits? Strip search everyone we meet in the street?"

She was angry now, gesturing wildly over her half-eaten food. Her bracelets made wind-chime noises, and she managed to capsize a yellow mustard squeeze bottle. God, this place depressed her. In Rhode Island, her parents had a diner just like this, never enough napkins in the dispensers. All that scrimping on supplies had sent her to college.

She kept fighting. "If your paper did a piece on this, it might stop the whole shark-pool syndrome. Why should people work for the feds if they're going to be betrayed?"

Eric flagged the waitress. "Separate checks," he told her and turned back to Darcy. "Here's an easy solution for Heywood. Quit dealing. How much does he need my help, Darce? What does he drive, and what do I drive?"

He looked at Darcy in a way that sent her fingers to the top button of her blouse. She could figure out the rest of the equation Eric was calculating.

They paid at the cash register and came out blinking into the light. There was a *Boston Globe* dispenser next to the luncheonette. Eric wanted a copy, but neither of them had the right change.

When Darcy came out of the luncheonette again with four quarters, Eric was staring down the block.

"Here they come," he said.

"Who?"

"Grace Stark, Huddersfield's very first bondswoman, and her husband, Phil. Ex-bondsman."

Now Darcy remembered: the *Crusader* office and the note for Eric, and the middle-aged woman with dyed bouffant hair. From the hand gestures, Darcy could tell that the older woman was arguing with her husband as they walked. The couple passed Darcy and Eric without seeing them. Eric, Darcy noticed, had drawn back into the luncheonette doorway. When he came back onto the sidewalk he was laughing.

"We did a job on Phil Stark, man. Looks like they're heading for court. She took over, but he's pulling the strings. It's like a George and Lurleen Wallace kind of thing."

Darcy ignored him and slipped a quarter into the newspaper dispenser.

"See, Darce, that was a case of a source who didn't know where the story was. It's the same thing with your idea. You got to leave news to the professionals."

Darcy handed Eric the paper, but not before she flipped to the business section. There it was, in big letters: "SynthIntellect May Revive Moribund Machine."

She tried to tell Heywood about it that night, about TallStory and the newspaper story idea. But he didn't care about computers anymore, said he never had, even when he was v.p. of the firm where Darcy had met him. And he wasn't interested in the *Crusader*. Except in a pinch, when a copy was handy and there was nothing else to roll up for a toot.

"A lot of leather tonight," she said, using her fake

flirtatious voice. "Pretty kinky." His brown cowhide jacket was old and familiar, but the couch was mint-condition. Its torn-off store wrappings were gathered in a Saran Wrap pool at Heywood's feet. He looked up at Darcy, surprised. He hadn't heard her let herself in.

She bent down and kissed him, unfastening her coat. It would be a short visit; she couldn't stay. Town was twenty unpaved miles away, and tomorrow she had to get to work early. There'd be a lot of activity about the SynthIntellect thing.

He hugged her and breathed something in her ear, husky if inaudible. But she could hear the squeaks Heywood's leather jacket made when it scrunched against the leather cushions. He heard, too, and made a joke about the bar in New York where the latex fetishists went, all vinyl chairs and people in wet suits.

The name was Hot Sounds or something, he said, adding, as he always did, "or so I heard." He hadn't been to New York since he was five years old and his parents took him on a planetarium expedition. Heywood was pure New England, born in Massachusetts, educated in Rhode Island. He always made a point of that.

Darcy laughed at the latex story and thought to herself: see, we can still have good times.

"How did the deliverymen get this monster up here?" She patted the sofa.

"They bitched plenty. The hell with them. That's what they're paid to do."

He was going to get nasty. He felt it, too, and opened a little drawer in the coffee table. Time to do a few lines. Darcy waited, wondering if he got mean with the deliverymen. There were three steep flights of oak stairs leading to Heywood's treehouse—the one his parents never let him have when he was a kid. The architect, however, was glad to oblige, and glad to include the big picture windows that gave him a sweep of the woods outside and one enormous heating bill.

Scattered around the living room were the harvests of earlier furniture sprees, a lot of big-ticket items that made the leather couch look right at home. The scoop chairs and L-shaped "conversation pit" had sleek, low profiles but plenty of upholstery. Heywood liked lounging.

The look here was more department store than hand-made, an anomaly in this neck of the woods. The area was a mecca for craftspeople, the successful kind. The ones who invested in oil exploration limited partnerships when they weren't busy at the potter's wheel.

Nearly everyone up here owned a monumental weaving or something of the sort. Not Heywood, that wasn't his style. Among his customers were some of the local artisans, but he didn't do business on barter.

There was, however, one item he had commissioned from a neighboring cabinetmaker. Not the type of thing you could pick up at Macy's, it was a hulking case with sliding glass doors, so low that Darcy was often tempted to set her coffee cups on the mahogany finish, but so wide that it spanned a wall.

Heywood's attitude had been improved somewhat by extracting what he needed from the drawer. He walked to the cabinet, slid the glass door open, and crouched, deliberating for a minute or so.

Darcy watched his back, dreading what would come next. Having selected the record he wanted, Heywood tipped it into his hand and propped the album cover against the carved rosewood stand that had been specially built into the cabinet top.

"Liltin' Martha Tilton and the Benny Goodman band," he announced, strolling over to the turntable.

He returned to Darcy's side as the first odd strains of the music began. Monaural, as usual. Darcy darted a poisonous look at the record jacket and the singer pictured on it, close-coiffed and crinoline-skirted. Big hips and short hair. Like most of Heywood's adored songstresses, she had triangular proportions—a pinhead.

Darcy loathed everything in the cabinet, as well as the cabinet itself. The carpenter was a big shot who exhibited regularly at the Rhinebeck Crafts Fair and got his picture on the cover of magazines, she was told. But this thing was a clunky, ill-proportioned work. Somehow it looked abnormally massive.

She spread her hand over the arm of the new sofa, measuring its width with her fingers as though they were calipers. Thick. Heywood liked mass.

It was a little chilly in here today, sign of a lowered thermostat. Heywood pretended the arrests didn't bother him, but he was taking fewer calls nowadays, sticking close to home, and budgeting things like heat. It wouldn't last, though. The bills would come in, and he'd rev up again.

Darcy tried to pull her coat around her shoulders, but Heywood pulled it off. He wanted to christen the leather couch, he said. She unzipped his jacket and his pants. He wanted to undress her, but she stopped him for a moment, sucking on his beautiful aristocratic fingers.

She rubbed them against her cheek, murmuring, "Nice, nice." The stereo was on full force.

"What's that song?" she asked. Though she didn't really care.

He named it. "Martha Tilton. Great singer."

"You want it so loud?"

"Listen to that. All those low notes she's got. God, is that terrific."

He was kissing her, but the music had destroyed her mood.

"How come you're buying couches now, when you can't do business?"

He smoothed her hair. "Don't worry about it."

But she couldn't stop. She sat up, waving her hand around the room to indicate the furniture, particularly the detestable record cabinet. "I thought you were fairly well-furnished already."

He sat up, too, refastening his clothing with impatient gestures. "Don't start."

"One thing I'll say for your taste, when the burglars finally catch on to the fact that your door is wide open, they won't be able to get anything out of here. Do you realize that everything you own weighs about ten tons?"

Heywood had his fingers pressed to his temples, headache position. "Burglars. That's the least of my problems."

"Just today at work I heard about a break-in in South Chumley. Everyone leaves their doors unlocked there, too."

He was on his feet and tugging on her wrist. "You want the door locked. Come on and I'll lock it."

Then he was pulling her toward the door. Clutching at her half-open blouse, though there was no one within miles to peek in, she stumbled behind him. His grasp was firm, almost painful, and she imagined for a moment that he was going to hurl her down the wooden steps outside.

But with his hand on the knob, he hesitated and released her. "Wait right there." He went into the kitchen, and she watched through the alcove opening as he reached onto a shelf and removed something.

Then he was back, opening the door and steering her by the elbow into the cold air outside.

"You want me to lock it?" Under the porch light, she saw him brandish a key. A turn and a click. "Now it's locked. See, I always had this key. Haven't used it since the builder gave it to me. Don't plan to use it again."

He pitched it over the stairs. "Now, watch this." He took something that looked like a Swiss Army knife out of his pocket and selected a blade. Darcy saw that it wasn't the usual kind of blade, and it wasn't one of those miniature screwdrivers or forks either. She got cold, and bored, standing outside, but she sensed that she shouldn't say anything.

"Voilà." It had taken about ten minutes. The door was open, and Liltin' Martha Tilton was singing, "For you, for you, for you, for you . . ."

"A scratch. Damn." Heywood rushed over to the turntable. Darcy closed the door behind her, glancing at the brand name on the lock. Medeco. Those were supposed to be good. Not the kind you could pry open with a credit card.

Back on the couch, she decided not to ask about it. Heywood seemed proud of his little stunt. Darcy had to admit it had snapped her out of her vicious cycle. They were beyond talking anyhow.

She slid her tongue and her hands across Heywood's body, trying to get lost in sex. Heywood was pushing up her skirt now, breathless. The phone started ringing. Someone looking to score. He ignored it, but it was a bad touch.

So was the singer who had replaced Martha Tilton on the turntable. "The Misty Miss Christie," said the album cover propped against the stand on the mahogany cabinet. At least this crummy music made Heywood happy. Maybe he'd even start singing again at parties, like he used to, Darcy thought.

Then she reminded herself. They couldn't go to parties anymore. It could be a setup.

She straightened up, smiling as she undid the front clasp of her bra. The couch smelled awful, like a hundred pairs of new shoes. She cradled his head in her arms. Lovely man, with lips that she called Neapolitan, though not too many Neapolitans were named Heywood and had degrees from St. George's and Brown.

That always stimulated her, thinking about his degree

from Brown. In Providence, she had been a townie, enviously watching the Brown students drive to football games in their sporty cars on the weekends she was home from her Brand X college.

"Ever go to the Colonial Diner when you were at Brown?" she murmured into Heywood's ear.

"What's that?"

"My parents' place. Maybe my mother waited on you, huh?"

"She look like you? I would've remembered. Would've asked her to tuck my napkin into my lap."

"It was kind of far from the campus. I know what diner you would have gone to. Haven Brothers."

Heywood was nipping her neck. "Never heard of it."

"Oh, come on. Everyone heard of it."

"Maybe it wasn't there when I was there."

"It's been there for like eighty, ninety years. Everyone in Providence knows it."

"Oh, yeah. A campus hang-out. I wasn't big on hanging out."

Haven Brothers was not a campus hang-out. It was a trailer that a truck towed to a downtown street every afternoon, and it stayed out there until well past midnight. Everyone who ever lived in Providence had tasted a Haven Brothers hamburger.

Darcy let it pass, more interested in other tastes at the moment.

"Terrific couch, no?" he said when they were finished. She pretended she agreed, though she really couldn't. There was the smell, and something else. It would take twenty, maybe twenty-five grams to pay for the damn thing.

Five

No going after the fancy stuff this time," Phil told Grace. "And sit down, will you? You're not supposed to traipse all over the place."

"I'll only have to get up again when the judge comes." Grace was near an open window, taking advantage. Once the defendants trooped in, that would be it for the sweet-smelling air.

"Drunk drivings only. Leave the Grand Larcenies to Isaacs. Please. You have no idea how to run a credit check."

"There's something I'd like to know. How are we going to make a living from all those tiny little bonds?"

Phil had an answer; he always did. But before he had a chance to say it, the judge walked in. Grace was up already, with her head halfway out the window. Pulling in from a good inhale, she saw Phil glaring at her. He lifted his behind off the seat by two inches, then dropped it. That was supposed to be respect. To Grace, it looked like a dog doing his business.

The defendants entered. Pretty good pickings today. Only about five were in shackles. Phil didn't let her anywhere near the Chain Gang. The others slumped into seats.

As usual, it looked like it'd been a rough night in the holding cells. The breeze from the window blew cold and strong, but it couldn't compete with this group. Grace gave up and sat down. She counted one, two, three, about twenty defendants, and the judge took his sweet time calling up the first one. Wouldn't you know, it was one of the guys with four others attached? They all shuffled forward, banging and clanging the whole way. This would take a while. Meanwhile, it was time to start wooing.

Phil had the clipboard and briefcase. "Give it here," Grace told him. She had to give a good, hard tug. "Fork over, mister. You've lost your license."

That always made him snap. "Go after the Drunk Drivings," he said, so loud that one of Isaacs' flunkies barked a laugh from a back row. Phil pretended he didn't hear. "Stick with the ones in the suits."

To Grace, it was like cleaning up after people at a party, watching them scoff down the hors d'oeuvres while you collected the toothpicks. The Isaacs gang got busy, running checks on the Burglaries and Assaults. Meanwhile, Phil winked Grace over to a guy you would have called respectable-looking about fourteen hours ago. Gray jacket, paisley tie, white shirt with something down the front she didn't want to look at.

"Grace Stark, professional bondswoman," she greeted him. "What are you charged with, do you know? Anyone here to co-sign a bond for your release?"

He signaled, and his wife rushed forward, nervous as hell. He worked for a food distributor. Drove around the state checking stock and displays, and got a little too happy at a Happy Hour. He fanned out a wad of cash, and his wife had a checkbook and credit cards. It was a first offense, so the bond would be small. Still, it was good that his wife was here. It was always good to have a friend or relative co-sign. Nothing like familial pressure to guarantee an appearance.

Once the defendant named an employer, the rest was almost unnecessary. But Phil was taking it all in from ten yards away, tuning in, like it was on the radio. Grace didn't dare skip a step.

She told the guy and his wife where she'd be sitting, so they could find her after the arraignment. Over in his seat Phil was winking and nudging, again toward a rumpled businessman type. There were a few stray hookers that Isaacs and Company weren't bothering with, probably figuring there'd be time enough when bail was set.

Grace edged toward one, just to watch Phil's reaction. She never saw anyone shake a head so hard. Couldn't be good for the blood vessels.

Later, at his office, she thought she'd ask once again. "Why no prostitutes? They're standing there, begging to give me a fee, and you give me the evil eye. They're good risks, they'll show, right? That's what you always said."

"Screw what I always said. You never understood what I was talking about anyway. Stay away from them. Their bonds don't add up to piss."

"Yeah? So it's the same thing with the Drunk Drivings. Penny-ante."

"You want to play around with the Rapes, the Armed Robberies, all that high-risk stuff? What do you think this is—mah-jongg? Jump rope?" They had been standing in the middle of the office, but now Phil turned his back on Grace, like he always did. It was the insurance he'd invented, to make sure of having the last word.

This time there were a few more last words to keep the other ones company, so he kept talking as he moved to the desk. "Who got you your license in three days when it's supposed to take thirty? Who went through hell and back to transfer my assets to your name?" He sat himself down and started shuffling through the drawers, as if they were still his.

"If you're looking for that filthy roll of heartburn tablets, I threw them out when I went through that rat's nest."

"Terrific. Now I have to buy another one. Who are we, the Rockefellers?"

"No, we're just a couple of bankrupt people, but that's okay. Because somehow we're going to pay our bills with the $25 fees I pick up from the drunks. And we're going to forget about all those coke cases that are jamming the answering machine, because who needs the money?"

Phil let out a belch. Maybe those tablets weren't just a habit after all. "Forget you ever heard of cocaine. I'm sorry I ever explained to you what it was. Forget you know where federal court is. You're not taking calls from there, you're not thinking about it, you're not going to *look* at it when you drive by. That's *big* risk. Big, big, big, big, *big*. You don't know the first thing about it."

There was one thing Grace knew that Phil didn't: if you took the broken blinds off the window, then you could actually see in this office. And when you saw, then you knew you had to go buy some Ajax.

She thought about that for a while, looking at the bare windows. It was better than listening to ranting. Maybe she wouldn't replace the blinds with the shades, after all. Grace liked looking at "BAIL" spelled backwards on the glass. She might enjoy standing here alone, looking at it.

"And stay away from those whores. They've got v.d." He wasn't through yet.

"Any of them ever come in here?"

"No. I don't know. Maybe. Before I kicked them out on their diseased behinds."

"Then there must be v.d. all over the place here. Because I know it's never seen a disinfectant bottle."

She had smuggled some plants in, after Phil finally started restructuring. As it turned out, he hadn't declared full-fledged bankruptcy. Barbara Lubin, daughter-in-law and investment banker, told him to file for Chapter 11. There was no denying what Ted said: if Barbara could rebuild some huge utility company that went bust and get her name in a magazine for it, then she could rebuild Phil Stark.

It was Barbara who convinced the court to go along with the idea. Phil was going to sell insurance at his cousin's agency to bring in money, and Grace would write bail bonds. Phil had fought hard with Barbara about it, but in the end he convinced her. Sure, there were other jobs Grace could get, but they'd only bring in pin money. Phil had a restructuring deadline to meet. Setting Grace up in business was the only answer.

"It's one of those in-name-only things," Ted said, when he and his wife came over to explain. They spelled it out very slowly, the way Grace had talked to Ted when he came home from kindergarten with some clay he wanted to bake in her oven. Everyone was good at explaining, but no one bothered to ask Grace's opinion. "Dad will be calling the shots from the sideline," is the way Ted put it.

But right now, Larry the range officer was calling the shots.

"Timed fire with five pounds load," he yelled. Larry was a big-chested guy with a large voice, but Grace could barely hear him through the ear protectors. She rolled nine cartridges into the borrowed .22 Smith & Wesson.

In the beginning, Grace came to the range half dead from bitching and balking. She had to pack a gun, according to Phil, but he couldn't list one good reason. He'd been happy as a clam without guns until a few weeks ago. Maybe he was getting crazy.

But by this time, she was enjoying the lessons, even if they did chew up her weekend. As it turned out, Grace was good at shooting. And it was a way to meet people she never would have, like Mrs. Mulcahey.

Grace glanced over her shoulder. As usual, Mrs. Mulcahey had already finished loading. First day of class, Mrs. Mulcahey let everyone know what an old hand she was, and how she shouldn't really be in a beginner's class. The range just placed her here because it was the only ladies' class at the moment, and that's okay, no hard feelings against the range. But she already knew how to shoot, because you couldn't own a grocery store on Five Corners without being a shooter. Main reason she was here was to perfect her semiautomatic technique. "Look at this piece," she said all the time, waving her Browning around. "My son got it for me. Isn't it a beaut?"

Right now, Larry was looking straight at the beaut. He bellowed, "Hold your fire," to the whole class and strolled up to Mrs. Mulcahey. She had a figure like a fire hydrant and furrows in her cheeks—the problem student of the Powder Puff class. Larry always pulled Powder Puff duty, asked for it, in fact. He was the kind of guy who got gruff sometimes, but he knew how to talk to ladies. Called them all "Mrs." out of respect, even the ones that weren't married.

"See that barrel of sand?" he asked Mrs. Mulcahey. "We've got it here for a reason. All students with self-loaders have to stick their muzzles in the sand before loading. I'm not going to tell you again."

Mrs. Mulcahey wasn't pleased. She was impatient to get past range shooting into the special-defense tactics course. "When do we get to shoot around corners?" she was always asking everyone.

At the moment, she was looking at the sand barrel and back at the beaut. "It's loaded already," she told Larry.

"Reload. You're not going to pass this class until you

learn some respect for that weapon. You've got a semiautomatic there, you know that don't you?" A beat later, he remembered and added, "Ma'am."

Five people waited while Mrs. Mulcahey thrust her Browning 9 mm. into the sand. Grace wasn't sure, but she thought Mrs. Mulcahey was moving her lips at her.

"What?" Grace lifted one side of the ear protectors.

"This is stupid," Mrs. Mulcahey was whispering. "Say some crooks come into my store, right? Say there's a shoot-out. I'm supposed to reload in a box of kitty litter?"

"Mmmmm," said Grace. It might be hazardous to your health to argue with Mrs. Mulcahey.

"Speed is the whole point. That's why I got this baby," she tapped the muzzle, "instead of a piece of junk like you got there."

"Ready on the right," Larry was yelling. Grace extended her shooting arm, locking the elbow. The excitement started pulsing through her.

"Ready on the left." She found the aiming area on the edge of the target frame.

"Ready on the firing line." Grace still couldn't control the startle reflex. The first shot hit the seven o'clock area.

When it was time to fill out the error sheets, Mrs. Mulcahey looked over Grace's shoulder. "Some jerking and heeling, but not too bad. Keep at it, and you'll be able to defend yourself."

Grace thanked her. Secretly, she was very proud of herself.

Mrs. Mulcahey had finished her own error sheet in no time, because she hit the bull with almost every fire. "Great feeling, isn't it?" She gave her beaut a pat. "They come into my store, and if it's war they want, it's war they're going to get."

When they finally got to special-defense tactics, Mrs. Mulcahey was in her element. All those quilted-looking parts of her face were glowing and shining.

Once she was teamed up with Grace for a barricade practice session in the range shack. You never knew when the little outline of a man was going to pop up. Usually it happened when Grace was curled up behind the big armchair, trying to peep through the bullet holes in the upholstery.

"Fire!" Mrs. Mulcahey yelled from behind the couch. "This is war!"

"All right, already," said Grace. She stuck her head up, and the target appeared. You got points deducted for exposing yourself too long, so she blasted before she was ready.

It hit, but on the outline of the leg. "The face, the face," shouted Mrs. Mulcahey. "Sink lead into that bastard's brain."

"Enough," said Larry, from the doorway. "I'm in charge here, ladies."

Mrs. Mulcahey couldn't seem to let up. "Aim for the face. Stop the attack. They'll keep coming at you, don't you understand? They're going to whack you. They're going to *whack* you!"

Mrs. Mulcahey left when she was asked to. But when Grace went to drop off her safety glasses in the equipment room, the grocery store owner was waiting for her.

"I guess I got a little carried away," she told Grace, "but this is serious. You've got possibilities, Mrs. Stark, but you've got one problem. You don't care enough about surviving."

It was like a flashback back there in the shack, she said. Her store had been robbed three times. So far Mrs. Mulcahey had clipped two—one in the leg, one in the hip. Next time, there'd be a clean finish.

"It's them or us, Mrs. Stark. Because the courts just put them on the street again."

Since she was feeling so chummy after a day on the barricades, she asked Grace what she did for a living.

And since Grace was never any great shakes at lying, she told her.

"You're a *what*?" The shrieking from behind the couch had been nothing compared to this.

The next lesson was night shooting. Larry put Grace in the shack with Mrs. Mulcahey again, this time in dim light. It was cold in the shack, but Grace was sweating. She kept wondering where Mrs. Mulcahey was aiming.

Grace got a silver medallion on her graduation certificate and a big gift from Phil: a Smith & Wesson again, but this time a semiautomatic .38. He and Ted took her out for dinner. Barbara stayed home—on principle, she let everyone know. Barbara didn't approve of shooting. She only approved of restructuring.

The gift came to the restaurant with Grace, but Ted wouldn't pat it or let her pull it out. From now on it would always be with her, in the handbag she bought at the range gift shop. It had a built-in holster. Very leather-like, too.

"Here's to self-defense," she said when the waiter finally showed up with her Pink Lady. She still wasn't sure why Phil had sent her to the range. But the shooting lessons put a spring in her step. She'd never be a Mrs. Mulcahey, because she never went in for dramatics. Still, it felt good.

You could trust Phil never to enjoy a dinner out without breaking the mood.

"Why talk shop after hours?" Ted asked, breaking in on a harangue. Phil had finally started selling insurance at his cousin's firm—behind schedule, Barbara pointed out. He arranged to work a lot of evenings so he could keep training Grace during the day. But sometimes he had to miss an arraignment, and Grace was on her own.

"A Grand Larceny yesterday. I still can't believe you."

"You told me Petty Larcenies were okay now. A few bucks less, and this would have been petty."

"Sure, sure. Listen to your mother, Ted. I don't care

about the charge. It's the bond that counts, the bond! You went two thousand over your maximum. What if you get a forfeiture, huh?"

"I had two final appearances yesterday. That's twenty grand back. Remember? No, you don't remember."

Ted tried turning on his p.r. charm. "No fighting allowed at celebrations, folks. Dad, just think about how great Mom's doing, picking up all that information so quickly. She's got all that jargon down pat. I'm impressed. I am really impressed."

Phil belched. A fake belch, in Grace's opinion. The food in this restaurant was not heavy.

Ted kept on; he was always careful about Equal Time. "Now, Mom, don't lose sight of the main point. We're trying to restructure Dad's business, that's what this is all about. He's an old hand who knows what he's doing. You've got to let him coach. I mean, we're all after the same goal, right?"

Dad never would have landed a job in p.r. "I'm in charge here," he told Grace. "Me! What I say goes."

"That's what *he* thinks," Grace told the office rubber plant the next day. As soon as she finished watering it, she was going over to court for the arraignments. Whatever was there, she'd take a little of everything. She knew how to shoot, she was settled in the business. It was time to diversify.

Wouldn't you know, there was practically nothing but Drunks. But this morning, Grace gave her card to everybody, including the spectators. Phil always did that, she knew. It paid to advertise. She even used the old jingle he made up:

In jail? Need bail? Call Grace.

What the hell. Twenty years of singing it in the shower didn't mean he had a patent on it.

The whore known as Midnight Mary came up to Grace after her bail was set and counted out the fee. Three

63

greasy $20 bills, meaning Grace had to tuck her clip-boards and briefcase under a shoulder while she hunted for change. She felt the Smith in the special compartment, still loaded with the Graduation Day cartridges. Why did Phil think she needed it, she wondered. And could dollar bills carry v.d.?

Grace wrote out the release form without asking for a co-signer. Just like Phil used to always say, they'd appear. The pimps saw to it.

Everything was fine until Grace made a mistake. She looked at Midnight Mary a moment too long, staring at the hair that peroxide had turned into cotton candy. That's how she got the nickname. It didn't look human.

If you stared too long in a fairy tale, someone would turn into a rock or a snake. In court, it made a whore open up her dirty mouth.

Midnight Mary told Grace how she'd have to earn back the money for the fee. Several body parts were mentioned. If Grace thought about it, which she didn't let herself do, they didn't seem like the right ones.

Grace was going to say, "I don't like that kind of talk," but instead she told the whore that she could do what she damn pleased. "Just show up for your court date." Worked like a charm.

The other whore was a skinny little thing with no nickname and no money. At least, not enough for the bond fee.

"Sorry," Grace told her, snapping her briefcase closed. That was that.

The skinny thing kept applying lipstick, like she'd been doing for the past half hour. Must have been some kind of nervous tic.

"I got it," said the girl. "All of it but ten dollars."

She said it so softly that Grace had to lean forward to catch it. That's why the spit hit right on target.

"No discounts," said Grace, turning around slowly. She

64

didn't want to dig for a Kleenex until she was out the door. She didn't want to give this pig the satisfaction.

"When's your husband going to come back here?" the pig asked Grace's back. Grace kept walking. All that did was turn up the volume.

"He used to give me a discount. Of course, I used to make up the difference."

Grace was in the corridor now, moving toward the door and dabbing away. The prostitute followed as far as the doorway, where the guard stopped her. He wasn't knocking himself out.

"I used to pay. You hear what I'm saying?"

This time, Grace turned around and saw the filthy, repulsive thing touching her crotch in the courtroom doorway.

Grace lifted her chin and continued on. Just like a queen, she told herself.

The queen had made the wrong choice. "He's got an ugly dick, your husband," the whore screeched down the hall. "With two little balls like gumdrops."

Right before Grace made it to the raw air outside, she thought she saw one of Isaacs' men, laughing his head off. But maybe she hadn't really. Who could see clearly with spit in their eye?

Six

Phil was watching himself on TV, himself and another guy. His skin tone looked bad, even with the blue shirt they told him to wear. He considered making a note of that in his Ray-Mar Insurance Agency looseleaf notebook. It was sitting in front of him on the conference table, opened to a pretty good doodle of Dagwood.

"You've got a four-year-old and a six-year-old," he was telling the guy. You had to crane your neck up to see the set, the way it was attached to the wall. "In twelve—no, fifteen—years that's two kids in college. See, this policy I've been—"

You couldn't hear the next few words. It all sounded like aluminum foil.

He and the guy dissolved into a horizontal line. Phil's cousin Marty kept his finger on the VCR button and turned toward Phil. "How many times do I have to tell you?" he said. "Don't rattle papers over the mike."

The set went on again. The guy was telling Phil that insurance didn't pay anymore. There was no use planning for the future, because there might not be a future, on account of the bomb. Anyhow, that was the guy's opinion.

"You're pulling my leg," said the Phil on the tube. He gave the guy a friendly punch on the arm. A big white streak followed his fist.

Marty shut it off again. Not the pause button. The stop.

"It wasn't like real TV," Phil said. "That streaking."

"Yeah?" said Marty. "That's okay, because you weren't like a real insurance agent."

He was going to be kept back in role-playing again. In a way that was bad, because it meant he couldn't go out in the field and make commissions. But it was good, too, because he got a salary even for training. ("Just like any other employee," Marty had said the first day, waiting for the great big thank-you.)

Eventually, Phil would have to get out there and sell insurance. The money Grace brought home was barely enough to keep him in blue shirts. But Phil wasn't looking forward to all that driving around and visiting clients. The Barkan killing still spooked him. At home there was the new security system, and the drive to this office was all highway. Calling on prospects in the boonies would be something else altogether. Lots of lonely roads.

Christmas was coming, and the cops who used to work for Isaacs were missing that extra dough. Either that, or the holidays just made people crazy. Those were the only reasons Phil could figure out for why the hate calls were coming in again.

Maybe he should tell Grace. She just shrugged when he told her to watch herself. Just shrugged no matter what he said lately. I-don't-know-suit-yourself, that's about all she said these days. Maybe the job was tiring her out. That's the excuse she gave at sex time.

Well, if she wasn't in the talking mood, he couldn't talk to her, could he? Let her go to work and not panic unnecessarily. At least they were meeting most of their bills.

Phil worked on his doodle. Dagwood needed a shirt

button. Phone threats were usually nothing. If the creeps were angling for Grace, they would have called the office instead of home, where he always raced to get to the phone first.

"You listening to me?"

Marty was standing in front of the TV with a rubber-tipped pointer.

"Instant replay, right?" said Phil. That's what always happened next. That's when hatchet-faced Marty with the liver spots could pretend to be Mr. Sportscaster.

"Yep. We're going to look at the body language."

Marty rewound the tape. In reverse, Phil heard himself making weird animal noises. His head was jerking back. Like he had been shot.

"Christ, it's getting dark out early."

Rob Quillan was standing at Heywood's wall of windows. He put a hand on the glass. "Boy, these get cold. Single panes, huh?"

Heywood stopped flipping through the pile of albums on his lap, and held one up, triumphant. "Bing Crosby doing 'Stardust.' What did I tell you?"

"Tremendous. Let me see it." Quillan walked over and picked up the record. He still had his gloves on. Those who say that fat people never get cold haven't met Quillan, Heywood thought.

"I had the same exact recording in New York. Before I got ripped off."

"I couldn't stand that," said Heywood. "Somebody ripping off my whole collection. Out here I don't even have to lock my doors."

"Sure. Out here no one's hip enough to appreciate what you've got."

Heywood put on the record. "Yeah? Then how come I'm hip enough to have this stuff? I'm from here."

"Your soul was made in New York, and you don't even know it." Quillan sprawled out on the new couch. Walrus on leather. Bing swung into "Cheek to Cheek" as Quillan hauled himself up on an elbow and grabbed for the drawer in the coffee table.

"Nothing like making yourself at home," said Heywood, coming over.

They did two sides of Bing and a couple of lines each. That shut Quillan up for a while, but soon he was bitching about the cold again. That wasn't like him. He usually bitched about how far they'd have to drive to get to the bar. Three years in Massachusetts, and Quillan still couldn't get into the car culture. Didn't want to. He was actually keeping track of the miles they had clocked looking for the p.p.b.—perfect piano bar.

There'd been that one in Jeffreyton a couple of months ago. Nice crowd, good decor, and a pianist who followed Quillan on a crazy trip through "Thou Swell"—legato, then on the beat, then back to legato again. Later, Quillan decided it was a lousy spot, strictly Hix-Stix. He blamed the good time on his drug buzz.

Heywood was sifting through albums. "Want to hear some Crosby-Sinatra duets?"

"Maybe. Maybe one or two. Where'd you say this Charades place is?"

"Masquerade. In Squanset."

"Wherever the hell that is."

"Route seventeen, near where it meets King's Highway. I called them last night. They've got a new pianist that they say used to be a music director. For a summer theater in the Berkshires."

Quillan stretched out on his stomach. "He'll suck. I'm telling you, any ten-block area of Manhattan has better accompanists than this whole tone-deaf state."

They went in Heywood's Saab. Quillan harped the whole way about people who lived in iceboxes.

"So it's warm enough in here, right?" Heywood's high was losing altitude and irritation was setting in. He made a big show of putting the car heater on full blast, hot enough to melt a Viking. "What's your problem?"

"What's happening? Is business bad? Hey, I didn't take your last lines, did I?"

Heywood kept his eyes on the road. He didn't like to talk business with Quillan. Sure, he supplied him sometimes, but they were singing buddies. Period. He said, "Don't worry about it."

"I heard about the busts. Who hasn't. A drag, no? Hey, if it's a marketing problem, I'll make some absolutely safe referrals."

"Don't bother."

"Why not? Remember LaPlante? That lox in M.I.S. who worked catercorner to your office? He's using now—can you believe it? He needs a supplier."

"I don't need him."

"You phasing out operations, laying low till this legal stuff blows over? Hey, come back to Digitronics. They'd crawl on their *knees* to get you back. You wouldn't believe the stock options they'd throw at you. Do it in time for the Christmas party. Chiarella can play piano, and we'll wow them like last year."

"Yeah?" A dog was standing in the road up ahead. Heywood could barely see it in the darkness. He felt himself hurtling toward it. "What'll we sing?"

"I don't know. A Sinatra-Crosby number. How about 'In the Cool, Cool, Cool of the Evening'? Christ, I don't know how you stand it at your place. What happened? You lost your connection? I couldn't believe that little bag in your drawer. It keeps getting smaller."

"I don't keep the stuff at my place. I don't lock the doors, remember?"

"So where do you keep it?"

At the last possible moment, Heywood swerved around

the dog. He could feel Quillan looking at him, but he didn't look back. He didn't want to hear any comments about how close it had been. He could calm down. It was easy. He could talk like a normal person.

"Those storage places off I-91. Different ones, wherever they drop it off for me. U-Store-It, Lock-and-Store, Tuck-It-Away. Places like that. Keep an eye out for a Getty station. I've got to hang a right soon."

"Tuck-It-Away. I love it." Quillan snapped his fingers and started singing. " 'Tuck, tuck, tuck. Tuck it awaaaaay.' No, wait. I'll take it down a step." He finished on a vibrato low C. The guy really did have a nice set of pipes.

Quillan was having fun. Good. And there'd be a men's room at the bar.

This Masquerade place turned out to be in a strip mall. Laundromat, video rentals, Chinese takeout, piano bar. The pianist was on a break when they came in and still on it when they emerged from the can, feeling good. It was strip-mall all the way here: black vinyl furniture and phony Tiffany lamp shades. About eight people were at the bar, twelve at tables. A nice-sized audience if it went well. Heywood ordered the Scotches while Quillan nosed around the piano.

"It's got a counter built on it, but no one's been on the stools," he reported. "No trace of cocktail napkins."

"Thank God," Heywood said. The drinks had arrived at their table. He and Quillan never sat around a piano. That was for the sing-along crowd.

"Here's the good news. He's got fake books."

"What did I tell you? It's going to be good."

"Maybe they're just for lyrics."

"Give up," said Heywood. "Anyone who can play without chords can really play. Fake books means he does his own arranging."

The pianist came back. As it turned out, it was a

woman. Mostly she knew modern stuff, but some of that was okay. Quillan went first with "Send in the Clowns." No fancy phrasing, just nice and expressive. After that, he tried "On a Clear Day." Heywood wondered if he'd take the second verse up-tempo. He did, and the pianist didn't miss a note.

People stopped talking and looked over. That always happened for Quillan, even on his froggy days. He had one of those legit voices that didn't need a microphone.

He did "Do Nothin' Till You Hear From Me," showing off his bottom register, but the crowd didn't get it. They wanted Broadway. So he tossed off "New York, New York," smirking at Heywood the whole time.

Everybody lapped it up. "She can play," he told Heywood, climbing back into his chair. The applause wasn't exactly deafening, but it was respectable.

"Have a drink," said Heywood. "The owner sent these over. I see you warmed up."

"Yeah," said Quillan, mopping his neck off with a napkin. The fat slob had all kinds of women winking at him from the other tables. Christ.

Heywood went up and made his request. The pianist didn't know it, but she found it in one of the fake books. He gave her a while to play around, and she managed a passable arrangement. The intro got flubbed, but she started cooking on the refrain.

It wasn't a swinging enough tune for Heywood's voice, which was heavier on rhythm than range. But his good interp worked well with light material, and he wanted to make Quillan laugh.

Ev-'ry kiss, ev-'ry hug seems to act just like a drug;
You're getting to be a habit with me.

Halfway across the room, he could hear Quillan cracking up, snorting like a rhino to show that he got the joke. No, the boy did not need a microphone.

It was Quillan's evening, they decided on the drive back. He had sung until last call, sticking with the schmaltz. He ended up with a pretty high opinion of the pianist—Marla her name was.

Walking together down Heywood's driveway, they agreed: it was no p.p.b. But close.

"In a strip mall," Quillan marveled, getting into his own car. "Who would have thought it?"

Heywood got up early the next day. Some D.E.A. agents walked right in through the doors he never locked, woke him up, and busted him. Charged him with conspiracy to distribute cocaine, delivery of cocaine, and possession with intent to deliver cocaine. They found his key to the U-Store-It right off Exit 32, where two pounds were waiting for him.

The agents had come in a crappy American car—a Fairmont or something, the kind of car you got as a rental. Everytime it hit a bump on his dirt driveway, Heywood was thrown back against his handcuffs. That hurt. Otherwise, the whole thing was almost a relief. It had been a long time coming.

They passed the spot where Quillan's car had been parked the night before. "Tuck, tuck, tuck it awaaaay." Heywood could still hear him singing.

It wasn't as easy to make a lyric out of U-Store-It. But Quillan had remembered the name.

Grace knew who it was right off, or almost. The girl had to remind her and then it came back. "We met at the *Crusader* office, I gave you a note," she said on the phone. Sounded a little shaky, but then they always did.

It was the Liz Taylor lookalike with the mink, calling from U.S. District Court. I'm coming right over, Grace told her. But fifteen minutes later, she was still in the office, hunting for federal bail release forms.

Okay. Phil hid them. Burned them or something. The court would have some more. She'd act very casual and ask someone.

As it happened, they had a handy directory hanging outside, next to the federal court entrance. Grace was able to sashay up to Room 127, Clerk's Office, without looking lost at all. The forms looked pretty much the same as at Superior Court. Well, what did you know?

Grace walked back into the lobby and looked around. Marble walls, iron fixtures. So, here she was at the Big Rock Candy Mountain, about to post a $30,000 bond for a coke dealer. What would Phil say? Not that she gave a damn anymore.

Darcy Kohler, that was the name. She came walking out of the ladies room, dabbing at her eyes with Kleenex. No mink coat today—just a business suit like Barbara's, except that Barbara didn't wear red. And the face didn't look so great this time. More like Liz after the tracheotomy.

She stopped short. "Grace! I'm so glad you're here."

"Mrs. Stark," Grace corrected.

"It's so awful. They've got him in a *prison cell.*"

"You don't say."

Grace led her back to the clerk's office, where she had spied a few vacant chairs. They sat down. Darcy blew her nose, and Grace shoved a clipboard under it.

"This is where you co-sign. Now you said something on the phone about collateral?"

"My condo. Where does my signature go? Will they let him out right away?" Darcy pulled a pen out of her clutch bag. The girl had about two rings on each finger, Grace noticed, some of them with stones that looked real.

Grace was trying to act cocksure, but the rings shook her up. They were probably gifts from the dealer. The mink coat, too, and maybe the condo. Should she ask to see the title, or would this Darcy look at her funny? Over at the other court, collateral meant that some relative had a job with the phone company.

"Now this condo—"

Darcy came to the rescue, ticking off facts so rapidly that Grace had a hard time nodding fast enough. It was in Westside Mews, she said, the place near the reservoir with the wooden sign: A Condominium Community. She was seven years into a fifteen-year mortgage, so there was plenty of equity in it. If Grace had any questions, she could call a certain vice president at a certain bank. They had personal banking there, after-hours service and all that. *You* know.

Grace steadied herself and walked out to the lobby, where she remembered seeing a pay phone. They said the bank vice president was in a meeting, but when she said it was about Darcy, he wasn't. He told Grace about Miss Kohler's assets and Miss Kohler's "net worth."

Grace got the signature and posted the bond. She left before the happy reunion, though she was kind of interested to see if the dealer looked like Richard Burton. But she figured she'd head home an hour early, maybe do some Thanksgiving shopping.

Why not? There was a check in her wallet for $3,000.

Of course, she didn't spend the whole wad at the Price Chopper. But you would have thought so, from the way the car dragged up the driveway.

A frozen turkey doesn't weigh *that* much, she thought. Must be shock absorbers or something.

Or something. It was getting dark, but you could still see in the rearview mirror if you concentrated. In the shack with Mrs. Mulcahey, Grace learned how to concentrate.

She had already pushed the button on her electronic gizmo, so the garage door was already halfway up. She let it come to a stop. Then she hit the button again.

As the door came down, Grace shifted into reverse. She

hit the accelerator hard, heading for the maple tree that she never cared much for anyway. Nothing but crabgrass could grow under that tree.

But the guy jumped off the rear bumper before she got there. He must have rolled to safety, because the sidewalk hedges were shaking when she got out of the car. A quick getaway.

The maple tree was in much better shape than her taillights, she saw. The porch lights went on at the Whelans' next door, and Bob Whelan wanted to know what the hell was going on.

So did Grace. Phil was home. He came out and started jabbering at her. She described what had happened in a few staccato syllables, shoved a bag of groceries into his arms, and walked right past him.

She picked up the phone.

"What are you doing?"

Really she wasn't talking to Phil. But with direct questions, you had to.

"Calling the police."

"Don't bother. They were here already. That was an officer on your bumper." Phil and Grace resumed talking that night. He told her a story about how he used to know a dry cleaner.

C H A P T E R

Seven

He jumped. The guy did, the guy with the cocaine. He didn't show for his court date. The judge didn't wait long. He flung himself out of court, mad, flicking his robe every which way. No one made a move for the water glass that fell. When the steno went out for a smoke, he crunched his heels right over it.

The fancy lawyer told Grace he was shocked. He was just shocked. He went out to the lobby phone with Grace, very much the gentleman. Stuck in his own coins, then let her make the call. Nothing. No answer.

Flaky, the fancy lawyer said. Maybe the guy was kind of flaky. He could be off somewhere. For a drive or something.

On the day of the pretrial hearing?

Okay, the fancy lawyer admitted. There'd been some concern about the judge on the bench, the robe flicker. There was a political thing with him. On drug cases he was very, very tough. Not a dealmaker. Heywood had expressed some concern.

"Excuse me," said Grace. "I have to use the phone again."

"The police?" asked the lawyer, sounding hopeful. He had a fee to collect.

"I'm canceling with my beautician."

The snow wasn't coming down hard, just dusting really. But two miles away from Heywood's house, Grace got stuck behind a plow. That's how it was in these rich towns. They plowed just about every day until July. It was good company, Grace tried to tell herself. Ever since the cop-on-the-bumper incident, she appreciated company.

She had one of those newsstand maps in a spiral-bound book. *Huddersfield and Outlying Regions,* glossy cover with a skyline on it: the big office tower shaped like a roll of pennies poked all the way into the upper-right-hand corner. The map went into detail, and Grace needed detail. Page sixteen showed Heywood's street. A dirt road, as it developed. The wooden steps to the door were something. Who would hear if you slipped and fell on your head? Country living, Ted called it.

Nobody living in this house, that's for sure. There were a lot of windows to look into, and they showed Grace that no one was home. Looking in, she got a panoramic view right through to the bedroom: open drawers, open closet, hangers all over the place. Someone left in a hurry. Why not? By now there was a warrant out for his arrest.

It didn't surprise her when the doorknob twisted freely in her hand. People out here had something against keys, which probably bumped up everyone's insurance premiums, including hers.

Maybe she should have insisted on meeting the guy before she posted bond. Phil was big on that, the eye-to-eye, said it had lots of intimidation value. Helped you with risk assessment, he said.

As if no one had ever skipped out on him.

Okay, she never met the guy. But she was damned well going to meet his furniture. She peeled her gloves off and stood in the center of the living room, ready to take a good look. Home furnishings could tell you a lot about a person.

There was more seating here than in a conference center. The conversation pit looked brand name, Henredon maybe. Plus a leather couch, and that wasn't cheap. Grace would have gone easier on the seating and plowed the money into building an addition. The house was puny, with just this big front room with a kitchen alcove and a joke of a little bedroom. Where would you stick a washer and dryer? Making guests comfortable didn't get your laundry done.

The subcompact range and sink were fairly clean, probably from disuse. Teeth gritted, Grace forced herself to peek into the fridge; no one home but a wine bottle, it turned out. The pantry held a few soup cans, lined up like tin soldiers. The guy hadn't knocked around in here to pack provisions.

The bedroom was where most of the grabbing and flinging had gone on. Grace sorted through some of the clothes spilling out of a bureau drawer. A button-down shirt with pink pinstripes. A button-down shirt with blue pinstripes—grown men wore baby colors these days. Caught on the closet doorknob were a pair of suspenders, which she would not have believed except that Ted wore them, too.

She felt around for empty ammo boxes. There weren't any. That didn't mean that Heywood wasn't carrying. Some people didn't know how to pack. They'd throw boxes into a valise instead of shaking out the cartridges and zipping them into a compartment or something to save space.

An end table in the living room held a telephone, one of those outer-space, push-button desk models that looked like a regular phone after a bulldozer had rolled over it.

Grace lifted it, hoping for a notepad with directions scrawled on it, some hint of where the fugitive had run so fast that he left his suspenders behind.

Nothing. Nothing on the envelopes lying on the coffee table either. Something caught her eye, a colorful illustration propped up on a mahogany bookcase. Grace picked it up. It was an old record album. Grace dimly remembered the singer pictured on the cover, some gal falling out of her push-up bra—what's-her-name who had been popular when Grace was in grade school. What would a young man want with this?

A look behind the cabinet doors showed her that this was no bookcase. She pulled a few records out. They were old, the kind of things people sold at yard sales in the summer. Well, someone had to buy them. Grace dealt a few of them out on the coffee table. Margaret Whiting, Helen Forester, some others in taffeta and crinolines. Very old-time music, what her parents used to listen to.

Personally, as far as oldies went, Grace sort of liked Roberta Linn, Lawrence Welk's Champagne Lady. She crawled along the area rug for a while, squinting at the printing on the album spines. Maybe she'd take something. Heywood definitely owed her.

She selected a Frank Sinatra for Phil, pulling out the record to inspect for scratches. An address sticker was glued to the center label: Arnie Kaplow, New York, NY. This was definitely from a yard sale, probably three for a quarter.

Enough of this. Grace gathered up the records that were fanned out on the coffee table and made room for them in the cabinet, pushing other records aside to form a gap.

A paper record sleeve had wedged itself into the rear. Neatening by reflex, Grace released her pile of albums and reached in to pull it out. Her fingers touched rough wood, the kind used to make crates.

She forgot the crumpled paper and removed another

foot or so of records. It was dark in the cabinet, but she could see that the back of the case was constructed of cheap material. Maybe mahogany wasn't as good as it used to be, but she doubted that.

She straightened up and circled the cabinet, noticing for the first time that it was twice as deep as the width of a record album. The rear was mahogany, all right. What she had seen before had to be a false back.

Meaning that something else was behind that cheap plywood barrier. Something Heywood didn't want people to know about. She eyeballed the luxurious dark wood that covered the cabinet's posterior in one solid slab. No hinges or sliding sections here.

For the third or fourth time today, Grace knelt. You're flirting with arthritis, she told herself. Beginning with gentle touches, she ended by pounding the rich, dark wood. One corner sprang out. She repeated the process and more corners loosened until the panel was ready for removal.

Maybe it's drugs in there, she thought. Maybe I should sell them and earn back the bond.

Or the compartment might hold some surplus ammo—nice stuff like shot-filled bullet jackets that rup-tured tissue upon penetration—or an extra carbine or two that was left behind in the rush. The bastard could be tooling around town with an arsenal in his car trunk.

She lowered the panel to the floor. More records.

What kind of screwball hid some of his records in a secret compartment? Maybe these were the *real* old ones, from the dinosaur age or something.

There were almost as many here as behind the glass cabinets, but not quite. To Grace's right was a one-foot gap, piled with dog-eared manila envelopes and loose papers. She sifted through. Old electric bills. A notebook lined for music composition, half of it filled with nota-tions.

The porn magazines nearly made her clap the panel back on, but then she noticed a photo underneath, an eight-by-ten glossy of a man, a professional shot. His long, dark hair was parted in the middle, a very bad choice for someone with such a long nose. The wise-guy face stared right into the camera, with the mouth wide open in argument position.

This guy wasn't arguing with the photographer to put down the camera, though. You could tell he liked posing, from the way he rotated his groin out. Most of it was covered with a guitar, thank God. The kind with wires.

The outfit was very tight patterned pants (looking like they'd disregarded a Wet Paint sign) topped with a vest made out of strips of leather in a loose basket weave. Grace clucked her tongue. A flabby body like that should not be flaunted. No one had to tell *her* not to wear stretch pants.

Unbelievably, there was something like a furry animal puppet on this young man's arm. And Grace had always thought puppets were wholesome.

Signed over this object of art were the words, "To Scotty, who beamed us up. They had to see us to believe us. Thanks for making it happen." The signature read, "Panzer."

Who was Scotty? Losing interest, Grace did a quick flip of the records. These were new, rock and roll, the kind Ted used to drive Phil and her into the poorhouse for. Maybe she'd pick up a few for him. But he was very picky about the ones he liked, and these days he didn't buy records anymore. He and Barbara had that thing with the laser beam.

Grace threw everything back into the compartment. It took some fiddling to replace the panel. For the life of her, she couldn't figure out why Heywood bothered.

Of course, you couldn't get rock and roll at yard sales, not the new ones. Even at K mart, these records cost plenty. Heywood probably wanted to hide the expensive goods. Maybe the tree huggers who lived out here believed in burglars after all.

The Sinatra album tucked under her arm, Grace pulled her gloves back on. She took a last weary look around. He was gone without a trace.

Her eyes lingered for a moment on the leather couch. It was worth a bundle, but no thirty thousand. And that's what the bond forfeiture would be.

Clutching Old Blue Eyes, Grace started down the stairs. It was still snowing, she saw. Just a little, like that presifted flour. Wondra. She began to slip and grabbed for the railing with her free hand.

That's when she noticed that someone else had driven up the dirt road, someone who didn't want to be seen by her. He was standing by his car, looking up at her. She swore, dropping the record and fumbling for the gun in her bag before she had even regained her balance. All that special-defense training at the range, and not word one about what to do under icy conditions.

It wasn't Heywood down there, she sensed that somehow. Maybe from the shoulder-length strands of stringy hair that had escaped from the ski hat he wore. Long, greasy hair wouldn't be Darcy's style. For another thing, there were Connecticut plates on the car he was hopping back into. She watched him pull away, and it didn't really matter. Most likely it was some drug freak looking for a sale, or for some conversation in the conversation pit.

It wasn't Heywood, because it wasn't going to be that easy. Heywood was gone, and she had no clue where to.

The guy who'd left in the Connecticut car reminded her of the guitar player in the picture, but she knew that was only because she was grasping for straws. Still, it was enough to make her turn back up the stairs and start pounding on the panel again.

Ten minutes later she was gripping the railing once

more, this time holding the photo, utility bills, and music composition notebook as well as the Sinatra record.

They probably wouldn't be much help. But she was remembering something now, had remembered it as she crawled along the record cabinet for the second time. She really didn't need any help. There was a logical, legal procedure for getting this under control.

Dusting the snow from her hair, she climbed into her car, cool as a cuke, reaching for the map book again. This whole thing couldn't have happened at a better time: she had blocked out the morning for a cut and a dye. In the afternoon there were a couple of odds and ends at Superior Court. Next stop after that would be Darcy's place. Grace would catch her coming home from work, back to the condo that she might as well kiss goodbye.

Sure it was a big bond, but there was a co-signer.

No use telling Phil about it until all the details were worked out. He didn't need the aggravation.

There was one thing Grace needed, though. A tweezer. The splinters on that railing were murder.

Eight

No wooden railings in Westside Mews, a Condominium Community. Here there were elevators. Grace was sharing one with the manager. Maybe he saw through her, maybe not. He was not the talkative sort.

You could tell that this place was for young people by the way the elevator closed. Zip, zap, hardly a chance to get your body through. "This way," said the manager, proving he could talk. He was young, too, like the couple with the skinny dogs that Grace saw in the hall, like the guys who entered the elevator and hammered on the "Solarium" button.

The manager was opening a door with his key when she caught up.

"This one," he said.

"Nice place," said Grace, looking in. "Just like my niece always told me. Long distance."

She was proud of herself; she made that one up in the elevator.

The manager flipped the light switch on. "Yeah," he said. "Now you can see it."

He went away, and Grace hung her coat up in the

closet. Good old Grace. Aunt Grace. Just got in from the airport to visit her sister's child, Darcy. Couldn't the manager let her in to rest her weary old bones? Her taxi was gone already, and the phlebitis was killing her.

She went into the bedroom, hardly glancing at the black lacquer furniture. If there was a mirror over the bed, she didn't want to see it. She was here for the walk-in closet.

A lot of shoes had walked in. About a hundred different pairs, she'd say, from a quick count of the ones on the rack and the ones still in their boxes. That didn't surprise Grace a bit. She had expected two hundred.

No sign of a man here, though. Not here and not in the bathroom. No pants, no ties, no razors, no big tan chunks of soap-on-a-rope. Walk-in closets were here galore, but not a live-in boyfriend.

Getting that squared away was the main thing. But Grace figured she'd stay awhile. She wanted this business with the condo cleared up tonight, so she could face Phil over the frozen manicotti. (Put it in the toaster oven, she'd told him. No need to heat up the whole oven.) Grace didn't want to wait till tomorrow to start the phone calls. One "Ms. Kohler is in a meeting" and she'd just about burst a blood vessel.

Following her plan, she flicked all the lights off. That reminded her. Too bad she'd passed that comment to the manager at the doorway. He'd swallowed the Auntie Grace thing up to that point. Sort of. An attaché case didn't really look like luggage.

But Grace knew about these kinds of places—and she knew even more after her walking tour, through the kitchen with all those tools hanging down, and over the living room's pastel rug that shouted "weekly cleaning woman." The manager wasn't going to call the cops. That would be too nasty (and he didn't know the half of it). He would only call Darcy.

When the key scratched in the door, Grace knew she was right. It was a lot of scratching. The hand on that key was nervous.

So was the voice. "Who's there? Who's in my house?" The hall lights went on.

"You call this a house?" Actually, that wasn't what Grace had planned to yell out, but what the heck. She sat tight in the dark. Come and get me.

"It's Mrs. Stark, right?" The high heels were clacking toward a door. Wrong guess—Grace wasn't one to sit in strange bedrooms. From the kitchen, where she was seated at a butcher-block table, she watched Darcy across the lighted hall. Grace saw her from the back, hestitating, afraid to walk in and turn on a lamp. That's the price you pay for indirect lighting.

Okay. It was the right moment. Grace got up and tiptoed over. "Not in a million years could I scoot under that bed," she said, inches away from Darcy's behind. "I was a very big failure at the Spa Lady."

Still on her knees, Darcy jerked her head around. She came up dusting. One thing about fur coats. You can't go rolling around in them.

"Are you crazy?" she asked, in a voice that sounded like she was. "Don't think I didn't know it was you. I knew it was you. The manager told me. What are you, weird? Hiding in the dark like that? I ought to have you arrested."

"Arrested, hah. You, young lady, are talking to the Law."

Making coffee around here was a whole production, it seemed. But during the grinding and the dripping and the filtering, Grace learned one or two things. Darcy knew that Heywood had skipped. The lawyer had told her. And she spat when she said it. Maybe she really didn't know where he was.

"Funny how you didn't come to court yourself this

morning," Grace commented, watching her. "The way he's your boyfriend. And the way you co-signed the bond."

Another funny thing was how this Darcy was holding herself very stiff. Grace noticed that, even under that baggy dress she was wearing, like from the days of that "No Chemise, Please" song. Darcy was holding her torso up straight and wouldn't sit down with her coffee cup. Maybe it had something to do with drugs.

"I was very busy at work," she told Grace. "I have a very pressured job."

"Looks like it pays off," Grace couldn't resist saying. Julia Child could film a show in this kitchen, no problem. Pots, pans, spoons, and things she didn't know the name of hung from a curled iron thing on the ceiling. How you could keep them clean in the open air like this was beyond Grace. Ted and Barbara were the same way. Somewhere along the line, cabinets got a bad name.

"Which brings me to the matter at hand." Grace put her cup down. She'd had enough anyway: two sips of this stuff, and your heart was flying. "I don't know if you knew that your boyfriend was going to take off. That's your business. I don't know if you know where he is right now. That's your business, too."

She reached under her chair for the attaché case. "But I promised the court I'd deliver your boyfriend, and he didn't show. And you were in on the promise. So you now owe me one condo." There it was, right on top of the other papers. The bond that Darcy had co-signed. Grace smoothed the creases out. Show and tell.

Darcy didn't say anything, but she looked damned uncomfortable. She just kept standing in that awkward way. Maybe she'd made a dumb mistake and worn a loose dress over a tight girdle.

In war movies, you never showed sympathy for the

enemy. But this wasn't really a war movie. "Sit," said Grace. "You look awful."

"I'll be okay. I've got this burn. On my stomach."

"Would an aspirin help?"

"It's okay. I've been to the doctor. I've got things for it."

Grace thought to herself: I bet she does.

The wall clock ticked. Grace glanced over at it. To her, it was ugly, big and plain, like something you'd have in a factory. A lot of things around here were like that, she noticed. Including a big disgusting wastebasket with a swing door on top. Like the ones in a public park.

Grace didn't know what to say about the burn. She'd never been very good with sickness. So she talked about the condo instead, telling Darcy that she'd take immediate action.

"I feel for you," she said, gathering her papers together and getting up. "It's your home, after all. Your ex-home. Rules are rules, and your boyfriend jumped. Do you mind if I get my coat? I hung it up in your front-hall closet."

"Wait right here," said Darcy. She disappeared into the bedroom and came out with some papers of her own. Something told Grace she'd better sit down again.

The condo was signed over to someone else. Anne Marie someone. A cousin.

Grace cleared her throat. "You did this a week ago. After you co-signed. The court's not going to stand for this. No way."

"I think it is," said Darcy. "That's what my lawyer said. And I have a very expensive lawyer."

Grace sat at the stupid butcher-block table—you couldn't wipe it up nicely like you could Formica—feeling hatred. So, this Darcy had a pressured job. Then how come she had every hair in place, swept up under those crazy clips that you should only wear in bed? How come she didn't have gray roots showing, like Grace did? Maybe because she didn't miss her beauty appointment to climb rickety stairs and sneak into condos looking for someone's drug-pushing, gangster boyfriend.

"I'll go after your bank accounts," Grace said, wishing she was still standing up. "The ones you need a private banker for."

"They've all been transferred into other names."

"It's a very simple thing to garnishee someone's wages."

"Try it. You'll find that there's no employee named Darcy Kohler at my job. There's just a new company— brand new, in fact—that consults with my boss on a contractual basis."

Grace looked into those odd-colored eyes. Darcy no longer reminded her of Liz, or of any other woman she admired. What kind of person said things like "on a contractual basis"?

It wasn't a beautiful face, Grace decided. What a waste of Ivory Soap skin. Lipstick was nice, but Darcy wore too much of it. Like her lips were wearing clothes. She wasn't someone waiting to be kissed. And she was young, so she should be.

"How the hell did you burn your stomach?" Grace was going to go ahead and be rude. She wanted to bring this girl down from Mars to her level. It was scary the way Darcy was, like someone in a silver space suit.

"Ironing," Darcy answered. "I was in this big hurry, and it happened. A second-degree burn."

"You must have been ironing nude, then."

"That's right." The clothed lips smiled. "You know what? You're the only person who had the guts to say that. Even the doctor didn't."

That made Grace feel all right. And she thought of a bit of advice, which made her feel even better. "You should never iron nude," she said, the voice of wisdom.

Herself, she never would have dreamed of it.

* * *

It couldn't have been better timing, Darcy told herself while she waited for the transquilizers to work. They were sure taking their time; the satin sheets were annoying her—she felt the need to get a good grip on herself instead of all this sliding around. Now that Heywood was gone, she didn't need these sheets anyway. They'd been his idea during the early, erotic period of the relationship. Way back when.

What period were they in now? Maybe the paperwork period, thought Darcy, who had taken the afternoon off to see her broker and her lawyer, in that order. The right order, as it turned out. Because the broker gave her a reason to think about leaving town, and the lawyer made that seem sensible. It wasn't, of course. Sense had nothing to do with it.

Maybe that woman was here in the condo somewhere, hiding in the dark like she did last night. But Darcy didn't think so, nor did it matter particularly. What the hell, they'd be seeing plenty of each other, so why not start now? And if she were here, chances were she'd be poking around in the living room, guessing the cost of everything, the way she did. They ought to put her on "The Price Is Right."

She was sharp though, that's what Darcy's lawyer said. Not that it took a genius to call Darcy's bluff. Signing the condo over to Anne Marie just delayed things; the bondswoman could get it in the end. Her cronies down at court had told her, of course. The messages from her piled up all morning. Darcy returned one of them, to set the travel plans.

They were going to go find Heywood. "Team up," as the bondswoman put it. She'd agreed to it, of course. She didn't want to go through a long process, putting liens on property and all that. And Darcy didn't want to lose the condo. If the woman was surprised, she didn't sound it, but then again that wasn't her style. She always seemed to be chewing gum, even when she wasn't. Kind of sluttish, actually, in spite of those elastic-waisted dresses and medium-height pumps. The type of middle-aged broad who invited the milkman in.

What did she say she and Darcy would be? Skip-tracers, fugitive investigators. "We'll get him," she said more than once, along with something about guns. None of it seemed to have much to do with Heywood.

The tranqs were working. Darcy didn't feel like she was sliding anymore. The satin sheets felt nice, in fact. On the road with Grace. She seemed pretty broke. Would they have to share hotel rooms?

Securities and Exchange Commission. The words worked like an alarm clock. The broker had gotten an inquiry from some S.E.C. men. Just hints so far, but Darcy better take them. Their computer was flagging an irregular trading pattern—an anomaly, they called it. Some heavy buying of shares right before public disclosure of previously unannounced events, the kind that sent prices soaring. If they asked again, the broker would give them Darcy's name. It's a federal crime, he said, suddenly talking to his wall calendar.

Time to take the first stagecoach out. If the S.E.C. wanted her, they'd get her, but it would be cleaner this way. Less embarrassing for the firm if she didn't work there anymore, and easier to find another job later. It was time to go anyway. That look her boss had given her when she asked to be placed on consulting status. . . .

They'd be sorry, though. Who but Darcy could convince a fresh-faced new M.B.A. to throw on a backpack and get an internship at the U.N.? It was the only way to find out about VCR penetration in Benelux. Nobody performed like Darcy. No one else could persuade contacts in ten key markets to line up Santa Claus jobs. And they wondered why the Garrison Group was always first to know what electronic toys were hot. It wasn't easy. Some of those Santas had to sing.

Grace Stark could bring the guns. Darcy would bring the brains.

Nine

I can't eat that stuff. What makes you think I can eat that stuff? Who the hell do you think I am?"

Grace just kept plugging away, tearing aluminum foil and pulling on rubber bands. It was getting to be like an assembly line job. The thaw-and-reheat instructions, that was the part where you used your mind. Otherwise it was strictly brute force: foil for turkey and meat, Tupperware for casseroles. Attach directions with elastics.

"Frozen food!" Over the past few weeks Phil had developed it into a wail. "I wasn't brought up to this. It's going to ruin my stomach permanently."

Grace was on rubber bands. She gave the one in her fingers an extra little twang. "Like I told you, just say the word. I'll have it all down the disposal in a minute. Maybe I should just freeze you up a couple hundred rolls of Tums. It would be a lot easier, believe me."

"Accch," he said, stomping out of the kitchen. The voice of indigestion.

Today's batch wasn't too bad. Just a matter of freezing the Thanksgiving leftovers that had been in the fridge for a week. No cooking today, except for a little gravy so Phil could moisten the stuffing. If he could be bothered.

The doorbell rang. Maybe it was Darcy. An hour and a half early? Sure, why not. She didn't have a husband to cook for. A single girl, that was the life. Just throw a couple of little dresses and pearls into your suitcase, and off you go. Ready to chase your fugitive boyfriend whose car was found two weeks ago outside a Connecticut motel. The state cops there and in Massachusetts claimed they were hot on the trail.

If they got any hotter, somebody would be out thirty grand or the condo equivalent thereof. Whether Heywood skipped for good or the cops brought him in, it all added up to the same thing: a bond forfeit. Grace had written the bond. She was supposed to deliver the goods.

But the state cops were just mouthing off for the media. They probably didn't have a clue. Grace didn't put much faith in cops. That was the one good point about this surprise trip—the reason why Phil complained, but not at top volume. Going after Heywood would cost a mint in expenses and lost bond business. But it would get Grace away from the Huddersfield P.D. and the slow burn the cops were still doing over the end of the Isaccs kickbacks. They weren't bluffing; the Barkan murder had proved that.

It was Ted at the door, alone. Barbara was boycotting again. She had boycotted cooking Thanksgiving dinner, too, so Grace had had that on top of everything else. Barbara wanted to pick up the tab for a restaurant meal downtown. No thanks. That wasn't American.

"Ready to go bounty hunting?" said Ted, kissing his mother.

"You bet. I'm bounty payer and bounty payee rolled into one." Grace wiped her hands on her apron. "You're talking to a lady who's got more powers than the police. I can threaten and pistol-whip. Hold him at gunpoint without reading him his rights."

"More power to you, Mom." Ted kissed her again, this time slipping two hundred-dollar bills into her hand. "Use them in good health," he said.

They had a good time at the kitchen table, Grace with her coffee and Ted with his tea. The subject was packing. Ted marveled at his mother, recalling the hundreds of items she used to jam into his camp duffel bag.

There was one thing she hadn't been able to pack neatly for this trip: her brand-new bulletproof raincoat. She'd have to lay it in the backseat of Darcy's car, next to the identical one belonging to Darcy.

The BMW pulled up right on time. Ted had stayed to get a glimpse of Darcy. Even Phil emerged from his lair to get a look-see.

"What's these growths she's got here?" he whispered to Ted, pointing to the side of his head. The women were settling whose garment bag should hang where.

"Ear cuffs," Ted answered.

Red wool cape, stockings with Oriental letters on them, huge brocade purse. Darcy was all set for a few weeks of fugitive tracing. She made a face as she placed Grace's raincoat on top of hers. "For the price I paid for these, you'd think they'd come in a few different styles. We'll look like a mother-daughter act."

That thought did not appeal to Grace. Darcy, in her opinion, could not have a normal mother. As for the crack about the price tag, did she think guns grew on trees?

"How gauche," said Grace, patting her hair and wondering if she'd pronounced it right. "We'll have to be careful to wear them on different days. But what happens if we get invites to the same shootout?"

Phil roused himself at the last minute, tapping the window on Grace's side.

"You remember all the ammo?" he asked.

Darcy, who already had the key in the ignition, peered around Grace's side wave. "Heywood is *not* armed and dangerous," she told Phil. "I *know* him."

"Yeah? Well, young lady, I'm sure he's got some very nice friends. Just keep your raincoat on. You never know when to expect a shower."

The car revolved on the driveway apron and descended into the street.

"Quite a turning radius," observed Ted, who had bought an Audi the year before and was beginning to regret it.

"Is that all you can say?" said Phil. "And to think, they pay you to talk."

Ted had to run. He and Barbara would be calling and looking in, he promised. He left with a smile and a shoulder clap. With Ted there were never any hard feelings.

But for Phil it was hard. He tramped back to the kitchen, to the coffeepot she'd left filled and warm for him. A year ago—less—he would have looked forward to this. A time to renew things with some female friends. Now look at him. A person who had to pinch every penny couldn't go to the tanning parlor. He was becoming a joke, noticing for the first time all the morning newspaper cartoons about insurance salesmen.

That's what he was now. A salesman, not a trainee anymore. There was a limit to Marty's patience, and no limits to his rudeness. He wasn't beyond threatening a cousin with the old heave-ho. Already Phil was making night calls in the boonies, traveling down those roads that were only little blue lines on a map. Like new varicose veins.

He still couldn't get himself to go to the cleaners. Grace did it for him. Phil looked around the kitchen, at the mysterious geranium plant (didn't he see her soaking it sometimes, in the bathtub?), at the yellow and green cleaning liquids in their plastic bottles behind the sink. Wasn't there some rule about never mixing them together?

He was going to stink and rot here, thawing and reheating.

They took I-91 to I-95, to the city, then the G.W. bridge. They were bound for New Jersey, where somebody Darcy knew thought he'd seen Heywood. Not a positive I.D., though. It was a four-hour drive, more if you hit bad New York traffic, but Darcy said she could do it in three. Grace said don't bother.

The BMW ran noiselessly, giving Grace the creeps, the way you couldn't feel it moving. By New Haven, she was asleep, tuckered out from the Family Disputes and Disorderly Conducts of recent weeks. She'd collected as many bonds as she could. A former clerk, a court hanger-on, would take over—for a price—checking on the no-shows. Usually they trotted down to court if you gave them a buzz. Most of your no-shows weren't conniving types like this skipper Heywood, with the girlfriend. By New Haven, Grace was really asleep. Even before that she'd been faking it.

She'd been getting mad, too, thinking of how she'd have to miss mah-jongg on Tuesday nights. In general, she'd only do that for an out-of-town funeral.

They pulled into the New Jersey motel at five o'clock. The room was big enough and clean enough, but there you had it: two double beds. Sharing a room with a stranger. Grace never thought she would sink so low.

"I undress in the bathroom," she announced, standing up straight so she'd be heard. Only fifteen minutes after check-in, and Darcy was already in her bra and panties, prancing around. This was going to be embarrassing.

"Well, I don't." Darcy sat herself down at the vanity. Her and her hundred-pound bag of cosmetics, making themselves at home. Nothing like asking if someone else would like to use the mirror.

Grace unsnapped her suitcase. Bathrobe, slippers, shower cap, and she was headed for the john. She snuck a look at Darcy first. Nice shape—small-boned but with just enough chest (not that Grace could ever wear one of those seamless bras). The narrow hips might be murder for childbirth, if that was on Darcy's busy schedule. Did the burn leave scars on the stomach? Maybe. You couldn't see them from here.

In the mirror, Darcy caught her eye.

Great, thought Grace, making for the shower. Now she'll think I'm queer.

Great, thought Darcy, getting up to answer the room telephone. Now I've got no time to get clean. She liked to set her makeup with some nice hot steam. From the sound of what was going on in the bathroom, there wouldn't be any left anyway. Was the woman trying to scald her skin off? Low-lifes were always like that, Darcy had noticed. Wild about showers.

It was Dave on the phone, all right. Her now-former colleague. Down in the lobby already, in the motel he had picked out for her. Right off the highway in Crenshaw, a lot nicer than Amarak, he said, but very convenient to it. As if she were touring New Jersey on an autumn excursion. Leaf-peeping, they called it in Massachusetts, where there were trees.

She broke a nail pulling the batwing blouse out of the garment bag. Where was the hip scarf for the purple mini? Under the belts, looking a little wrinkled. The granny slippers were okay, though. Not as smashed as she had expected. They looked a lot like the ones Grace was holding when she shuffled into the can. Well, thought Darcy. I like them anyway.

The sound of water running gave her an urge, but she didn't suppose Grace would ask her in for a pee. Probably a confirmed door-locker. So was Dave, Darcy remembered. Something to look forward to.

Her cape was over her shoulders and her hand was on the doorknob when she decided to be nice. She opened some drawers expecting to find hotel stationery. After a moment's hestitation, she crossed to the vanity and uncapped a lipstick. "Bye," she scrawled, with a smeary red tail on the "e." If the bitch liked staring at mirrors, that would give her something to read.

Dave was in the lobby, jingling keys, conscientiously casual in neatly pressed jeans. Who ironed them now that his wife was gone, Darcy wondered. But he was the one who'd left, he said as he drove toward A Nice Place for Dinner. He had a studio apartment now, the rents were unbelievable, there wasn't enough room for the kids when they visited. The divorce would be final in January. Then he'd get something better and maybe be in shape to enjoy it. The thing had to happen, but it had been hell. It really had.

No sooner had he and Darcy settled into the exposed brick and seventies rock music of the Whittier Winery than out came the snapshots. Two boys, nine and five, just like business hours. They were nice-looking enough; the older one had his father's deep-set eyes. It was the divorced man's spread-the-guilt ritual, a signal sent to Darcy so that she'd know what sacred ground she was treading on. Later, he would want to take her to bed, ambivalence in every caress. Slide in the crack and break your children's back.

Darcy complimented and cooed. They ordered drinks, and she got down to business.

"What exactly was the problem with doing an I.D. on Cahill's representative? The guy you saw didn't fit the specs I gave you? I had it all spelled out down to the cleft chin."

"You said five pounds overweight. The one I saw is chubbier," said Dave. Darcy sipped her Bloody Mary, relieved. That would be Heywood, putting on pounds out of nervousness. He was a real oral guy, she thought, crossing her legs with a pleasant feeling. Not like Dave, who was thin enough, yet had ordered a light supper. "Divorce melancholia," he'd explained, asking for Salade Niçoise. It had shocked her slightly. She'd thought dishes like that were for women only, like the understood distinctions in the want ads: Gal Friday, M/F, must type 65, an equal opportunity employer.

The drink made it easier. Oh what a tangled web Darcy had woven. Dave was in her debt because of the TallStory incident. In the end, he had counted the shipments, the good foot soldier in a major Garrison Group coup. He was glad, he told her afterward, that she had twisted his arm. He would get a bonus and a good report.

Now Dave had to swallow another TallStory, one of Darcy's making. She had sent him to spot Heywood in an Amarak after-hours club. He was there, of course. Darcy knew all about it, had been there once. Dealing in Manhattan wasn't his speed; he wasn't about to hang out on street corners in Washington Heights, and he had no in with the big city club and party scenes.

But there was a good market for his type of operation in suburban New Jersey. The bridge-and-tunnel crowd, as New Yorkers called them, were getting tired of crossing those bridges and tunnels on the weekends.

Heywood had also been eyeing Rockland County. He might have opened shop there. It was in the southern portion of New York State, a short hop from Jersey. Darcy might have to look there, too; she hoped not. Here, she had a contact: Dave, who owed her a freshly minted debt. Not a drug user, it had cost him plenty to go to those clubs. In his shape, he didn't need any mood changers. He wasn't in the mood.

"But you liked it all right, didn't you? The coke?"

"It was okay. Actually, I felt very excited, but I knew it was fraudulent. I found the whole thing upsetting." The salad arrived, and he complained about too much dressing.

The good soldier Dave had followed her directions, even though he hadn't like them. No, he couldn't merely go to the club and "soak up information." He had to show up with cash and ask about buying. If he didn't want to buy, he wouldn't meet the dealer. And he had to meet the dealer, an emissary of Roy Cahill—the Cahill who headed up a very large, very important computer company—sent down here for secret merger talks with SynthIntellect.

"This will be the biggest thing we've ever done," said Darcy, sawing away at her steak.

"Why a dealer? Why didn't they just send some guy to go to parties? I mean, isn't this more illegal than it has to be?"

Darcy drank some wine. "Because a dealer has the perfect excuse to mingle with all the top people at SynthIntellect. Everybody from the whole high-tech strip down here goes to those parties. We're not the only ones listening in, right?"

"I don't know. I don't think too many people at that club were fully conscious."

"Come on. Remember how Track-It Associates scooped us on the Pulsor? There's always someone watching. And if they see this guy, this right-hand man of Cahill's, hobnobbing with SynthIntellect execs, they'll know what's cooking. They probably suspected you, but they wouldn't suspect him. He's got a role. He's a dealer." She took another swig of wine. She was making it up as she went along.

"I'll take it from here," she said. "You did a great job of spotting, but I can handle the eavesdropping. I don't mind making that scene."

"Didn't you use to do a bit too much of that?" asked Dave, the father. "I thought I remembered you saying you got into financial trouble for a while there."

True, but a little stock trading based on inside information had fixed that. Too bad it was a federal crime.

The check came. Darcy was all set to jump for it when Dave whipped out his credit card. The business one, she saw, her heart sinking. "The Garrison Group should be happy we didn't eat in New York," he said. "Wait till they get my expense report with cocaine costs on it. I bet that'll be a first for them."

"Don't do that!" Diners at the next table turned around. Darcy lowered her voice to a taut whisper. "I'll pay you in cash before I leave. You can't leave something like that on the record." And what about this dinner he was expensing? "To consult with D. Kohler," who is no longer employed at Garrison. He'd find out sooner or later anyhow. As soon as she left New Jersey, he'd start those weekly calls to her at the home office. He was going to hate her.

But now his breath was close to her hair as he helped her on with her coat, suggesting they go back to his place in a voice that made no assumptions. His neediness appealed to her; they held hands across the stick shift. Once in his apartment, he seemed more at ease, offering her liqueur and piling logs in the fireplace. A homebody, Darcy thought. She saw toys in a corner, not quite put away.

The first kisses were gentle but tentative. Most of the fire was happening behind the grate. Darcy ran her hands over Dave's sides, his chest, the hard plane of belly over his belt that she kept buckled, since he showed no interest in her buttons. Here was a guy who took care of himself, she thought, trying to savor it, angry at Heywood's flab. Why did she bother with him, she thought. The only cokehead in the universe who sends as much down his mouth as his nose. He claimed it had something to do with singing.

And that music! A relfex made her cringe as Dave got up to change the tape. She was expecting strange, moody melodies, nasal singing and blaring trumpets. Instead it was pleasant—Dave was playing upbeat songs she knew from her car radio. Here and there, she could even name the group. Heywood's records had always defied her, their rigid white-and-pastel covers seeming almost aggressive. Darcy was unsure about music, buying for herself strictly by the Top 20 lists she saw posted in stores. Except for the Betty Carter records (those were hot, she knew, since the singer was always mentioned in magazines), Heywood's taste eluded her.

"Shall we move over to the bed?" Dave asked. Shall. She wondered how long he'd been putting that sentence together. There was entirely too much thinking going on here.

The bed was just a few steps away, behind a rattan partition. Once there, he was suddenly avid, tearing at her blouse. A place for everything, she supposed. Her place, he apparently thought, was under his hastily opened zipper. She held his sides, still in their Oxford shirt, loving it. Dave, her colleague. It was like sneaking it in at work.

Grace snapped the switch on the headboard lamps, still thinking about what she'd seen on the eleven o'clock news. They showed a business report on the station down here, with a big yellow dollar sign on a blue background that came flying out at you. Then the guy on the tube started yakking. That wasn't the part that Grace was going to think about all night. She was going to think about the dollar sign.

Towels like tissues, carpets like you'd play miniature golf on, and they were charging forty-four a night for this place. Halfie-halfie, of course—though it took some doing to get Miss Silk-and-Mink to agree on sharing a room—but it still added up. Spending without earning could be very tricky, and worse if a bankruptcy court snatched your husband's credit cards. Ted was helping out, but only in a limited way. Barbara didn't like it. Dangerous, she said, wrinkling her nose up to those crazy eyeglass frames she wore, the ones that looked as if she had them on upside-down. Terrible, she said. Guns.

The Smith was in the Samsonite, unloaded. There was nothing to point it at yet, and Miss Gold-Chains-and-Velvet didn't like looking at it either. A bunch of lily livers, these career women. Though they didn't mind sticking it to your bankbook.

Were there footsteps outside the door? Grace grabbed for the light switch, pulling herself up to sitting position. The cable TV listings were still on the night table. She reached for them, posing. "I was just seeing if anything was on," she'd say. No one would catch her tucked in early, like some old lady.

The noise moved down the hall. Grace hit the lights. For a moment, points of light formed before her eyes, like the dust motes falling in her house in Huddersfield. She imagined them softly covering Phil as he sat at the kitchen table.

Grace tossed from her right side to her left, wishing she could clean long-distance. She'd take some nice strong ammonia to her kitchen floor, like the bottle she'd found in a service closet out in the hall. Industrial strength. It had sure done a job on that filthy lipstick on that goddamn mirror.

Ten

Breakfast with Dave was in a restored brownstone in Amarak's booming downtown. The
management had knocked down walls and added windows. How nice, everyone said, when the restaurant first
opened, its hardwood floors gleaming in a sunny, cav-
ernous expanse. How *Victorian.*

Darcy held Dave's hand as they waited to be seated.
Nine o'clock on a Friday, and there was a line. She rubbed
his fingers against her face briefly, noting that her smell
was still on them. Two people in a shower don't really do
a thorough job of washing. He'd been conversational in
the morning, if a little brisk—it was a workday. She still
suspected he'd own a rowing machine if there were room
for one. One man she knew had left her to read the
newspaper while he climbed aboard his, grunting and
flapping over metal and springs with a zest she hadn't seen
the night before.

The waitress led them to a table covered in a tropical
print. The early December sun struggled in through the
window behind them, trying hard to fit in with the motif.
They ordered elaborate omelettes and Mimosas, because
you always did in these places. The menus were enor-

mous, shielding diners from one another when opened, like dressing screens. The prices were jumbo sized, too, Darcy noticed. She'd have to be quick on the draw with her VISA card.

A glance around told her that this was an expense-account mill, a place for "power breakfasts" before people hit the nearby office buildings. People were grouped in threesomes and fivesomes, with briefcases bristling around their feet.

Dave, too, was in a commercial frame of mind. His fork moved through the eggs like a fork with a motive. They were expecting him at the Garrison telesurvey office where he administered one of the tracking studies, his job between spy stints. Twelve hundred randomly selected American households, contacted once a week. Hello, do you own a VCR? Can you tell me what brand, where you bought it, what you paid for it? Who in your family made the decision to buy it?

To Dave's credit, he didn't talk shop with Darcy. Instead, he made arrangements to drop by her motel. He was going to be her escort to the after-hours club. Nice gesture, and a useful one. It would be very conspicuous if she went alone. But what if Heywood was there and greeted her? They were supposed to be total strangers. Weren't they?

She was going to have to talk shop.

"Did I ever mention to you that I know Cahill's rep?" She paused for a moment, and added, "Sort of."

"No," said Dave, knocking back a coffee. From Venezuela or Veracruz, whatever it was they'd settled on from the exhaustive list.

"Well, I do. Slightly. I ran across him on another investigation a while back."

"I'm surprised they put you on this, then. When he sees you won't that blow the whole thing?" Dave sent his

Mimosa where the coffee had gone. Would they mix down there, like a Kahlua drink?

"Yes. No, rather. I didn't tell them, actually. It's a terrific assignment. I wouldn't want to pass it up." She was floundering now. A drowning woman. "Anyway, once I see him, it's confirmed. That's all we need, basically. What would he be doing down here except talking mergers?"

"Making money from coke, maybe. Don't those guys mark it up about a thousand percent?"

"Be serious. He doesn't need it. He's Cahill's right-hand man."

Dave was waving for the check. "Well, you'll be able to make the positive I.D. I'm still not sure it was the guy."

She was. It was the guy she wanted to see.

She beat him to the plastic, and they relaxed for a minute. He told her he liked her lips, her earrings. The loopholes in her story were plastered up with a mixture of cologne and Lancôme. He dropped the talk about business, and she thought that was sweet of him.

He couldn't do very much tomorrow. "The kids are coming." Oh, *that* business. But a neighbor, another parent, would be taking them to a Muppets movie in the late afternoon. Dave had been planning to join them, but now he wanted to slip out and see Darcy. "A motel quickie," he said, sitting across from Darcy in his Brooks Brothers suit, trying for sleaze.

How incredibly endearing. Missing the Muppets movie for her. Now why was she looking for Heywood? Oh, yes. Her home was at stake.

So he'd be at her motel tomorrow. At 4 P.M. sharp, one dyed-blond bondswoman would have to do a vanishing act. Garrison Group analysts did not bring their aunts along on business trips.

* * *

Grace was placing the receiver in its cradle when Darcy came in. "Why are you using that phone?" she shrieked, pulling the door closed behind her. This was going to be a very private conversation. "Didn't I ask you not to?"

"Not even to call my husband?" said Grace. "Am I the Prisoner of Zenda?" She had watched that movie once with Ted, when he was a kid and it was on the "Walt Disney Hour." A very enjoyable program, as she remembered.

"Oh, no, of course," said Darcy, shedding her cape and feeling a little silly. "Outgoing calls are fine. Incoming is different. The guy I told you about, the one who may have seen Heywood, thinks I'm alone here on business. I just left him, but he could have been calling from the house phone or something. You could have blown the whole thing."

"That, as a matter of fact, was incoming," said Grace, walking over to the dresser to see if the heat-indicating dot on her hot rollers was black yet. Darcy *would* have to come back when she was all plugged in, an immersion coil in her collapsible cup and the curlers trying to heat up.

"In that case, why did you answer it?" Darcy was straining for the friendly touch.

"Could be something that concerned me. Like maybe a hotel fire." One might start right here in the room, if this girl didn't leave her alone. Grace walked back to the cup. Just bubbles so far. These coils were not approved by the Underwriters Laboratories, someone once told her. Yet they were on sale at every drugstore. It went to show that the law is what you make it.

"Actually," said Grace, jiggling the connection, "it was a call for either of us. From your boyfriend's lawyer. He had some mail from him. Postmarked Chicago."

"It came today?"

"No, yesterday. But he couldn't reach us because we weren't here yet. So he called bright and early today. Some

110

people work very hard for a living." Grace wasn't sure why she had thrown in that last crack. This was work for her, too. Even for Darcy, she guessed. "Heywood writes that he has not really jumped bail. That's his opinion. He is only biding his time until Judge Ritenauer, the soft one, comes back. He told his lawyer not to worry."

"Is that all?"

Grace shrugged. "Maybe he sent hugs and kisses. From Chicago. While here we are in New Jersey. I honestly don't remember. Personally, I've got a black dot on my rollers and some coffee going, so I've got to get busy. You got questions, go ahead and call the lawyer. And I don't know how good your spotter down here is, unless maybe he has X-ray vision and sees all the way to Chicago."

She stuck a spoon into a zip-lock bag and dug out a teaspoon of instant.

Darcy paced the room. A Chicago postmark. Well, you could buy any postmark you liked through those forwarding services, those hole-in-the-wall places that rented out postboxes. But Chicago—there were a lot of Hispanics there, Colombians maybe. Heywood's suppliers might have moved there. Maybe Dave's I.D. was way off, and Darcy was here for nothing.

Grace answered a few questions, keeping those huge hot-roller pins in her mouth, like a hooked fish. The lawyer had thought of those forwarding services, too, but who knows? No, the lawyer had not called the police. But he had talked to the *Crusader,* off the record.

Eric will have a ball with this, Darcy thought. She could see it now: The Chicago Connection. Or maybe he'd do something about Our City and the Second City. Or he'd put "Chi" in the headline, however you pronounced that. A lot of good Eric's rag did. If he'd taken Darcy's advice and reported how the D.E.A. ditched its informers, maybe Quillan wouldn't have ratted. Sung, that's what Quillan did. Heywood called him his singing partner.

When Ritenauer was back on the bench, is that what Heywood would do? Turn in one of his buddies, make a deal? Darcy fumbled in her bags for a change of underwear. She needed another shower.

Eleven

Dave played footsie with her in the Volvo, his loafers cuddling her Trojan boots, on the way to the club. Grace, when last sighted by Darcy from a motel window, was bumping around the parking lot in the BMW. "All this money for a car, and you don't have automatic?"—those were her actual words. She was at the ready for a call from Darcy with the news that Heywood had been spotted (permission to answer the phone having been granted her for the evening). If it turned out he was in Amarak and not in Chicago, Grace planned to come on over and "round him up," as she kept insisting on saying.

Darcy, who had no intention of calling her, could visualize it. Grace in the BMW, intently following the directions to the club, clutch-popping all the way. Would that damn loaded gun fall from the seat and go off? "It's riding shotgun with me." That was Grace's big joke.

Dave was on the right street now, searching for a parking space. It was a warehouse district near the Amarak-Crenshaw line. The club entrance was on an alley. Darcy remembered the damp hallway, the mailboxes with typeset labels for the graphics studio downstairs, the cracked concrete steps, the unmarked door. She also remembered the pretentious Marx Brothers in-joke. Knock three times and say Swordfish.

Dave did not, thank God, attempt Chico's accent. Heywood would have. Not that Heywood needed a password to get into this place.

At the membership check, she was curious about what name Dave had chosen. He was a member already. They had arranged that before she arrived.

"Brit Reid?"

"A fantasy from my youth," he apologized. "The Green Hornet's real name."

"Why not use The Green Hornet?"

Dave blushed. "It would seem . . . fake."

They had to pay a guest charge for her. It was enormous. She imagined this listed on his expenses, along with his membership—in what? The no-name Amarak dive? Club Swordfish? The Garrison Group would take a very dim view of all this. She visualized Dave's house, his children, his apartment, his car, all with a large eraser dragging through them. Would he ever be trusted again with the twelve hundred randomly selected American households? They always sounded so sunshiny. "Households." Even when that meant a bachelor eating over the sink.

There was a live band in the big room. A rock ballad performed by a female vocalist, electric guitars and vibes. Dave and Darcy ordered drinks. The music wasn't especially loud, but they didn't talk to each other. This was no Happy Hour, this was work. And one of them would never get paid for it.

"All the action's in there," said Dave, motioning to a side door with his drink. A Martini. He had actually ordered a Martini in a club like this.

Darcy asked for time. She wanted some booze under her belt to lubricate things. But Dave shook his head. The children were coming tomorrow, and they needed a bright-eyed, bushy-tailed dad.

She took her drink with her. It was dim in there, with a boom box going. A mirror-topped table—how clever—and someone had just finished a coke creation on it. One long serpentine line, the profile of a woman's breast oddly topping a series of squiggles. Crudely done, very crudely.

Only three people in the room, so they'd all be invited to partake. The breast artist was a short, moon-faced man with drooping eyelids. "Join in," he said, with a congested laugh. Undoubtedly, he wished Dave and Darcy to hell; he'd been alone with two women before they walked in. But if you were going to play host, you had to do it up. That was the price of buying your friends.

Predictably, the snort tube was a rolled-up hundred-dollar bill. It had gotten so that Darcy wouldn't accept those at the bank. You never knew whose mucous linings had been on it. The host went first since it was his wedding cake, then the women. One wore her hair shaved short on the neck and back of the head, but with a long strand over the eye like a pony's forelock. This piece loosened as she bent, dusting away part of the squiggle.

"Sweetheart," said the host, pulling at her hair and licking. "You now have the most expensive do in Amarak."

He's going to swallow a cupful of hair gel, thought Darcy, disgusted. She was glad she was out of this filthy scene. She'd seen people's tongues go places she wouldn't touch with tongs. What would happen when her turn came? Bad luck to walk in now.

"Go for the nipple, man." The host was waving the bill at Dave. She saw a moment's hesitation, slight movement of his shoulders under the blazer, but then he went to it. He was a pro. He knew that one of them had to do it.

Her turn. She muttered something about nostril burn.

Turning it into a joke would have been the wrong thing. No one here had a sense of humor. She did what was natural in these clubs and acted affected, talking in a spaced-out voice. The poor man's existentialism. "Thanks. I can't."

Fortunately, the group had too much of a buzz on to inquire why not. Leaving them to their jabbering, Darcy and Dave retreated to a corner. Making out was always apropos in these situations, and she was glad to oblige.

"I've got to find out where they work," she whispered to Dave between ear nibbles. "Maybe they're SynthIntellect." She was proud of herself, keeping the story straight during all this. "In a little while, we'll ask if they've seen Heywood. That round little guy got his stuff somewhere."

It was a chore to eavesdrop on the group at the table, but Dave would be watching her. A talky bunch, they turned out to be. Maybe because neither of the women wanted the host's undivided attention.

The topic was real estate. From the sound of it, all of them very well could be from SynthIntellect. Dollars and interest rates were bandied, the way young people with big money bandy them. Darcy detected too little shrewdness for banking or law, too dull a vocabulary for advertising. In this stretch of the terrain, that left high tech or chemicals.

"I tell you I *know* that section of Brooklyn. That neighborhood—"

Darcy took time out from listening to move her lips down Dave's neck. He had discovered how wide her sleeves were, she noticed. Wide enough to give his hands some traveling room.

"If I pay one-fifty for that co-op, it's going to be worth—"

He was exploring under the elastic of her camisole. Nice.

"Transitional? Hah! That's realtor talk." The host was speaking. "You know what that means? Jigaboos."

"What?" asked a female voice.

"Jungle bunnies."

Somebody changed the boom box tape.

"Oh, wow," said the host. "You gotta listen to this. This is Miles."

Later, when the talk had run out of them, Dave asked about Heywood, saying he wanted to make a purchase. "A dealer with some fine Peruvian powder," was the way he described him, not quite bringing it off in his serious voice. Brown hair, he described him as having, barrel chest, and "kind of a gut." This was a masculinized, loose translation of the information given him by Darcy. An out-of-towner who touched base here quite often, he said.

"Oh, *that* guy," said one of the girls. "He's cute."

Okay. Dave had done his mission. Chicago was ruled out. Cute, the girl had said. Yes, thought Darcy, he still had that face, the modeled lips, the lovely eyes. Not fat, *husky,* he always insisted.

He wasn't around now, everyone agreed. But tomorrow night there would be a private party in Crenshaw where he might be, and You Are Invited. Apparently, Darcy had passed the test without even inhaling. No matter what anyone said, good clothes helped.

"I bet he'll come," said the girl. "That guy."

She said it with an eagerness that made Darcy take a second look at her, as she sat cross-legged on the floor in her boring sweater and pants. The face wasn't bad, though. Darcy hadn't noticed until now the babyish lips and nose that looked doll-like or porcine, depending on your point of view. Men never stopped and thought how a face like that would sag when it was older.

She had a full head, a lioness' mane, of shoulder-length curled hair. A permanent, of course, but Heywood wouldn't notice that. Darcy wondered how much of her he had noticed, and at how close a range.

The mouth actually ended in vertical dimples when it smiled, which it was doing now, because Doll Lips and her friend with the wet strand of hair were still giggling about the cute dealer.

"It *isn't* like bedding the bartender," the one with the bi-level hair was saying, or that was as much as Darcy could pick up between the laughs and sniffles.

Dave suggested that they move back to the corner, but Darcy shushed him. She knew where this girlie conversation was going.

So did the moon-faced host, now almost totally eclipsed in shadows as he lay prone on the rug. "Did you plug into the supply line, Kath? I didn't know that."

"He plugged into her," said Doll Lips. Giggle, giggle.

Darcy listened, fascinated in a horrified kind of way, as the two girls refined the distinction between screwing a dealer and a bartender. A bad scene with the bartender might preclude going back to the bar, they agreed. Dealers were different, it was argued. They came and went.

Darcy was amazed to learn where Heywood came and went. Doll Lips would have been one thing, an error in taste but a common one for males. This freak with the tail on her head was something else entirely.

Doll Lips suddenly straightened up and addressed herself to Dave. "Are you into rock?"

"Huh?" said Dave.

"I thought maybe you were a musician."

Kath, the freak, whispered something behind her hand to Doll Lips, punctuating it with shrill, short laughs.

Doll Lips pouted at her, defending herself against being thought stupid—something she'd undoubtedly had an opportunity to practice. "I asked him because your dealer guy is so heavy into music."

Darcy snapped to attention. "What do you mean?" she said, and damned herself. Too eager.

Kath sized her up. "I kind of know this guy. I knew him for a night or two?" She sounded unsure.

Darcy held her breath a little before asking, "What's his name? Do you happen to know where he's staying?"

Kath narrowed her already narrow eyes. "You tell me his name, if you're looking for him. I don't give out dealer's names."

"Heywood," said Darcy.

"Nope, that's not it."

Kath looked sly as she said this, as if she were challenging Darcy to accuse her of lying. Darcy would have liked to do just that.

"He's not the only supplier around here. What makes you so interested in him?" But the fight in Kath's voice was deflating now. The drug lift was over, and she was starting to recline, tired perhaps from the weight of this conversation. "Sometimes he's in town, sometimes he's not," she said, supporting herself on one elbow. "We saw each other at my place. We were going to go to a concert at the Civic Center, but he couldn't make it. Motorhead."

"Motorhead?" repeated Darcy. A heavy metal group. For someone so wary of divulging names, Kath was giving out plenty of information. Darcy had lost her chance to press for the name, but she didn't need to anymore. This could not be Heywood.

"He's really into guitar. Played my Steve Vai and David Lee Roth albums about fifty thousand times. Told me I should get some other stuff, I forget who. Said I was too heavy into Van Halen clones."

"He plays the piano, too, right?" This from Doll Lips. I heard him play at the last Crenshaw party."

"He was there. Someone else was playing."

"He was a riot there." Doll Lips' opinion.

"That's to twit us all, that stuff," said her friend, almost mumbling into the carpet now. "Because the Crenshaw place is that kind of place."

This was incomprehensible to Darcy. However, she did understand one thing: she and Grace were here for nothing.

Doll Lips volunteered that someone else had been looking for this same dealer, a greasy guy with long hair who looked "real old, real Led Zeppelin." She wrinkled her fetal nose when she said it.

Darcy was no longer interested. Dave was touching her, but she felt cold and closed up, unable to respond. He had fumbled the I.D. True, he'd had to work without a photo—Darcy didn't have one—but she'd gone into such detail with the description. He was a lot better at spying on machines.

Kath's head had popped back up to coffee table height. She was licking the mirrored top for any stray grains of breast sculpture that might have been neglected. Looked like she needed them badly.

"We thought the Led Zep guy might have been a fed," she said between licks.

Which could have been code for telling Dave and Darcy that she thought the same of them. But Darcy didn't get that feeling. Kath's initial smart-ass remarks were probably from sexual jealousy. Even that wasn't in the air anymore.

"Hey, Kath, put away the mop," said the moon-faced man, reaching for his pocket. He was ready to play host again. She stopped licking and gave him a weak smile.

"I still don't trust that guy," he said, shaking out some powder. "Looks like he rode here out of that sixties movie. *Easy Rider.*"

"He strikes me wrong, too." This was Doll Lips. "You know how they're always older? And they try to look cool, but they don't know how to do it?"

No wonder Dave passed muster here. He certainly didn't fit the profile.

Darcy's analyst's mind started clicking. If the unsuspecting group in this room suspected that Led Zep guy, he must be simply oozing suspicion. Actually, that did sound like an undercover agent, wearing clothes that were about twenty years off the mark. Which could mean that she was going to be caught in a bust, in addition to her other problems, and Dave along with her.

They had said that this sixties type was asking after the dealer. The dealer didn't match up with Heywood at all, except for one point, and it was a big one: Heywood had people after him.

Darcy remembered what Grace had told her, that the two of them weren't the only people on Heywood's tail. The D.E.A. in Huddersfield could have sent local New Jersey agents out for him.

That heavy metal bunk could be nothing but a cover. That would be just like Heywood, to goof on everyone by pretending he liked music he really hated.

Why would this club still be open if a D.E.A. agent had been here? Maybe because the Led Zep fellow was a cop. A cop who was looking for a fugitive, leaving the drug stuff to the feds. That's another way they did it, Grace said. The police up in Huddersfield—or maybe the U.S. Attorney—contacted the police down here.

If the cops got him first, Grace would lose the bond money, and she'd come after the condo. Grace was supposed to get her man without remedial assistance.

The party in Crenshaw would decide everything, if this dealer even showed up. In the meantime, Darcy didn't know how much to tell Grace. She'd spit nails if she thought they'd come down here on a wild goose chase.

On the other hand, if Grace could be convinced that the dealer in question probably wasn't Heywood, she might relax her trigger finger. Part of Darcy's mind had worried all evening that Grace would somehow follow her here and jump the gun—literally.

Saturday morning cartoons start early, so Dave couldn't stay any later. The coffee table klatch scarcely looked up when they left. They were bent over their work, happy not to have to share.

"You get what you wanted?" he said later, in the car.

"She gave you a negative on the name, but she had such a sneaky look about her, I don't know whether she's trustworthy."

"That's the understatement of the year."

"You didn't find out whether these people work at SynthIntellect."

"I wanted to press for other information. The important thing is to locate the guy. I'll know him."

"You think the one with the strange hair really works for Synth?"

"Computer types can be pretty odd." And leaks could spring fast in Darcy's story.

"I can't believe an important exec is wasting time posing as a dealer—no, actually dealing—and talking about Van Halen to a bunch of coke freaks. None of them looked like they'd be on the decision-making level."

"They're young these days. Look at Bill Gates at Microsoft. I heard Cahill's henchman is some hacker who used to head up a garage software operation. One of those hot, coke-fueled little California companies."

"Why don't they just do merger talks in private homes. In a desert resort or something?"

"That's too obvious. They know that Garrison and Track-It are watching. It's changing the whole way business works."

"It's certainly changed it for me. What if that guy they're suspicious of turns out to be a fed? Will Garrison fix federal charges for me? Maybe I ought to call the legal depart—"

"Leave it to me," said Darcy, sharply. She caught herself and honeyed her voice. "Trust me. You didn't want to count the TallStory shipments either, remember? This is going to be good for us. Good for our careers."

And it would feel good, too, she reminded him, stroking his leg as he drove.

C H A P T E R

Twelve

Grace was propped up in bed, too engrossed in a paperback to look up when Darcy came in. Darcy took a peek at the cover. It looked new, perhaps bought in the motel lobby, and was apparently a bodice-ripper. Grace herself had no bodice in sight. Her night-gown was gathered at the shoulders, billowing far from her body. About three layers of nylon, was Darcy's estimate.

"I hate to interrupt any bawdy seductions or spine-tingling rapes," she told Grace, "but we may be shadowing the wrong man."

The book slammed down on Grace's thighs. "What are you talking about?"

"My contact here did an I.D. the best he could. It sounded right, but now it doesn't."

"I take it you didn't run into him tonight. Or else you let him get away and you don't want to tell me."

Darcy sat down on the chair in front of the vanity, pulling it around so she faced Grace. "I didn't let anyone get away. You surprised me, though. I thought you were so anxious to run over with guns blazing if I saw him. You look packed in for the night."

Grace shrugged. "Two minutes and I'm in my raincoat."

She really is the type who asks deliverymen to have a cup of coffee, thought Darcy. Running around in a coat over lingerie.

Darcy turned to the mirror, smoothing her hair. "Well, we missed the turn for the O.K. Corral. By about a thousand miles."

"Meaning he's in Chicago?"

"I don't know that."

"What do you know?"

Darcy reached for the mascara she had left earlier on the vanity and began applying it. It was silly, because she was headed for bed soon, but she didn't want to look straight at Grace.

"There's a guy here who fits Heywood's physical description. But I heard more about him at the club tonight, and I don't think it's him, all right? So we'll stay one day, and I'll go to a place the dealer's going to be tomorrow, just to make sure we can rule him out. If we rule him out, we leave."

"Just like that, huh? You can stop putting that goop on and tell me just what you heard, Miss Millionairess. For myself, I'm ready to check out right now if we're down here to twiddle our thumbs. I can do that at home, without a motel bill."

Darcy leaned forward to check the mascara job. She'd already put three layers on, but she took the wand out again.

"I think it's better to do a final verification. I'll go to this party tomorrow night and do it."

"A party. And I guess I can assume it's like the club tonight? Again I can't go in with you?"

Darcy's eyelashes began to take on the appearance of a bottle brush. "Yes, it's like the club tonight. I'll phone you if anything happens. You can't come with me. It would seem strange."

"What's this verification you plan on doing? You heard the guy down here is five-foot-one instead of six-foot-two, and you want to make sure he's not walking on his knees?"

Darcy turned around, weary. "I know this isn't going to mean much to you, but it's about musical taste."

"You're right. It doesn't mean much if you don't tell me what you're talking about."

"Heywood has very specific ideas about music. He sings, I don't know if I told you that. He likes old songs a whole, whole lot, he's very into his record collection, and he can't stand rock and roll. The dealer down here is into rock. A couple of people told me that tonight."

Grace ran a fingernail along the embossed muscles of the man pictured on the cover of her paperback. She was thinking.

"So he couldn't be Heywood?"

"I can't see how it could be. You probably think all of us like rock, but—"

"What's this 'old' music you're talking about? Give me an example."

"I can't even remember the names. People I never heard of. Okay, Frank Sinatra, that's one."

"And it's odd to like Sinatra?"

Darcy sighed. "It's late. I don't want to have this argument. I'll go to the party, I'll check it—"

"It's impossible to like both Sinatra and rock and roll?"

"Okay. For young—for people my age, it's odd to like Frank Sinatra. Take it however you want."

"If a person your age liked both kinds of music and was ashamed, which one would they hide?"

Darcy rolled her head back. In low impact aerobics class, they said that this would help tension. It didn't. "Why even discuss this? The old stuff, I guess."

"Wrong!" Grace told her about the record cabinet with the false back.

Darcy was surprised to hear how much snooping Grace had done around Heywood's place. About the music, she was surprised but skeptical.

"That cabinet always did look pretty clunky. So he keeps his old records from college in the back. So what? Maybe he had the cabinet made for storage. You always need places to keep things. Sounds pretty neat, actually. Maybe I should have one made. Heywood didn't say he had never in his life liked rock. The dealer down here is into it *now,* and into a specific kind of music. Heavy metal. You wouldn't even know what it is."

"I know new merchandise from old merchandise."

"Five years old? You can tell when it's five years old? He got out of college just five or six years ago, you know."

"Some of this was that old. A lot of it was brand new. It smells different. And it was that metal kind. I'm not as out of it as you think. I've got a son. Watch this, I'll prove it." Grace grabbed the phone from the nightstand, slapped it atop the novel in her lap, and began punching buttons.

Darcy watched, incredulous. "Who are you calling at this hour?"

Which is more or less what Ted said when he answered the phone, but that was okay. At least Barbara hadn't picked up.

Grace told him to go over to her house tomorrow and ask Phil for the picture she showed him when she gave him the Sinatra album.

"I want you to do this tomorrow first thing, and I want you to call me here, and talk about it to the young lady that answers the phone for me. That's right. Darcy. She's the one that answers because I don't have permission to pick up the phone in my own room. She wants to talk to someone *her age* about this picture, because someone *my age* could not possibly understand what it is."

Grace placed the phone receiver back in its cradle. "Now that you're all made up, mind turning that light off over there? Time for some shut-eye."

Darcy kicked her shoes off. "I don't know why in the world you bothered your son. I can resolve the whole thing at the party."

"This way, you'll know that you better stay on your toes instead of giving up so easy. I can't make you take me to the party, and if everybody there has your attitude about age, maybe you're right and we wouldn't get in, because they'd call the zoo on me or something. But you let me know the minute you see him. Because I'm going to barge in and round him up."

Darcy rose from her chair.

"I'm going to round him up, you hear?" And Grace clapped the phone back onto the nightstand, right next to her Smith & Wesson.

Darcy shuffled slowly toward the bathroom.

"Just as well you didn't close in tonight," Grace yelled at the crack of light coming from the bathroom door. "Tomorrow we're renting a real car for me. A Plymouth Reliant, maybe. Something that goes in reverse. I don't want that car of yours, and maybe you're taking it yourself. You getting a ride to the party? No, right? And you didn't even think of how I was supposed to follow."

The bathroom door now closed with a decisive click.

Grace leaped out of bed and, crossing the room on tiptoe, turned the vanity lamp back on. She easily found what she wanted and riffled through it. A minute later she was making a note on motel stationery. She'd found a nice stack of it shortly after check-in, and it had been in her suitcase ever since. Then she clicked off the vanity lamp, crawled back between the covers, and switched off her bedside light. Let that night owl find her own way back to bed, she figured. Maybe by radar.

* * *

Okay, renting the car at the Brand X rental place where Darcy had dropped her off took about a half a second. Okay, driving it around to get the feel of it took fifteen minutes—it was a lot like the car at home. Now what? It wasn't like there was anything to do in this town. So, time to go back to the room. Everyone was right. New Jersey stank.

Nope. The sign was on the doorknob. "Do not disturb." Better than "Please make up this room," Grace supposed. Where to? The lobby, if you liked sitting around with a couple of snake plants.

Imagine that, screwing in the afternoon. Nice behavior while you're looking for your boyfriend.

Of course, it wasn't clear anymore whether they were looking for Darcy's boyfriend, or just hanging around for a lost cause. Ted had called this morning to talk to Darcy about the photograph. He didn't recognize the musician he said, but the signature on it, Panzer, sounded familiar. He didn't think it was someone who was hot now, however. Probably a guitarist he had heard of some years back, before he got married and lost touch with that scene.

"Thanks a lot," Grace had told him when she grabbed the phone. She had been leaning into Darcy's ear, catching the whole thing.

Ted said he'd check around with friends at work, but Darcy felt pretty smug about her theory being confirmed. It was college stuff from college days. People change, she said.

She was going to have to change her attitude about Grace being born in the Stone Age. One thing Ted set Darcy straight on: the picture was of a guy who did that type of music. Heavy metal. Probably, Ted said. Ted was very big on saying things like "probably."

People change, so maybe Heywood had changed back into rock and roll. People totally redecorate their houses.

Grace sure wanted to redecorate hers.

That seemed more and more impossible. She was sitting here, $30,000 in the hole unless they caught Heywood. It was looking less likely, she had to admit.

Still, Grace was not going to give up the ship. Just like Mrs. Mulcahey said on the shooting range, *semper parata.* Not *paratus.* Always prepared. Mrs. Mulcahey had asked a priest how you said it for women.

Meanwhile, there were these hours to kill. Grace wished she hadn't left her book in the room. She was just getting to the part where Anthea, heiress to a West Indian plantation, was trying to run the place by herself following the death of her father at sea. She was out at the stables now, attempting to harness a rebellious stallion. Eusebio, the mulatto slave, had just shown up. He was naked to the waist.

That room was going to have an odor. She didn't suppose Darcy would bother to air it out. Sickening.

If she'd had the book, Grace would have sat in the lobby. But damned if she'd buy another one. All the others in the rack were celebrity sob stories anyhow. Rich people who thought they had it bad.

So I'll have a drink, she thought. It's after five o'clock and I'm over twenty-one. She headed for The Grotto. That's what they called the bar.

It was nice with Dave, but not *as* nice. He had things on his mind this time. He had to head off the neighbor and kids at a certain ice-cream parlor. Movie ended at 5:35, five minutes to find hats and mittens, fifteen for bathroom visits, short walk to ice-cream place with time out for dawdling and nose-blowing. He had it all figured out.

"My, aren't we cuddly today," said Darcy, watching

from the bed as he pulled on his ankle boots and buttoned his cuffs. All locked up for the evening.

She decided to stay nude, grabbing one of his hands with two of her own, dragging it over her thighs. It was mean, but here they were, sharing a day-rate motel stay. You had to get into the part.

Not Dave. Before his hot fudge sundae, he wanted advice on an investment. And Darcy, with her hair premeditatedly splayed over the pillowcase, was the person whose opinion mattered. He told her that, seriousness in every syllable. She knew that he considered it a compliment; he was waiting for her response. She got up and put on her clothes.

"Usually I stick with low-risk, low-yield," he said. "Money market funds and C.D.s."

She considered the loose, boatneck dress in her hands. How self-sufficient our clothes are, she thought, noting the lack of fasteners. Grace wore tailored things—sheaths or something—with miles of back zipper requiring spousal participation. The Sunday-supplement gadget ads sold hooks for the purpose: "Widows, do it yourself." For a wild moment, Darcy imagined walking to Grace's closet and putting on one of her dresses. She'd call Dave over for help. . . .

He got to the point quickly. It did seem that Cahill's representative was down here. Therefore, it did seem that SynthIntellect was going to be acquired. The stock was selling at a low price-earnings ratio. The merger offer would probably be way over book value. Dave wanted to buy some shares, lots of them.

"I need cash now. More than I ever did in my life. Leslie's lawyer is going for the jugular. I've got rent to pay, plus car payments, plus the mortgage."

Darcy was thrusting her head and arms into the dress. She stayed inside a while, ostrich-style, hiding the horror on her face. SynthIntellect may have parlayed a dud machine into a temporary success, but the market was soft. The stock was a turkey.

"I don't know," she said, reaching for a hairbrush. "The deal may never come off. Many a slip between the cup and the lip."

"Oh, come on. If Cahill is courting them, going through all this trouble with the drug dealing stuff, they'll roll over and die for him."

"Maybe he'll change his mind."

"You know how tenacious he is. A bulldog."

She tried various ploys: the old man's getting senile, his second looeys are really running the show, they'll probably stop this in its tracks.

"Especially when they find out how he did it, with the cocaine and all. He's losing it, you know."

"That's not what you were saying yesterday. You thought it was a clever way to keep the news from leaking out."

"Never mind what I said yesterday. I was assigned to this, so I came down. That doesn't mean I think it will come off. We have to know what's going on whether the deal gets done or not."

But Dave held fast. Why? Because if the Garrison Group had sent Darcy out on this assignment, that was proof enough for him that the deal was serious. "I know how chintzy they are about expenses."

He was going to know a lot more soon.

What could she do to stop him? Give him some unspoken signals, telegraph him with her eyes? But already he was beyond cabling distance, searching for his jacket, his mind on his watch.

She didn't need his information anymore, the I.D. that he probably bungled. There was no reason why she couldn't come out with it now, announce that she had set him up. In his puffy down jacket, Dave was no Green

Hornet, but Darcy with her deceptions could pass for the Dragon Lady. She didn't tell him. She wanted it to last a little longer, the sweet goodbyes and preoccupied kisses from the guy who'd always gone low-risk, low-yield.

He stepped into the hallway. The sign on the doorknob made him laugh. He flipped it over to "Please make up this room." Soon all traces of their afternoon would vanish.

She waved as he walked to the elevator. As soon as she left town, she'd take care of it by phone, the way he and she had always conducted business. Until then, the stock should hold steady or dip just a few points—the price of a year's worth of ice-cream sundaes and Muppets movies.

She closed the door, unsure where to walk or sit. Maybe she'd send away for one of those zipper hooks from the gadget manufacturers. "Widows, do it yourself."

Thirteen

The man had one of those long upper lips, like that puppet Charlie McCarthy. Held it tight, too, like he'd just got a shot of novocaine. That's what happened back in Huddersfield to people who got dentures from Aaronson, the butcher, instead of paying a few dollars more for Corelli, the D.D.S. with the golden touch.

Drunks. Drunks were the other people who looked that way. Stiff faces to control the tremors. Well, this drunk had the wrong idea if he thought he could start in with Grace Stark.

He was standing right over her now, a drink in his hand, probably his seventeenth in the last half hour. She was braced for it: Mind if I join you? Holding her Daiquiri so that her wedding band caught the light from the fake coach lamp over the table, she got ready for it.

Mind? she'd say. Speaking of minds, if you've got half of one, you better beat it out of here. My husband's due downstairs soon, and he can't stand crowds.

Or maybe she'd say, Join you? You mean *you* like the *two* of you? Because that chair you're sloshing your booze on is reserved for my husband.

"You've got your coat thrown down over my briefcase."

It didn't register at first. The way that if you bite into an egg salad sandwich, only it turns out to be peanut butter, you can't place it at all for a minute.

"What?" she said.

"Just lift it up." The man was motioning toward her coat with his drink hand. Idiotically, she obeyed, removing it from the seat next to her, where it was supposed to keep drunks from sitting down. Seems like a briefcase had gotten there first. A big fat one, but dark brown. Very dark. Who could see anything in this cave? She considered herself lucky for having spotted the tables. There were few of them, very few, and damned if she was going to step up to the brass rail.

Now he was snapping the briefcase open, for God's sake. Balancing it up against his chest, juggling the drink from one hand to the other. Looked like the Fuller Brush man, back when they had them.

"Okay. Put it down," she said, shoving her Daiquiri to one side. "If you think I took a walk in there, you're very much mistaken. Go on. Check and see if everything's there. If it isn't, frisk me."

He ignored that, but accepted the space on the table. Grace watched him flip slowly through envelopes and file folders. What did he have in there, a bomb recipe? The upper lip never moved, the mouth didn't open to say anything.

Snap, snap. He was finished.

"Everything there?" She might as well ask.

"Yep." The briefcase was off the table and at his side.

"Hey, it was an honest mistake. I didn't know anyone was sitting here. So I put my coat on it. To err is human." Ted had said that, during the thing about the cribs that strangled babies. Grace remembered thinking it added a nice, educated touch.

"Mind if I join you?"

"Not at all," said Grace.

* * *

Darcy was taking a tour of suitcase compartments. There were quite a few of them in just three pieces of hard-sided luggage. Beige, of course. Beige was Middle America's camouflage.

She ran across a six-inch gash on the outside of one piece. She would have thought it was a defect—Grace buying manufacturer's rejects on the cheap—except that she'd seen a suitcase with this feature before, a TV game show prize. It was for sticking in last-minute items. Grace, of course, wasn't the type to leave things unpacked until the eleventh hour. It was probably more for Hubbie, always forgetting his razor or his corn pads and spoiling the trip. Darcy could imagine Grace producing them with an ah-hah! on the point of departure . . . for where? Lake George or the Catskills. Bermuda in a good year.

Five little luggage pouches and nary a Valium bottle. Nothing in the motel medicine chest (Grace hadn't used it, probably because it had no paper band proclaiming it sterilized), and nothing in her bathrobe pockets. Darcy concluded that the pills had traveled with Grace to the car rental place in the big black pocketbook. It was not possible that Grace didn't have any; women over forty always got their prescriptions. It was like the voting age.

Aside from a halfhearted stab at putting the right items back in the right compartment, Darcy left her signature on her handiwork. Served Grace right, after she'd let her fingers do the walking through Darcy's handbag, probably late last night. If she wanted to try the Purple Sage eyeshadow, why didn't she just ask? The mess at the bottom of the bag wasn't Darcy's mess—imagine, shoving a comb into a boar-bristle hairbrush like that. And the brazenness of walking around with that shadow on. Darcy could see from a mile away that it wasn't Grace's usual ninety-nine-cent spread.

Maybe it was just as well, about the Valium. No mood changers, that's what they'd said at the Narcotics Anonymous meeting where she'd gone for some follow-up support right after she kicked her habit. Somebody had actually asked if sex was all right. Now that she'd double-crossed Dave, Darcy wasn't too sure when she'd score some more of that.

Mood unchanged, Darcy lay down on the rumpled bed. She wondered if Grace would bust in and start spraying her Gardenia Air Freshener. Darcy had located it in a vinyl bag, next to the one trip's quota of Q-tips, neatly tied in a garbage-bag twistie. In a mind that thought of such things, what else went on?

It would be good to sleep for a while and gird up for the Crenshaw party. It would also be good to obliterate the image of a *Wall Street Journal* page, with a certain O.T.C. stock ticking down, a point at a time. Another fine idea would be to stop wondering where Grace was. Surely she'd managed to put the rented Reliant in "drive."

She was a hard one to pin a tag on, Grace. In any market study of consumer products—washer-dryers, say—she'd fall smack-dab in the Mass Market. Made purchase in a conventional store, decision driven by both price and brand, highly aware of current promotion, had seen the product in a neighbor's home.

Then again, there was that pistol she toted. Fairly amazing, especially when one considered her demographics.

Guns and Gardenia Air Freshener. Where did she come from?

Grace still said he looked like a lush, the way he had no facial expression. But he did have a name. Deppen. Bob Deppen.

He was talking about how you just couldn't lose. Not

these days, not with the market for prerecorded video the way it was. You made the picture in Spain, right? No unions to worry about, right? It still could bomb at the box office. But with video you'd always recoup.

Grace nodded, seizing the opportunity to lift her hand up and fiddle with an earring. She was still trying to flash her ring. But Deppen beat her to it, waving for the waiter. She caught the glint of a gold Rolex watch. With diamonds.

Maybe she didn't need to adjust that earring after all.

"Just a club soda for me," she said. One drink was her limit, and she'd just finished her second. That had to be the reason why she was sitting in this bar with this Bob Deppen, who claimed he was into oil and film. Or oily film. Well, why not? If he got fresh, she could dump the Smith on the table. See if *that* changed his expression.

It was sort of a challenge, the way she couldn't tell what he thought of her. He'd been very much the gentleman, so far. No sexual innuendos, no suggestions about getting a bite to eat. Very nice, except that her stomach was starting to rumble. In a minute, she'd excuse herself and get some dinner. One club soda from now.

He told her that one of the films had bombed in Peru, but done very well in Argentina. He told her that you wouldn't believe the amount of video piracy in Mexico. He told her that the best way to drink club soda was with a twist of lime.

"I like it this way, thank you." She gave it a thoughtful stir. Lime, huh? He was beginning to get personal. Time to put a little distance between them.

"I never cared much for foreign films myself," she said. "All that stuff to read on the bottom of the screen. The way I look at it, you want to read, you go to the library."

"These pictures aren't shown in the U.S. Only in Latin America. No subtitles required. Except, of course, in Brazil."

"Of course," agreed Grace. Brazil? Probably had something to do with the crazy laws in those nutty dictatorships.

"You're probably thinking of art films. I make trash. Grade Z. Shoot 'em up, kissy-kissy, blood all over the place. Maybe a little nudity."

Grace checked. Yes, the top button on her dress was buttoned.

Bob Deppen drank his drink. "One thing we'd love is car chases, but not on our budget. They ask about that a lot, the backers do. I hear it about ten times a month, 'Any car chases?' Sure, if they want to up their investment. But they never do."

He took another sip. "Car chases," he said. It was the first time she'd seen his face change: yearning.

Grace took a good look at those fake coach lamps in this Grotto place. They'd be just right for a summer cottage, if she and Phil could ever afford a summer cottage. Which they probably never would. Some people, everything they touched turned into money. Like Bob Deppen. She admired that, especially now that he'd explained. No subtitles, that was a good idea. And no art, that made her feel more at home.

"You want to hear Grade Z?" she said. "How about if some broad asked you out to dinner?"

Darcy turned off the Stones tape and cut the engine on the BMW. She had just driven into a history book. This was the section of Crenshaw that had the same fame as Levittown, New York. Sociologists had scoured these ticky-tacky houses, these neat little lawns, searching for the bones of Ozzie and Harriet. Books about it had been written by urban anthropologists. Or were they called suburban anthropologists?

Thirty-odd years after this subdivision was subdivided,

it was so far out that it was in. That's why the party was being thrown here. Quite a few get-togethers were going on, judging from the number of cars on the street. Darcy had to park blocks away from the address she'd been given.

She found the house and rang the doorbell, squinting at the window awnings in the glow of the front-porch light. Yes, they were pink, running the length of the picture window. And they did have free-form designs on them, dark blue, or probably black. A punk touch on the splanch, the split-level ranch, just to prove it was all a joke.

A woman with a ponytail and pedal pushers took Darcy's coat. The lady of the house.

"Make yourself at home, except for the upstairs." She pointed to the place where the second level started. "That's where the kids sleep, and it's No-Drug Land." Darcy wondered briefly if the kids were a one-night rental, to carry through with the motif.

A man with a flat-top haircut, dressed in a checked big-shoulder shirt and pleated cotton pants—very The Cape for this time of year—slouched up to Darcy. "I'd like you to meet my friend Bernice," he said. "A nice girl. She grew up south of here."

"You've got a bad case of the sniffles," Darcy told him, suspecting that he wore his runny nose like a badge. "Maybe from those summer clothes you've got on."

He laughed, positively delighted, as she knew he would be. (Christ, nobody called it Bernice anymore.) A few false remarks, and she'd hired herself an escort. She walked with him past the dinette, where she caught a glimpse of wrought-iron chairs, ice-cream-parlor style. They moved into the den. It was the wrong room, no piano.

She was looking for a piano, because those girls last night had said something about how the dealer had played piano, or sang with a piano, at a Crenshaw party, because it was "that kind of place." At least, Darcy thought they had said that, though they might as well have been speaking pig Latin.

Really, she wondered why she bothered. Heywood did not play the piano. He sang. And the parking problem outside proved this wasn't the only place in Crenshaw where people threw parties. There apparently was no piano here.

They probably meant the kind of piano that rock bands used. Weren't they little jobs that folded up? Stevie Wonder seemed to play the regular kind. Darcy wasn't sure what she was looking for, but she looked, because she didn't know what else to do. It had probably been a mistake, coming here. To think that Grace had wanted so much to come with her.

Poor Grace. She never did come back to the room and try to get directions to the party. Maybe she had gotten lost somewhere, in that rented car of hers. Too bad, thought Darcy. She would have felt right at home here, idling that sedan beneath the maple trees of Circular Drive.

It had a nice atmosphere, this restaurant. Fishnets, lifesavers, a couple of anchors here and there. It didn't have a rug, though. To Grace, that made it seem like a place without tablecloths.

But it did have tablecloths, and she had Shrimp Scampi. Soup came first. She was tempted to try oysters, but she couldn't remember the saying about when they'd make you sick. Something about months with a certain letter in their names. Probably "o" for oysters.

They talked about their sons. Bob Deppen had two. One was in college, the other lived in Spain, helping out with the film business. Grace pulled out her wallet photo of Ted, the one she'd taken with a Pronto camera right off the TV set.

Where there were sons, there were spouses, but nobody talked about that.

Nice place, Grace thought, taking another look at her watch.

Now Bob Deppen was talking about a problem with the Spanish government. Something about permission to blow up part of a stairway in a castle. "We've got the numbers on tourism," he was saying. "The place doesn't even rate as an attraction."

Grace had some stories ready, too. She'd been thinking them up through the soup course, choosing the ones she thought he'd like best about the Disorderly Conducts and the Bad Papers. She wouldn't tell him any Prostitutions, because that would be in poor taste.

Somehow, none of it ever came up.

The piped-in music was piping "Strangers in the Night." If it had been Phil in this situation, he would have made a funny crack about that. Phil was a kidder. Bob Deppen didn't say anything. He was a drinker, and he kept getting to be more of a stranger.

He flagged for another Scotch.

"You've been putting those away," Grace remarked.

Bob Deppen straightened in his chair, slowly. He did everything slowly, maybe so he wouldn't knock things over. But his voice had just done a quick-change into hard and distant. He used it to ask Grace if she wanted to come back to his room. "I think we both know that's where this is leading," he said, like someone two tiles away from a winning mah-jongg hand.

Grace removed her napkin from her lap and folded it on the table with a nice crease. "I'd like to swing back to the motel all right," she said. "To my own room where I left a pair of navy shoes under the bed, size seven-B, and they don't need your clodhoppers to keep them company."

"Relax," said Bob Deppen. "So I got it wrong. Sorry."

The waiter came and prepared to place the Scotch on the paper coaster. Deppen plucked it from the air in mid-flight.

Grace had her pocketbook clutched to her chest like a shield. "Time to go."

"Right after this drink."

"You got so much alcohol in you already that if someone got mad and sliced you up, I wouldn't worry about infection."

"I'm a very high-strung type with a terrifically pressured job. A man has to unwind sometimes."

"No kidding," said Grace. "I guess we gals just can't put ourselves in your place. But if you don't get me out of here and on the highway fast, you're going to find out what real pressure is. You're going to feel like the kidney beans, the time I tried to do them at twenty pounds in the Mirro Cooker."

When she got back to her motel room, her phone was ringing. She took her time removing her coat. Let them ring, whoever they are. The hell with everyone.

On the tenth or eleventh ring, she reached for it.

"Hey! How are you?"

Her son. Grace felt filthy, remembering how she had responded to the twinkle of a diamond Rolex.

She could tell when her little boy was excited, and he was right now. Something different slipped into those pear-shaped tones.

He'd checked around about Panzer, that guitar player in the picture. The guy had a past that Grace might want to look into.

"Drugs," Ted said. "Cocaine dealing."

"So what. So they all do that, all those guitar players in tight jeans."

"This was different. I've been thinking about it, and it might have some bearing on your search."

He talked and Grace bustled around the room, stretching the phone cord as she went for her stationery supply, hunting for a pen.

"The band was AFZ? What does that stand for? A drug?"

"AFV. Armored Fighting Vehicle. They broke up, I believe. They were never very big in the first place, but according to some guys at my office, they were heavily involved in a scandal that nearly ruined Sound TV."

Grace knew what that was. The weird cable television station with everyone acting like perverts while music played. It came with your basic service whether you liked your TV programs to make sense or not.

"I don't know how AFV came in exactly, but it had something to do with payoffs to the people who decide what gets shown on Sound TV."

It surprised Grace that payoffs were necessary. It looked to her like everybody's garbage got shown on that channel.

"It was like the radio payola scandals that you may remember."

"Alan Freed."

"Exactly," said Ted. As usual, she liked how he said it. He knew how to make a person feel smart. She could use some of that tonight.

The payments had been in cocaine as well as cash, he said. He wasn't sure how AFV had fit in, but it had fit very tightly, he was told. According to him, the incident had made public relations history.

"Don't tell me public relations people were buying these drugs, too. Not your friends, I hope."

"I mean that one of the big New York p.r. firms

smoothed the whole thing over for Sound TV. One of the giants. They did a really incredible job. It was buried within a few weeks."

"Alan Freed should have gone to the same people."

"I'm not sure this is going to help you, but the man you're running after is a drug dealer, and this photograph of Panzer has what looks like a pretty personal inscription. If your man was involved in the videola thing with AFV, that could be why he fled. I don't know the details, but the feeling is that not everyone got fully prosecuted."

"So if I bring him back, they'll give me a medal. I've got enough things to dust already. I just want to not lose thirty grand."

"This could help lead you to him. It's always good to have as much deep background as possible."

"Maybe in your line of work. Myself, I use other equipment." Grace looked over at her purse, which she had carefully placed on the bed so as not to jar the contents.

"You did think it was strange how he had fled, when it seems from the pattern of prosecutions up here that he'd get off easy."

Grace stopped her note-taking. She realized she'd been seduced, for practically the second time tonight. "Teddy, I love you, and it's all good information, except that the photograph is signed to Scotty. This guy's name is Heywood."

Ted paused for a moment, the way she had seen him do only once before the cameras in the crib-strangling days. He had forgotten her fugitive's name, but he wasn't going to admit it.

"I wouldn't discount it," he said. The good old mumbo jumbo. She could go into p.r. soon herself. She was catching on to his tricks.

Grace wanted to ask how Phil was doing, but after her evening out, it didn't seem proper to mention his name—

not that she was at all convinced that Phil was acting proper. She chatted a while, and hung up, knowing that the phone probably wouldn't ring again tonight. She hadn't run for Ted's call because she had known it wasn't Darcy. Darcy, she knew, was not going to call. She didn't want Grace at that party.

Fourteen

Darcy's companion of the last ten minutes, the man in the flat-top and the summery clothes, cut four lines on the stackable end table. Darcy extended her regrets. An operation for a deviated septum. She couldn't join him.

"A nose job, huh? Let me see." He took her chin in his hand and cocked it into profile. "Very professional. They gave you small nostrils, which they usually forget, and that little bump right here looks authentic. I could bring you home for Christmas, and the 'rents would never guess. You look like a real-live Gentile."

"You should hear my version of 'Amazing Grace,' " said Darcy, a real-live Catholic who only knew it from a bagpipe record.

Her companion laughed, a brief preppy laugh that was a long time coming, and started working on the lines. "Maybe we can score some rock around here. You don't need a septum to freebase."

That could mean that a supplier was expected. Darcy excused herself to resume the piano search. She'd been thinking about it: there really should be a piano in this house somewhere, with a metronome and the sheet music for "The Spinning Song."

The den flowed into a living room with a sectional sofa and flocked wallpaper. She flowed right along with it. There were no musical instruments here, unless you counted the console phonograph topped with doilies, where 45s sat stacked on a fat, spinning cylinder. "Get a Job" was going at the moment. People talked over it, drinks in their hands.

An arm waved to Darcy from the depths of a tilted-back La-Z-Boy. She approached, wondering who could possibly know her. A head arose from the Naugahyde, smiling a moon-faced smile. It was the coke host of last night, the one who'd invited her here. He apparently was unaware of the bill protruding from his nose.

She moved toward the bottles arrayed on a wheeled cart.

"Can I pour you something? I'm Jonathan. I live here." Someone in an argyle V neck was at her elbow. Husband of the ponytail, who was nowhere in sight.

Jonathan, who lived here, asked if she'd ever seen this subdivision before. He spoke its name as if it were between quotation marks, as if it were Patagonia or Shangri-La, those other places that had inspired literature.

"Some of this is vintage," he said of the house. "Though Maribeth and I also did restoration. Here, watch this." He guided her by the elbow to a card table in the corner. She still hadn't gotten that drink.

"Just watch." He reached for a chain-hung ceiling fixture, two layers of green glass, like one upturned mixing bowl floating over another. There was a tab on the bottom of it, and Jonathan took hold of it. He pulled, and the fixture came down. A push, and it resumed its original position, blinking for a moment before it subsided into complacent ugliness.

"There's an elastic thingie inside." By now Jonathan had

gathered a small audience. A couple across the room had interrupted their sneezing and squeezing to take a look, and the woman seated at the card table had whisked away her compact.

"We found it at a Bergen County tag sale," he added, more quietly, just to Darcy. The couple abandoned him, and the woman at the table began hunting in her purse. "It's just the kind of thing they would have had here. The original owners I mean. Of course, we can't be sure, since we haven't met them, but we may sometime. We tracked them down through a realtor, and we've been corresponding."

Darcy glanced longingly at the bottles on the cart.

"This is what you call the vernacular architecture of the fifties," Jonathan informed her. "The lamp has to be here, so does the card table. They played a phenomenal amount of bridge in those days. Did your parents have a lamp like this?"

Jonathan pulled it down again, to the level of Darcy's face. He scrutinized her, the suburban third degree. "No, you're too young. Barely made it into the Baby Boom, I bet. Maribeth and I are '47. For us, this lamp is childhood. The card table, the couple coming over all dressed up to join our parents for a few hands and some Bridge Mix." He thought better of it and translated. "Assorted chocolate candies."

End of seminar. He pushed the lamp up again.

"Do you mind?" The woman at the table was trying to readjust a slipped contact lens.

Jonathan excused himself to check up on the kids and left through a door that was cut into the wallpaper. Darcy made a beeline down Memory Lane toward the cart. Bridge Mix would have been welcome at this point. There wasn't any.

Jonathan and mate hadn't done it up as well as they thought. There should have been a frosty pitcher with a glass stirrer. Darcy thought of Dave last night, ordering his Martini. He was her age (as unfashionable as Jonathan thought that was); where did he get such tastes? Dave lived like this, really, except that the split ranch had been replaced by the split family. A long relationship with Dave was unthinkable, but she thought about it anyway. You couldn't live like Dave unless you were Jonathan. Then you could say it was Retro, and it would be all right.

Dave, of course, was more honest. Darcy looked around her, at the man in the reclining chair balancing a tray on his stomach and cutting lines, at the group in front of the record player shuffling through 45s. She hadn't ended up here by mistake. At some point, she'd made a decision. Irony, that was interesting. Alienation, that was interesting. Honesty? Like clean hair, it squeaked. Someone like Dave would be bound to keep embarrassing you.

It wasn't going to be her choice, though. Dave wouldn't wait for the merger forever. When it didn't happen, he'd think back about Darcy, and he'd know exactly who had acquired whom.

Something was cutting through the backup vocals playing on the console. Darcy put her drink down and moved toward it.

Music, live. Voice and a piano, from the wall that Jonathan had exited through. She searched for the door, feeling over the flocked wallpaper with her fingers.

"Lonely and confused?" a voice called out to her from the depths of the La-Z-Boy. "C'mon over and we'll fix you up."

She ignored this, finally spotting the doorknob. It opened on a hallway with a staircase that led up, probably to the children's rooms. To the left of the stairs was another door, half-opened. Darcy passed through. It was pitch-dark in here. Carefully she descended one step to what her feet told her was a landing. She fumbled for a light switch among the mops and brooms hanging against the walls.

The music came up strong over the darkness, past the pogo sticks on clips that Darcy was now dislodging as she groped her way down.

> *Let it rain and thunder,*
> *Let a million firms go under.*

A pogo stick slipped loose. Darcy pulled to one side, letting it skitter down a step or two with a tinny, twanging sound. It wasn't enough to be heard over the voice below. Heywood's voice.

> *I am not concerned with*
> *Stocks and bonds that I've been burned with.*

Darcy righted herself. A few more steps down, a dozen or so, and she'd be in the light. She could see a light down there. She had made it past the landing now, with its treacherous hanging objects. No banister on the open left side of the stairs—she felt for one, but it wasn't there. Best to hang near the concrete wall on the right.

"Take the tempo up, here." Heywood was saying. And the piano player listened.

She was doing all right, one step at a time. This was one day when she wished she were the type who wore sneakers.

Something on the wall, made of rubber. She pulled her hand away, but a moment later she'd lost her balance and grabbed for it. It came loose, bounding down the stairs. Her knees buckled, and she followed it.

The piano stopped.

"What the hell?" Heywood was over her, she could see that when she brushed away her hair with her left arm, the one that didn't have pains in it. Next she saw the triple runs in her tights and the kid's bicycle, bent crazily on the floor beside her.

Another voice. "Are you okay?" A man was behind Heywood's shoulder. This had to be the pianist.

"They used to keep bicycles in the *garage*," she said. "Not on utility hooks. There wasn't any such thing in those days."

"Darcy!" Heywood had only just now recognized her. By the vocal chords.

Three minutes later he'd scooped her up and carried her over to a curious little recess where a bunch of sheets lay tangled on the floor. Just like the Red Cross, except that these sheets smelled tangy. The pianist having been sent upstairs in search of iodine, Heywood knelt next to her, kneading her arms, her legs, her ankles. No broken bones, they decided. Heywood wanted to play doctor, but she slipped out from under his smile and stood up.

"Where's the fire?" he asked.

"You know why I'm here. We're going back together. You've got a date in court."

"Not until the hanging judge goes off duty. Didn't my lawyer call you? I sent a letter."

"From Chicago. Nice of you to keep in touch."

He was tugging on her hand, trying to get her down in the sheets with him again. She yelped with pain and pulled free.

"Sorry—"

"You're going to be real sorry if they pick you up here. I know you're dealing. You've got to be out of your mind. Don't you remember your night in jail, how much you liked it? Wait for the soft judge. Fine. But wait at my place. The cops are looking for you here, you know. You'll have a much nicer ride back with me."

"A man's got to make a living, doll. I'm what you'd call overextended, and the Organization likes to see a man pay his debts." He stood up and grabbed her shoulders. "The collection agency can get very, very unpleasant. Just as unpleasant as jail."

She removed his fingers. "I'll pay the debts." Then, thinking of her situation, she added, "Eventually. Just come back with me now."

"I couldn't have you do that."

He couldn't? "Heywood, the only reason you're a free man is because I signed my condo over to bail you out. And then you didn't appear in court. Where do you think that leaves me?" It happened: her voice was quivering—a small voice, as he always said.

Then he had her folded in his arms, hurting her aching muscles with the touches he meant as soothing. Have faith, he was telling her. He was going to go back. He wouldn't let the court take her condo and all her nice records, the ones that would make such neat candy dishes if she melted them over a flame.

She snapped to attention at that. "I've got some David Lee Roth records in there. You want to melt them? I bet you don't. I heard you were into heavy metal. I wouldn't have believed it, but I got it from a source very close to you."

He opened his mouth, then shut it. Darcy wanted to shut hers, too, but it kept going.

"Seems like you have a lot of tastes I wouldn't have imagined."

"Most people here are into that crappy music. I go along with it. It's good for business."

"You didn't back home. Most people are into it there, too."

"It's different in Huddersfield. I'm a stranger here."

"Yeah? But somebody is hanging around, eager to make your acquaintance. I heard that from the girl you invited to a Motorhead concert. She thinks a fed is after you. If you get busted again, it won't matter what judge you get. You'll be locked up for years."

"What fed? The greasy-haired guy who looks like a hard rocker? She's imagining things. I know who that probably is. Don't worry about it."

"If you come back, it'll save my home, and I can borrow money against it to help pay your debts." The big emotions were making Darcy's voice smaller than ever. "How can you be so selfish?"

Heywood looked away. Brace yourself for a lie, she thought, but instead she saw the I'm-in-control facade slip away from his face. It was replaced by something she would have called sadness. That is, she would have done so last week, back when she felt she knew him.

When he spoke, it was to the air. Pulled close to him, Darcy could feel his voice vibrating in his singer's chest. "Yeah, I'm selfish. That's the one thing I didn't change when I started over."

"Started over?" she said, but he was meeting her gaze again, cocky and familiar. Ready to bullshit.

"You know, Darce, if I went to your place, we'd have a very nasty bail bondsman at our door raring to haul me in. I don't think he'd want to wait till the court flipped through its calendar to get me an appointment with my favorite judge."

"She."

"She who?"

"It was a female bondsman. Grace Stark. She came here with me."

Heywood darted his eyes around wildly. "Where?"

"Not here, though she wanted to. She's at a motel in Amarak. I'm traveling with her, and believe me, it's been hell. She's got the foulest mouth you ever heard, and she runs around with a gun."

Heywood cleared his throat. "Darce, I'll tell you what we're going to do. You're going back to the motel, and you're going to tell this Grace woman I took the last boat to the Lower Volta. Meanwhile, I'm going upstairs to shake some money out of some pockets. Soon as I settle with my suppliers, I'll be home. Honest. Right on your doorstep. And I won't squeeze the toothpaste wrong this time."

Darcy opened her mouth to say something.

"Not with the bondswoman. I'm not coming," he said.

"All I could find was Mercurochrome." It was the piano player, descending the stairs. He had switched on the light over the staircase, so Darcy had no difficulty climbing them, leaving with no word of farewell.

She pushed past the people in the living room and located Jonathan in the den. Maribeth had never again materialized, or perhaps she'd spent the evening stacking coats. Darcy asked for hers.

"God, how did you bang yourself up?" Jonathan asked, handing the coat over.

"Fell into some quicksand. It was the biggest fear of the fifties, after the bomb."

She hurried out, into the cool wind that was whipping up the front walk. It felt good against her aching muscles and the tears on her face. She stuffed her painful wrist into her coat pocket, because they always said you should immobilize injured parts. Immobility sounded like an inviting idea right now. Darcy hustled past the late-model parked cars lining the gently curving road. She longed to get into hers and reach the motel bed.

Morning would be hard, she knew. It had been that way before, the times she'd grabbed for Heywood and noticed the distance. He was like one of those people she'd seen on a TV special about airplane crash survivors—the people who made a dash for the emergency exits while everyone else was fumbling around for luggage, eye-glasses, loved ones.

Fifteen

A car was coasting alongside her. Someone leaving the party, Darcy thought. But they were going awfully slowly. Either they were observing the Slow Children sign at 1 A.M., or they were following her.

Experimentally, she halted. The car stopped. There was the smooth sound of an electric window opening, then a rough voice yelling, "Okay. Where is he?"

Darcy walked over and told Grace Stark to keep her voice down.

"Bet you want to know how I found you," said Grace in a rasp that was the best she could do for a whisper. "It took two minutes flat to dig the address out of your purse. Wrote it on a charge card receipt, didn't you? You ought to take care of those things. Sears tried to stick me with an extra forty dollars once, but I shoved the receipt in their face."

"You've got some nerve to look through my things." Darcy was leaning into the driver's side, her hands on the half-rolled-down window.

"Don't play Emily Post with me." Grace lightened her brake foot, and the car began to roll. "I was back in the room a while ago, saw your paw prints all over my valises.

What could she want here, I said to myself. Maybe she thinks I've got a spare tube of diaphragm cream."

Against her will, Darcy followed along with the car. "Just trying to even the score."

"Yeah? Took you all that to get back at me for swiping eyeshadow? Because that's all you thought I took, I bet. I did that to throw you off, kid. Like in the Sherlock Holmes movies, if he wasn't before your time. The Cherry Heering." She gave it some gas, and Darcy let go, standing helpless in the street as Grace nosed into a distant parking space.

Then they were both on the sidewalk, heading back to the house with punk awnings. Darcy didn't need to point it out; Grace was drawn there as if the aluminum siding were a magnet.

They rang, and Maribeth opened, eager for the coats.

"Did the breath of air do you good?" she asked Darcy, apparently uninformed of the exit speech.

"I'll keep mine on, thanks." Grace pulled her raincoat tighter around herself. It was, Darcy noticed, the bullet-proof number.

"You don't need your armor," she hissed, when Maribeth had retreated. Curiously, no questions had been asked about the new guest though she hardly seemed the type to be carousing the night away, looking for some blow. Maribeth might have mistaken her for the ghost of a former inhabitant, back to haunt the knotty-pine walls.

Indeed, she seemed uncannily familiar with the house. Once she understood that Heywood was in the cellar, she made her way there with confident steps. While Darcy hesitated, Grace was plunging ahead, into the living room where no one looked up and Grace paid no attention to the noses traveling over mirrors. The flocked-wallpaper door held no surprises for her, and in moments she was throwing open the staircase door.

"Heart and Soul" was being played down under.

"He's alone," Darcy said.

"Congratulations. You can see around corners."

"There was a pianist before. But the pianist plays with more than four fingers."

She began to warn Grace about the elusive light switch, but Grace interrupted her with a flick. A square glowed near their feet, the landing light. The stairs remained dark. It was, obviously, how Grace wanted it.

"Keep it down," said Grace. "I'm going to stake this out."

Darcy watched, fascinated, as Grace slid her hands expertly over the wall at the top of the stairs, searching. It was dim there and dangerously close to mop-and-broom territory, but Grace disturbed nothing.

She paused, crouching slightly, reaching. Her fingers were tracing something. "Did you see dirty clothes down there?" she asked. "In a pile, maybe."

Darcy told her about the sheets in the corner. "Why?"

Grace sprang into action, pulling an unseen object. Darcy heard the sound of sliding metal, then Grace was down on her knees.

"A laundry chute," she announced over her shoulder. Then Darcy saw her head disappear into a hole as her hand went deep into her raincoat pocket.

"Knock off the piano," she was yelling.

"Heart and Soul" came to a dead stop.

"This is Grace Stark, bondswoman, and you're coming up here with your hands up. I'll give you to the count of ten." Grace kept her head in the hole, and her right hand in her pocket but moved her left over the wall, in Darcy's direction. A click, and the stair lights were on.

Darcy had a very strong inkling about what was in that right pocket. She crawled up behind Grace, telling the back of her head, "There's no need for—"

"One!" Grace bellowed. The echo in the chute transformed Grace's voice—so suitable for yelling in a store aisle, "What's the price on this?"—into a terrible rumble.

The numbers came out clipped and staccato, like passes of a guillotine. By "six," Heywood had started playing again, "Chopsticks," rushed and sloppy. So, thought Darcy, he's panicked, too.

"Ten!"

"You really can't—" It was Darcy's last try. As the hand jerked out of the raincoat pocket, she scrambled backward, out of the way. A shot exploded in the laundry chute, screaming its way down to the basement.

Darcy gasped, air sucking into her throat like paper clips down a vacuum cleaner. Grace fell back, almost against her, propelled by the kick of the weapon. But soon she was back in position, her mouth against the mouth of the chute and her gun poised for more action.

"There goes a pile of good percale," she called down. "And that's just a taste of what you could get. I'm serious, mister. Come on up."

Grace raised herself up, knees cracking. She planted herself near the lip of the landing, feet spread wide in their brown wedgies. Not knowing what else to do, Darcy stood, too.

Early rock and roll could be heard faintly through the cellar door. People were dancing.

The gun was pointed downward, and Heywood was on the bottom step.

"Hands over your head."

"Give me a break," he said.

"I said, hands up. Unless you want the front of your shirt to match a certain set of sheets."

He lifted his arms and walked up the stairs muttering, "Brother." He had put on weight. Darcy noticed that now.

One step from the top, he halted, unsure what to do. He was almost chest-to-chest with Grace.

"Keep coming," she said.

"Where? You and I are about to become bosom bodies."

Grace hesitated, and Darcy saw Heywood's face change. The fear was supplanted with something else.

"Just step behind me. And no false moves. I'll be right at your back." The same tone, but she was improvising now, and he knew it.

"Could you give me a little room to squeeze by?"

"There's room enough. Squeeze."

He began to step up, then his knees buckled and he was clutching for the banister. A fake fall. Very fake.

"Don't!" cried Darcy, and she darted forward, pushing Grace's gun arm up in the air.

If Heywood had been lighter on his feet, if Darcy hadn't released her grip, they could have done it and foiled Grace. But it took him too long to correct his position and dodge past the struggling women. By the time he was knocking past them, Grace had freed her arm and had the semiautomatic trained on him.

There was no time to take careful aim, but it didn't really matter in quarters this close. She would have gotten him, but instead she got a tiny, silly click. Heywood flung the door open and was gone.

"I emptied that gun," Darcy told Grace's shocked face. Then she slid to the landing, grabbed hold of her bruised knees and started rocking. This was as close as Darcy Kohler would get to hysterics, a crisp, professional inner voice told her. "When you fired, I thought you loaded the whole thing again. Thank God you didn't."

The brown wedgies approached her face. "You emptied my gun."

"I got a book at a newsstand near the motel, *You Can Learn to Shoot*. I did it when you were in the shower. I pulled out the magazine and emptied it. I don't know why it still had one bullet."

"Cartridge," said Grace. "Not bullet, cartridge. You're really smart. Except that one cartridge was in the cham-

ber. Your book didn't tell you about that, huh? You could
have blown your head off."

"Oh."

"*You Can Learn to Shoot.*" Grace spat the title out in
derision. "A lot you know." The wedgies were pacing the
landing. "Do you have any idea how dangerous it is to be
unarmed when you think you're armed? You could have
got me killed."

Darcy looked up. "I can't believe you said that. I really
can't, after you almost murdered Heywood."

Grace stuffed the gun back in her pocket and glared
down at Darcy. "He had his warning. And don't you *ever*
rush at me again when I'm aiming." Darcy expected a
finger to start waving in her face. This must have been
what Grace's son was nursed on.

The door, half open, moved. Jonathan was at the
entrance, sniffing.

"Did I hear something explode a few minutes ago?"

"No," said Grace. "Yes," said Darcy. It smelled of hot
gases; they had to say something. "There was a guy down
there, playing the piano. Actually he was playing a
synthesizer. He brought it with him. It shorted out or
something. Maybe you heard it? They can make it sound
just like a piano."

Jonathan looked dubious. He examined both women
closely, then seemed satisfied. "Okay. Just as long as you
weren't freebasing. I'll have no freebasing in my house.
There are kids here."

The two women set off for their cars. They had parked
in the same general direction, so they couldn't help
walking together.

Grace's rented car was closer. Darcy complained about
the tightness of her shoes and the distance to her BMW
until Grace agreed to give her a lift to it. It had been a long
day for both of them. They strolled slowly to the Reliant.

You could hardly see the stars here, they agreed. Probably because of the pollution. It was different in western Mass, where the same bright blanket of sky spread over Darcy's Condominium Community and Grace's Orchard Grove single-family. Two homes still in danger of expropriation. The two women didn't have a lot in common. But they had that.

As they walked, Darcy confided to Grace that she was beginning to doubt whether she knew who her own lover was.

Grace shrugged. "I guess it's hard to keep those one-night stands straight. Maybe you could try a pocket organizer."

Darcy explained that she meant Heywood. She told Grace his comment in the basement about how he "started over."

"It's going to be damn hard for me to start over," said Grace. They were at her car now, and Grace unlocked the passenger side for Darcy. "He knows I'm after him. He's going to run hard."

"I don't know." They slid into the car, brightly illuminated by a streetlight. Darcy extracted long leather gloves from her coat pocket, and Grace watched, fascinated, as she used the pantyhose technique to pull them on. "He said he owes a ton of money to his suppliers. They're around here somewhere, and a big creditor like that might not want him to go too far."

"His suppliers are around here where?"

"Someplace in the Northeast."

"Oh, that pins it down."

"He didn't tell me, okay? And I didn't want to know about it. In the beginning, back when I used, I was happy he was loaded with stuff. I didn't ask questions. Then when I stopped I wanted him to, too."

She stopped adjusting her fingers inside the gloves and let her hands fall into her lap. "I thought that was very odd, that business about starting over. He never mentioned any radical changes in his life before. He said the one thing that didn't change was that he stayed selfish."

That reminded Grace. She asked Darcy to fish a pad and pencil out of the glove compartment so she could write a note to herself.: "Load gun."

She turned on the ignition briefly, but cut it after a glance at Darcy.

"That seat belt goes on even for just a couple of blocks, or we go nowhere. I believe in safety."

Back at the motel, Grace asked to hear about this starting over bit one more time. She mentioned that Ted had called again. She asked if Darcy had ever heard about monkey business with that wacky Sound TV, something called videola.

CHAPTER

Sixteen

DeSimone from the U.S. Attorney's office thought he was smart, calling Phil at seven in the morning. He said no, the federal government wasn't in the wake-up service business, but it liked to catch people before they went to work.

That's how smart DeSimone was. But if he was a little smarter, he wouldn't be so low on Uncle Sam's totem pole that he had to bang away at phones at 7 A.M. If he was even smarter than that, he'd know that Phil worked afternoons and nights. But Phil wasn't going to tell him that. He wasn't going to tell him anything.

DeSimone wanted to know where Grace was. The U.S. Attorney had a right to know, he said. The United States had a case against the prisoner she'd bailed out. It wanted him back.

"Not as bad as my wife wants him," Phil said. "I haven't seen her want a guy so much since we went away to the country, and Tom Jones sang at our hotel."

"Take off your horns for a minute and cooperate."

Phil didn't particularly want to meet DeSimone, but if he did, he'd have some advice for him: don't apply for any jobs where they want a pleasant telephone manner.

Phil said come to think of it, he'd got a postcard from her. A picture of guys playing bongo drums and something about a hijacker. You get on a plane these days, that doesn't mean you get where you're going, he told DeSimone.

"Where *was* she going?"

"To work," said Phil. "She had a job to do, and she's doing it. Women have changed a lot, they do things they never used to do. Bus driving, meter reading, skip tracing."

"Call me when you want to get serious."

DeSimone hung up without leaving his number. Very nasty. It was no mean feat looking up government offices, the way they stuck them on those mixed-up blue pages.

For the second week running, Phil was a failure at his sleep schedule. One day it was the paperboy, thwacking the thing against the house like a wrecker's ball. Another time the neighbors blasted Christmas carols from their roof speakers, in broad daylight. Just a few bars, to test the connection they'd rigged up the night before, but it was one of those honky-tonk ones. "Hark the Angels." Worse than the Chipmunk songs, at that hour at least.

Today it was the feds. Phil considered rolling over again, but his nervous system was already dancing all over the room, so he decided to join it. He switched off the electric blanket and started the slipper search.

Would DeSimone call anyone else, he wondered, and did anyone else know Grace was in Jersey? If the feds got wind of that, they'd start closing in for the forfeit immediately. No one but Grace would believe a story about her prisoner sticking so close to home. That guy had credit cards; he was probably on some Frequent Flyer plan. He'd be flying.

Phil's lips were sealed, but he felt pretty hungry. Dinner last night had been lousy—soup and clam strips at a roadside place, midway between the man who didn't want a life insurance renewal because he was pissed at his beneficiary, and the couple who heard that Sears gave a better deal on car policies.

Breakfast, that was the hard meal, the one she didn't leave in the freezer. She did leave the cereal, though. Cheerios, Raisin Bran, what a thing to wake up to. Maybe Phil would go to the Price Chopper later on and pick up some of the sugared kind. It would probably go down easier.

Everything was ready to go on the kitchen table, but after he sat down he remembered the napkin, and after he sat again he remembered the milk. It was a wonder that women could put on weight, with all the running around the kitchen they did. The milk carton had a photo of a missing child on one panel. Angela Grimalt, age seven, brown hair, brown eyes, last seen three years ago wearing a gray pleated skirt and red sweater.

Phil sat and poured. Only two drops came out. He crumpled the carton into a butterfly and walked to the trash can. Angela Grimalt's brown eyes stared through a space in his fist. What the hell, they'd never find her in that skirt and sweater. Kids outgrow clothes. He hurled the carton in.

Plan B was oatmeal. Oatmeal came with directions on the box; eggs didn't. As soon as he was through with that, it was time to work on lunch. Everything left in the freezer looked like meat loaf, but some of it turned out to be tuna casserole. The labels Grace had stuck on were all frosted over. Phil pulled out a foil pan and left it to thaw on the counter. He hoped for the best: tuna.

Now he could head for the TV set. At least there you had a choice.

Watching TV in the bedroom wasn't normal, not in the morning, but Phil went in there to get the blanket. It was cold in the den, and he couldn't push up the thermostat, because he wasn't the Rockefellers. Changing into clothes would be warmer, but Phil kept his pajamas on. He still didn't have this schedule figured out, but some early dozing seemed all right. Sleeping meant you were falling apart.

The weather report was bad, so he zapped it and strolled back to the kitchen. Mallomars were one thing Grace hadn't thought to freeze up for him. He had a nice stash laid by, ten packs in fact, the limit for the supermarket "express" register. The other lines moved so slow that people got restless and stared at your cart.

The house plants over the sink didn't seem to like sixty-two degrees, or maybe they needed water. Phil parked the Mallomars on the counter and looked for a glass. None on the shelves, so he fished into the dishwasher. Had he run it already? Clean or dirty, you couldn't tell, so it couldn't really matter. He stuck the glass under the faucet.

Hovering over the plant, he noticed something different. Out in the Whelans' yard, there was another goddamn reindeer. That made one, two, six, all of them alike and one uglier than the next. Last year he thought they were papier-mâché, but that's when they kept their distance. The herd was growing and multiplying, marching ass first toward the Starks. Close up, Phil could tell they were made of cheap, hard plastic, like those tiny little Kewpie dolls they used to give out at amusement parks. If you pushed their noses a little, the whole face would collapse. Phil would have loved to give that a try with the reindeer.

Christmas carols blasting from the rooftops was one thing; he'd been all through that with Bob Whelan some years back. The compromise was to cut the hours down so they were bagged after 10 P.M. But that didn't stop Whelan from doing the test-run the other day at dawn. And as Christmas drew closer, curfew always crept up a little past ten, then a little more. By Christmas Eve, all hell broke loose and it went on until midnight. Whelan knew he had Phil by the balls on Christmas Eve. That's when he went extra heavy on the Chipmunks.

Phil couldn't be sure, but he expected more reindeer. Dancer, Prancer, Vicks, he couldn't remember how many more there were, but none of them out there had a red bulb for a nose. That meant that Rudolph was on order. The Whelans must have been buying them on layaway, or like those pearl necklaces Phil's nieces had. Start with one pearl, and hit your relatives up for more every time they turn around.

Phil toyed with the idea of phoning, but Whelan was a big guy. He sold pantyhose wholesale, or maybe distributed it, and Phil couldn't think of much to say to him besides what everyone said: So, up to your ears in women's hose? The guy had been looking at him funny ever since Phil's name got in the papers. The time Grace kissed some tree bark with her car's behind hadn't helped either.

There was someone else Phil could call. A surveyor. If he wasn't mistaken, that newest deer was over the property line by at least a hoof. It depended who did the surveying, but Phil knew just who to call. A guy who got picked up for driving while intoxicated every so often. A bad habit, but bailable.

Phil went for the phone, then stopped. He could convince the guy to survey to specifications, but he couldn't convince him not to send a bill. Phil had too many of those already.

The phone went into action on its own. Phil picked it up fast, and the other party hung up. That happened sometimes after one ring, or it happened when disgruntled Huddersfield cops felt like being threatening. Phil stood by for a moment, but there were no rings. The cops hadn't bothered with the blower for more than a week, but with twenty-odd shopping days left until Christmas, they'd be missing those coins from Isaacs. Phil grabbed the Mallomars and went to wrap himself in the electric blanket.

He clicked the remote control, touring the channels. The exercise show looked interesting. The very good-looking instructress was in a very interesting position. The "V" she called it. Keep that lower back pressed to the floor as the legs come up, she said. Now spread those feet apart.

Eight chimes. The front doorbell.

Phil put the Mallomars down with the blanket and TV still going. If it was a charity selling Christmas cards, he'd come out with it and say Christmas was against his religion. If they didn't see reindeer hopping all over the yard, or a wreath at least, couldn't they get the picture?

As soon as Phil knocked the stuffed cloth snake from the foot of the door, he felt it. A cold snap was on. There was a young guy on the porch, hopping around like an Amtrak commuter who's waiting for the "free" sign on the bathroom. He had a big down jacket on, like the ones Ted used to order from Maine, but it didn't appear to be working. Only a few inches of head stuck out over a muffler—enough to show the red hair.

The kid's teeth weren't really chattering, but his voice came out like he was talking through a snorkel. It said: "You're Phil Stark, aren't you?"

"Could be. Who are you?"

Phil didn't catch the last name, pronounced through the bottom of the muffler, but he caught the important part. The kid, Jason someone, was a *Crusader* reporter.

Funny how you could stand in a bathrobe and slippers in ten-degree weather and feel extremely warm. When Phil closed the door, it wasn't because he needed the insulation.

The TV exercise girl was on something called the Swan and the blanket thermostats were clicking away, seeking a lower setting, when the chimes rang again. Phil let them. The Swan was nothing terrific, and the Bird wasn't much either, but the Plough was something else again. Hold it to twenty, *slowly,* then let your knees drop. Chime, chime, chime.

The knocking came on with the commercial. Phil dusted chocolate shards from the blanket and got up. The kid was short, he noticed, like the salesmen who bothered Dagwood in the funnies. Dagwood always got a rise out of kicking them. Maybe there was something to it.

But the kid threw him off-balance, because he had one glove off, and with the other hand he was pointing to his fingers.

"Frostbite," he said. "It's an emergency. Will you please let me in for just a minute?"

"Drive yourself to the hospital." Phil was poised to slam.

The kid pulled his muffler all the way down, and started shaking his hand in the air. "My car heater doesn't work. Please, Mr. Stark. I think I need an ambulance."

Later, Phil would tell himself it was because he didn't want to land in *Crusader* headlines again: Mean Man Fails to Aid Citizen. Really, it was because of something his mother had taught him. What did his mother know? The only time she had a gripe with the press was when her brother died and they left her out of the "survived by's."

Phil let Jason in, and he let him see his back. He even shoved the draft-stopper back in place with his heel— pretty tricky. Phil walked to the kitchen with the kid trailing and pointed to the phone.

"Dial 911, and hope to hell your insurance covers it."

"You're in the insurance business yourself now, aren't you, Mr. Stark?"

Phil turned around. The kid wasn't shaking his hand in

the air anymore. "Are you dying or aren't you?" he said. "Because if you aren't, I want you out of my face."

Flustered, the kid started the hand-flapping again. "Thanks a million for letting me in. They feel better . . . a little. I got this once before. Sailing. They almost had to amputate."

He had his eyes on his hand, not on Phil's face.

"Sometimes running water helps," the kid said. "You mind if I use your sink?"

"Long as you don't piss in it."

Phil felt embarrassed that the breakfast dishes were still waiting for a rinse, but the kid pushed them aside looking right at home. He probably lived with a dozen others like him, in one of those houses near the college. One of Phil's friends had some nice property there, until he rented it to kids. Students have no respect for a beautiful house, the friend said. He had to paint over the wallpaper twice to cover the filth.

Phil didn't know much about frostbite, but the kid seemed pretty nimble with his fingers. He played with the single faucet, dialing it around like he was from India and never saw one before. Finally, he got it turned off, and his eyes darted around the room and fixed on the paper-towel rack.

"Would you have anything I can dry my hands on?"

"I would," said Phil from the doorway. "Air."

The kid wiped his fingers against his scarf. Then he walked over to Phil, finally looking him in the eye, but with fear shimmering all over him. Phil lounged against the door frame, burying his chin in his chest so he could look down. Dagwood had the right idea; this was more fun than the Plough.

Jason spread his feet apart, trying to look tough, but looking more like the neighborhood bullies had dared him to do something while they hid nearby, checking up. "Don't be angry because we reported the facts," he said. "If you didn't forfeit bonds when people jumped bail, that isn't our fault. We do what we have to. We inform the public."

"Go inform them outside of my house, squirt, unless you want to take another trip to the sink. Head first, this time."

"I don't think you'd do that, Stark."

"*Mister* Stark."

"I'd have you arrested for assault. And I have reason to believe that the cops don't like you."

Phil wasn't enjoying it anymore. He was mad and wanted to kill the kid, but he couldn't. And he didn't want the kid seeing the color that was rising out of his intestines and searching for his neck.

"Out!"

"We know your wife is searching for a coke dealer, and that she's doing it with Darcy Kohler. Has she been in contact with you?"

"Out!"

"Are they in the U.S. or Latin America?"

Phil gave him to the count of ten. He figured it shouldn't take as long as the Plough. That took twenty.

"There's no need to get angry. The *Crusader* admires your wife, you know. A bondswoman. We dig her. You wouldn't happen to have a current photograph of her we could use? Black and white, thirty-five millimeter would be preferable."

Phil was counting, unaware that Grace had done the same on a strange staircase in New Jersey. They had never counted for one another. They didn't know they had this in common.

"How is she getting on with Darcy, anyway?"

Phil counted.

"Our editor-in-chief happens to know Darcy. I do, too, a little. Have you met her? Do you know what we say about her around the newsroom?"

Phil stopped counting. "What?"

Jason alluded to several parts of Darcy's body, obscenely. Phil laughed.

A flood of questions was unleashed, one tumbling on the other. What airline did they take? It's Colombia, isn't it? Heywood's product was always Colombian. It's the Colombians who are after your wife, right?

Phil wasn't laughing now. "What are you talking about. Who's after my wife?"

"Someone called us at the paper. A guy with an accent. We ran a story about how Heywood jumped bail and mentioned your wife. This guy wanted to know more about her. He made some threats, but we're used to that."

"Get the hell out," said Phil in a voice that was strange even to him. Maybe it sounded like a rattler just before it strikes, because a moment later the kid was flinging the stuffed calico snake away from the front door and hightailing it out. He wasn't so used to threats after all.

Wire hangers clashed and played ominous chords as Phil grabbed for his jacket in the front-hall closet. The freezing air pushed up his pajama legs and clutched at his ankles, but he raced across the lawn toasty with wrath.

The kid's car was idling, chugging and spurting, when Phil hammered on the driver's-side window. If it wasn't such a secondhand piece of trash, maybe it would have responded when the kid popped it into gear. But it was garbage, and it stalled.

Phil kept banging on the glass with a bare hand, watching the kid turn the ignition key. The motor thudded and caught, but Phil knew it would need time to get going. This beater was a Ford, '79 or '80, with one of those two-bit carburetors. It would probably die again while Phil played knock-knock.

The kid rolled the window down a few inches. Just enough so he could say, "Don't fuck with the press, Stark," and enough so that Phil could feel the blast of the car heater against his naked face. Then the window was up, and the car was down the driveway. Somebody must have dicked with it and replaced the original carb with a modified Holly.

It was almost lunchtime, and the frozen food—meat loaf, as it developed—was still glistening with ice crystals. Maybe Phil should have asked the kid to take it for a spin, warm it up with that car heater. He threw some water in a pot, boiled it, and threw it over the meat. He was learning to be domestic.

While it heated up he wondered about that call to the *Crusader,* asking about Grace. Someone with an accent. It wasn't DeSimone because he wouldn't have made threats. The farthest he went was rudeness. He didn't have an accent anyhow, not that Phil had noticed.

And this accent was very noticeable. Phil found that out, three bites into his meat loaf, after the phone rang.

The accent didn't ask questions. It told Phil he'd better get his wife back home.

"You dumb cop," Phil said. "I can hear it from ten miles away, you're one of the affirmative action hires. Who is this, Mendoza?"

The accent chuckled. "I am not a cop."

"Villareal, is that you? I'm going to report this. Learn English better before you make any more creep calls. How many of you guys do you think are on the force?"

"This is not the police. We have more deadly methods than your police."

The dial tone came on, and Phil listened to it for a while. He walked back to the table and, after a moment's hesitation, grabbed the plate and hurled it and its contents into the sink.

When was he ever going to guess right and find the tuna in the freezer?

Seventeen

A few hours after the kid left, Phil was finishing up his paperwork in the den, watching the snow fall. It always snuck up, waiting for you to turn on a lamp so you could see it outside, already revved up and in full swing when you didn't have the slightest idea it was happening. Of course, it had been cold enough to snow all day. That's what the mailman would have said if Phil had bumped into him, and he would have said it the way he said everything: giving Phil The Look to make him feel peculiar for not working days.

"With these small flakes, it can keep going." That's the other thing the mailman would have said. They were real small. Phil saw them spinning in the night outside when he jabbed the button on the garage wall with his elbow, too loaded down with his briefcase and flip charts to free up a finger. The overhead door lifted on a bona fide winter wonderland. It was pretty, like the curtain lifting on those Christmas plays Ted was in at Coolidge Elementary. They were fine except for the year they had him playing St. Joseph. That was going too far.

It was a whole lot like a play, sound effects provided courtesy of the Whelans next door. As soon as the sun had set, they'd started in with "Silent Night." And the people who lived near the airport thought they had it bad when the jets started coming in.

Twenty-seven miles out on Route 5A, Phil checked his notepad under the coach light. "Leads supplied," that's how Marty advertised this job to the poor saps scanning the want ads. "Leads" meant people who let their policies lapse, usually on purpose, and might be talked into a renewal. Or it meant somebody who called the agency with a vague question about rates and got railroaded into leaving a name and number. Sometimes it was a person who had circled a want-more-information number on a reader's response card in a magazine. The insurance firms sorted the cards by city and doled them out to the agencies. By the time the name filtered down to Ray-Mar Insurance of Huddersfield, the reader wasn't responsive anymore.

Phil switched the light off. For a change, Marty had ganged addresses located in the same neck of the woods. Last week half the bunch had been northeast, the rest was southwest. With a twenty-two-cent-a-mile gas allowance, that hurt.

The new list brought Phil back southwest, to the more affluent towns full of transplanted Bostonians and New Yorkers. God only knew what they wanted with this area. Phil was going to have a rough time finding dinner down here. Restaurants were scarce, usually named Lord This or That or after some Indian, their windows all glued up with American Express and Diners Club insignia. The only other buildings lining the highway were farmhouses pushed right up to the road, the way rich Yankees liked it in the days before car horns and busted mufflers, and tourist-trap shops. "Shoppes," they always wrote it.

If you needed candles or some lumpy balls of soap, you were all set. But try getting a grilled cheese or a Reuben out here.

He turned the light back on for the directions. Turn right at the Wonder Bar. He squinted at it through the snow. It didn't look too fancy, but probably all it had in the way of solids was pigs knuckles in a jar. Dinner was a problem, but it was better than work. Phil was drawing closer to the people who knew he was coming, but didn't know when. The folks who hadn't said he couldn't come, but wouldn't be delighted to have him.

The wooden frame house was the same blue color as the old museum houses. They used to get that blue out of iron filings and berry juice—you'd hear that over and over if your wife dragged you to one of those restored places and hauled you on a tour. Some savvy paint company had matched it in exterior latex. The New Yorkers who moved here were snapping it up. Made their homes look just like the Witch's House.

The little girl who answered the door in a sweater and jeans didn't listen to Phil's name or look at his card. She just twisted her head and yelled, "Insurance man." Even kids gave Phil the neck.

The couple sat him in the living room, but didn't bother with too many lights. Maybe they thought they could flush him out that way, like getting rid of a moth. It was going to be bad for the flip-chart presentation. Another bad thing was the position the wife chose, right next to her husband on a loveseat. That ruled out the Divide-and-Conquer thing Phil had learned: roll your eyes up at one when the other says something foolish, give those "get a load of her" nudges.

They had filled out a card with the years, makes, and models of their two automobiles, expecting to receive an estimate in the mail. Instead, they got Phil.

The man puffed on his pipe while Phil worked the flip charts. There was an anxious moment when he yanked the Life-Pac out of his briefcase instead of the Car-Pac, but soon it was all straightened out. He handled his colored grease pencils with a flourish, circling liability levels, keying them to rates, then erasing it all with a rag and starting all over. When it was over, he thought he'd spoken convincingly and well, and he felt like panting.

"I remember sending in the request for an estimate," said the husband. His pipe wasn't drawing, so he spent a while tapping it. "Since then, I've gone down to Sears and taken out one of their policies."

Phil was armed and ready for this response. He offered to do a comparison, with grease pencils.

The man shrugged. "The money isn't all that important. We're always going to Sears for one thing or another. Now we'll drop off premium payments at the same time."

"It's simple," said the wife. "We're great believers in simplicity."

Phil could see that from the cars they'd listed on the estimate request: a Land Rover and a Porsche Audi.

The snow was accumulating now. A plow and sander had already been through, he saw, but drifts were forming against the white picket fences erected along 5A for the tourists' benefit. Phil had steel-belted radials and no fear, as long as the leads lived on paved roads.

There were two small children at the second lead's house, and a wife who stayed out of the way while Phil talked insurance. The husband had called the agency about a life policy, but that, he said, was before he bought a home computer. He led Phil into a spare bedroom where the thing was set up and showed him a flat, plastic-coated box. On it was the photo of a cocky young man, a financial columnist for a big magazine (*big,* the lead said), with the title: *Finances on a Floppy.*

The lead demonstrated it for Phil. The computer asked about his age, sex, smoking habits, and other things Phil didn't even catch, they flicked by so fast. Then it came up with a snap judgment: You are overinsured.

The man pointed to the words on the screen, looking

very pleased. "I just punched in the amount of coverage you offered me. You see the result. Actuarially, I don't need it."

"Punched in, huh? You call it punching?"

The third guy lived on what you'd call the wrong side of the tracks, if the Baltimore & Maine came out here, which it didn't. He was way off 5A in the flats, where everybody had satellite dishes. The blueberry-colored houses never had those.

The fellow who came to the door wore work boots and a flannel shirt, and he didn't give Phil the neck. He gave him some lip and got ready to slam.

"Could you let me in for just a minute? For an emergency phone call?" Phil had his hands waving around in the air. "My car heater's not working. I think I got frostbite."

An hour later Phil came out to find his car stuck in its parking spot. The couple shots of Wild Turkey that the guy had poured into a couple cups of coffee made it seem not so bad. He was a nice guy who didn't know you could buy your own hospital coverage during plant layoffs. First he balked at the price, but Phil explained. Actuarially, it made sense.

Whistling while he worked, Phil knelt in the snow to snap on the jiffy chains. He had to give the rusted-up clasps a couple of kicks before they closed. But they stayed on long enough to get him unstuck, or at least the left one did, and that's all he needed. He got out of the car and removed it, because these things weren't sturdy enough to drive with. He would have liked to have searched for the right-hand one, but the snow was so deep it seemed hopeless.

The plows and sanders were busy on 5A, so Phil decided to give the Wonder Bar a try, even though it was still snowing. No jars of pigs knuckles in sight, but they did have microwave pizza and fries. Eat now, pay later,

Phil figured, giving his order. He had the bartender rip two packets of Alka Seltzer off the display, in case Grace had the home supply in Jersey.

The mailman was right: those teeny little flakes could go on forever. Traffic had thinned out to almost nothing as Phil made for home. There was a Bronco or something like it behind him. Maybe a Blazer, he never could tell the damn things apart.

The fun began at the Huddersfield city limits. It looked as if the plows might have been through, but only once and not too recently. Too bad, but that's how it had to be. Phil voted that way whenever the bond issue came up, and he'd do it again. Better to fish tail a little than see the tax rate go up a few mills.

The car skidded, but there was nothing to hit except utility poles and streetlights. Phil got stuck several times and wished for the other jiffy chain, but rocking managed to pull him out. The Bronco or Blazer kept right behind him. That surprised him; whichever one it was, it had four-wheel drive. It should have made better time.

Phil was nearing the turnoff for his neighborhood, five hills away with tricky lights on three of them. In a region where it snowed hard every winter and cars needed momentum to keep moving, you wouldn't expect to find lights at the bottom of a hill or halfway up, but there they were. Either it was for a post office or a school, or on the intersection of a side street where some politician lived. The city put them up in July and forgot about them.

The one at the foot of Temple was green, and Phil breezed through with no problem. He chugged up the incline, hung a right at the corner of Arch and stayed level for a while. Next came Elm, and if he hadn't slid, he would have had a yellow three-quarters of the way up. As it happened, he caught it more red than yellow. Elm was a piss-poor excuse for a hill, a slope really, so Phil decided to stop. You never knew when cops would pop out of the woodwork, and Phil was not in good with the cops.

He was on the wrong side of someone else, too. He'd been thinking about that hate call with the accent. Phil had gone over the list of law-enforcing Latins, and he couldn't think of a one who had done trade with Isaacs. They were all new, plunked into the police force in bulk after some kind of discrimination suit. Isaacs hadn't gotten to them yet.

Why was the accent so interested in Grace? Phil remembered what the bastard reporter had said about Heywood's dope being from Colombia. Maybe this Heywood kid had real good reasons for skipping.

The Bronco-Blazer idled right behind Phil, sitting there as the light turned green and Phil's wheels made Mixmaster noises. Funny, because there was plenty of time to pass. Phil took a rearview stare at it. When the wind blew its hood clear, he noticed the chains draped over it. That was the kind of thing Nazis would do.

Weren't Nazis always showing up in places like Colombia?

Phil was zigzagging down Arbor now, approaching the bottom of Fountain. This was a real hill; from the foot, the traffic light for the library crosswalk wasn't even visible. His neck rigid, Phil kept his eyes fixed on the top of the arc that his wipers cleared every few seconds. The car held a straight course, and he knew he was at the point where the light could be seen. The wipers passed, and he saw it. Red. It held that way until he was almost beneath it, the Bronco-Blazer at his rear.

He ran it, and the four-wheel drive vehicle followed him. If it was cops, they weren't interested in sticking him with a moving violation. But whoever it was, they wanted to stick him.

Phil had dressed the way Marty liked him to dress when

he went visiting leads. A brown suit, a yellow shirt with nice buttonhole detailing—and drip-dry, too, so he could handle it without Grace—and shoes that he'd recently slapped some liquid polish on. No Colt, because he was wearing the pants that fit right instead of the loose ones that accommodated the holster. Dressed to be killed.

Naturally, a man with other men on his tail wanted to hurry. Naturally, in a snowstorm he couldn't. He should keep cool and use the time to figure.

The floodlights would be on up and down the street, including at his house. That was good. The neighbors would all be shut up indoors. That wasn't so good.

Phil thought while he sweated. Beating and pistol-whipping was probably what was on the Yuletide agenda. Shooting? They'd threaten him at close range, maybe kidnap him, but they weren't likely to take potshots across the lawn. If it was people who wanted information about Grace, they'd be more interested in keeping him alive for questioning. He wouldn't want to bet on it, though.

Phil was drawing close to his house now, with his pursuers clinging as close as a U-Haul trailer. He considered the automatic garage door opener; he could use it without alighting from his car, but they'd be right behind him, blocking the garage door from closing. Then he'd be a pig in a poke. Better to park and make a run for it, though they'd be ready to follow.

When Phil pulled up to the garage door, the Bronco-Blazer was practically locked on his bumper. They were waiting for him to make a move. He used the time to breathe deep and steel himself. Soon, he saw that he'd hesitated too long. One of them was emerging from the passenger side. They were going to smash the window and pull him out, and no one would hear. Christmas carols were screaming from the Whelan's loudspeaker. More effective than a silencer.

Now the other one was getting out, but Phil had already

flung himself across the seat and out the door. He was running toward the sound of "Oh Holy Night," and the lights that were trained on the lawn display.

The one who'd alighted from the passenger's side was almost even with him. The driver, Phil knew, had to cross behind the car, a maneuver that would take a few seconds. Already he had the first reindeer, the newest one, unplugged from its flimsy aluminum pedestal.

About four feet high and grinning, the reindeer weighed almost nothing, but Phil added body English, and it caught the lunging man by surprise. He didn't fall, and he didn't drop the ugly tool he had in his hand. But he stopped. By then Phil had the next one ready. Dancer. He threw it at the tool bearer, now recovered and closing in on him. Out of the corner of his eye, he saw the second man, still several yards away, slip and tumble into the snow, then rise quickly.

Prancer he held before him like a shield, as he ran up the six concrete steps to the Whelan's door. The first man followed and reached around the celluloid figure, landing blows on Phil's body but not his head. Prancer was hoisted in front of it protectively.

Phil had already leaned on the doorbell, and his two enemies knew they'd entered a DMZ. They lit out, tracing a wide loop around the remaining reindeer as if they feared them, and lurched away in their Bronco-Blazer.

No one ever came to the door. Maybe Phil hadn't pressed the button right, or maybe the bell couldn't be heard over the music. The Whelans might have decided to hole up for the duration. The telephone and the door be damned, they might have figured; they were going to bust out with those carols.

Phil thought, but wasn't sure, that his body was aching. The wind tried to block him as he lumbered back toward his house. He'd reached his driveway before he realized that Prancer was still in his arms. Turning to heft it back into the Whelans' property, he crashed down with it. He was eye-level with Prancer, who leaned rigidly against an antler, as in death. Several yards away lay Dancer, hoofs stretched out toward the sidewalk, flanks already dusted with snow.

The warrior lay with his deer. He could get up any time, he reasoned. There couldn't be any internal injuries, or he'd have seen blood oozing from his mouth into the snow. Phil couldn't hear it over "It's Beginning to Look a Lot Like Christmas," but he believed he could feel the beats of his heart. The heart that Marty said he wasn't putting into insurance sales.

Eighteen

Grace was in this cab of terror because Darcy and Ted said she should be here. Yes, Ted, God bless him, had a voice in this decision, even if it was just a long-distance voice hundreds of miles from Park Avenue, New York City, where Grace's life was in the hands of a crazed taxi driver.

The driver was calmer now that the buses seemed to have disappeared. It was the buses that had made him particularly crazy all the way from the Port Authority terminal. Grace didn't have many kind words for buses either. The one she took up here from New Jersey had made her carsick, and it wasn't like they sold Dramamine on that rainy street corner where she waited for it.

It was still raining and dark, and Grace pitied the hundreds of people scuttling along the sidewalks under umbrellas. New York, you can have it, she thought, as she always did in the days when she went on those bus tours for a dinner and a show. Now that Huddersfield had the Coliseum, the shows all came there sooner or later. So there definitely was no need for New York.

She needed it today, though. This taxi was taking her to

a public relations firm named Carson-Heller so that she could infiltrate it and nab the file on Sound TV.

Egg her on as they did, Ted and Darcy didn't like it when she told them she was going to play it mostly by ear. None of their business. She had butted out when they did their bits; now she'd do hers.

Their bits had been a lot easier than this. Darcy pretended she still worked at the job she'd left and called up Brown University and St. George's Prep. Said she was considering hiring Heywood and needed verification of his graduation.

They never graduated him. They never even heard of him.

That and the music thing meant he wasn't who Darcy thought he was. He'd even admitted as much when he told Darcy something about starting over. So they took Ted's advice and decided to do some digging. Deep background, Ted called it.

Or the way Darcy put it, how are you going to find Dr. Jekyll if you're looking for Mr. Hyde? And all this time Grace had thought she was looking for Mr. Right.

Ted found out which p.r. firm had smoothed out the videola scandal at Sound TV, and Grace was going there to discover how Heywood worked into it.

It was a piece of the puzzle, Ted kept saying, and they definitely needed to solve it, because Heywood had skipped Amarak without a trace. They expected him to be real careful about traces now. That scene on the cellar steps at the house in Crenshaw showed him that Grace meant business.

Grace was going to do her part, but she put the whole thing in the cockamamy category. All they had was one photograph, autographed for the wrong person. Maybe Heywood picked it up at the yard sales where he got those old records.

Okay, she had to agree with the others on one point. He

was keeping the records and the picture hidden, and that looked suspicious. Face it, if you needed storage, you got some organizers from Closet Maid. You didn't pay to have hidden compartments and spring panels built into a mahogany cabinet.

Even if they found out about his past, Grace worried that it wouldn't help. All they were doing was looking in the rearview mirror. Which is more than her cabbie was doing.

In spite of all his zigging, zagging, and horn blowing, it was getting late. The plan called for Grace to arrive at Carson-Heller shortly after nine. Red lights were one thing; nothing you could do about them. But the people who kept crossing after the light changed, maybe they needed a tap with a fender.

Cool it, she told herself. Calm down. The cab got stuck once again in front of a pedestrian parade, and she forced herself to look out the window. One of the buildings had fountains going in front of it, spraying up into the rain. Dumb. Yet eat in a restaurant here, and see if they give you a glass of water.

Before she was really ready, the driver was letting her off. Grace became one more moving umbrella on the sidewalk. But maybe this umbrella was more anxious than most of the others.

Finding the address she wanted was easy. The lobby floor had a shine you could have skated over if they hadn't rolled out a rubber mat. There were guys in gray uniforms, security guards. She saw them staring at her as she scanned the directory under the clock.

Carson-Heller, floors twenty-two through twenty-four. The bunch of floors didn't faze her one bit. Ted had warned her that just one wouldn't accommodate this monster. She was to go to the lowest number.

The banks of elevators threw her off; there were certain ones for certain floors. She had to go elevator hunting, feeling the guards' eyes on her. That also could be because she was the only person in this lobby without a paper bag. Lunch, she thought, until she saw some people sipping out of them. She hadn't noticed, but there must be a Dunkin' Donuts on Park.

The elevator kept filling up. Someone even wheeled in a little cart full of folders, just to make it cozier. Squeezed into the middle, Grace waited for the doors to open and thought about the Coconut Grove fire.

If she had wanted out on twenty or twenty-one, she didn't see how she could have made it. But at twenty-two the cart moved out and she followed. A glass door opened into a reception area, staffed by a girl in a red dress with her hair raked back into a braided bun. Grace wondered if the telephone headset she wore helped keep the hairs in place.

The console in front of the girl was buzzing nonstop, so she motioned for Grace to take a seat. About thirty buzzes later, she asked Grace how she could help her.

"They sent me over from the temp agency." Let her ask which one. Grace had memorized a whole list from the Yellow Pages in the motel phone book, learning them jumbled so as not to blow it with alphabetical order. If one name didn't accomplish her purpose, another would—assuming the temp agency brands here were the same as in Jersey.

She didn't have a chance to try them out. The receptionist said she'd have someone from Human Resources come and get her. Then she went back to her buzzes.

Great, thought Grace. I might never even clear the reception area. One of those carts wheeled past, en route from the elevator, and she noticed this time that a man in a uniform was pushing it.

A security guard, she thought for a panicked moment, until she took a better look at the guy's greasy hair and skinny build and the safety pin holding his glasses together. Well, everybody needs a job, even if it's only pushing carts. His green uniform had a Carson-Heller insignia on one shoulder. Nice way to represent yourself. And they call this public relations.

They hadn't spared any effort on this reception area, though. While she was gauging the depth of the maroon rug with her heel, a thirtyish man in a four-hundred-dollar navy blue suit emerged from an entrance to the receptionist's left and walked toward her.

"You're the temp?" he said.

Grace rose, her heart pounding in an arc from collarbone to stomach. "That's right."

"Hi. I'm Hal Rosenstein. It looks like there may have been a mix-up. We've checked through the log, and it doesn't seem that anyone called for a temp today. What agency sent you?"

"Manpower." If that didn't do the trick, Grace was all set to reel off the speech Darcy had helped her with: I work for all of them, the call woke me up this morning, I'm not sure which one it was, I'm positive they said Carson-Heller.

Hal Rosenstein looked at her kindly. "Are you sure they said Carson-Heller?"

"I'm positive they said Carson-Heller."

Furrows appeared in the executive brow. "Why don't you come back to my department with me, and you can have a cup of coffee while we figure this out."

She followed him through a maze of dividers covered in orange fabric. Some people worked hidden behind them, their voices muffled but audible, while others were visible in little cubicles that opened onto the walkway.

Like working in rabbit warrens, Grace thought, and each warren seemed to have its own set of file cabinets. Orange, every one of them.

They walked for miles, it felt like. Rosenstein kept up the patter for most of the trip, talking about how a company directive had asked all supervisors to notify the H.R. department before calling temp agencies.

"We've got our own temps lined up. It eliminates the middleman and makes things better for everyone concerned. I'm sure you realize that you don't get the entire fee we pay the agency. I hope we get you straightened out today, but you might want to consider registering with us directly."

Grace murmured something that she hoped made sense. She was trying to get the lay of the land.

It looked bad. Multiply the orange file cabinets she had seen here by three floors, and there was no way she was going to find the Sound TV file.

They reached a real office with a real door, all the way in the corner, and Rosenstein plunked Grace down on a coach and pointed out the Mr. Coffee machine. Besides Mr. Coffee, this area was occupied by a young girl dressed in a knit top, slacks, and maybe a half dozen gold chain necklaces. Looked like she waltzed past the clothing stores and ran straight for the jeweler's. She appeared to be pecking at a huge gray typewriter, though Grace didn't hear any typing noises.

"I'm sorry. I've forgotten your name," said Rosenstein, who had never asked in the first place.

"Marion Buchsbaum," said Grace, figuring it served the real Marion Buchsbaum right. Tonight was mah-jongg night, and Marion would probably have a field day dishing the dirt on Grace.

"I'm going to call Manpower and try to track down where you belong." He disappeared.

Grace asked the girl for directions to the ladies' room, and was given a key attached to a big wooden paddle. As she took it, the girl pushed a button and the typewriter went into action on its own, making machine-gun noises.

"One of those new kinds," she said to the girl, pointing at the typewriter.

The girl shrugged. "I guess so. All of them around here are electronic. Some of them are newer than this."

The telephone was new, too. It looked like the one at Ted and Barbara's house, the one Barbara dialed by pushing the buttons with a pencil. That one had a memory for storing numbers. Grace was Memory Dial No. 1. Ted had shown her.

Grace really needed the ladies' room, but long after her needs were fulfilled she stayed there thinking.

All right. Her plan hadn't been so great. Even if the best possible thing happened and they let her work here for a day—putting her someplace where they were short-handed and figured someone had called for a temp—no way could she handle a modern typewriter like that. It had been about thirty-five years since she got her "C" in Business Typing. Back then, typewriters didn't work by themselves.

Manpower was going to say they didn't know any Marion Buchsbaum. She could use the early-morning-confusion ploy and venture a few more temp agency names. It would buy some time, but the time would be useless. She had wanted a whole day so she could ask questions and nose around.

Better nose directly with Hal Rosenstein. Like he said, who needed a middleman?

Even the stalls are orange, she noticed as she finally exited from one. Combing her hair, she read the hand-lettered sign taped to the mirror: "Beautiful crocheted sweaters for sale every day this week noon to 1 in the 23rd-floor cafeteria. Ideal Christmas gifts. For more information, Laura x481."

Next to this was a smaller notice, typed and more official looking: "Ladies. Due to a rash of thefts over the past weeks, we are asking your cooperation in keeping track of your handbags and valuables at all times. Please report any thefts immediately to Security x257."

Grace peered at the date on that. Recent.

That was New York for you. Thieves all over the place. She took a deep breath, busied herself with one more detail, and went back to Human Resources. She was ready to steal the Sound TV file.

Rosenstein had been looking for her, the girl said. She buzzed the intercom, and he popped out.

"I'm really sorry, Marion. Manpower has no record of sending you here. They say they don't have your name in their files—I'm sure that's a mistake. Could it have been some other agency?"

Grace said what she'd decided on saying in the orange bathroom stall. "No, it's Manpower. Definitely. This isn't the first time they've gotten it backwards. They called me bright and early, said I was going to work for someone over here who does p.r. for a TV station. Maybe if you could track down who does the media accounts, you'd find out who asked for a temp."

Accounts: she knew all that kind of lingo from Ted.

The brow furrowed once again. "TV? I can't think of—"

"They mentioned Sound TV. I remember, because my daughter watches it all the time." The real Marion Buchsbaum had a daughter. Might as well be consistent.

At the mention of Sound TV, the girl at the desk looked up from her silent typing. "That's Nancy Ortega's boss. Mr. Chapman."

"I thought Bill Chapman was out of town," said her own boss, whose furrows were deepening. "Get Nancy on the phone."

It went as Grace knew it would. This Nancy said no one had ever sent for a temp. They never needed temps there, period.

The furrowing gave way to a forced smile. "I'm terribly sorry about all this," Rosenstein said to Grace, who had risen, knowing that this was goodbye. "Maybe it was some kind of a joke. Listen, I've got to get back to some other things, but I hope you can fix it all up with Manpower. Let me know if I can help in any way."

He said those last words with his back already turned, walking away.

"So long now," Grace said to the girl, who shrugged. "I thought I better tell you that I left the key in the ladies' room. Sorry. By the time I remembered, it locked behind me."

With a sigh, the girl flicked off the machine, withdrew a heavy key chain from her top desk drawer and left for the lavatory.

Grace darted over to the desk, lifted the telephone handset, and scanned the buttons in its center. There it was: automatic redial.

She depressed the button, and the numbers 673 flickered into the read-out window. The last number dialed had been x673. The office handling the Sound TV account.

"Nancy?" Grace said to the person who answered. "This is Hal Rosenstein's new assistant in Human Resources. Turns out that Mr. Chapman asked for a temp before he went on his trip. She's coming over now to help you do the filing."

Grace hung up on a sputter of protest.

At the first cubicle where she asked, no one knew where Mr. Chapman was located. But a passerby heard the request and stuck his head in. Chapman was up on twenty-four.

She got on the elevator and got herself steered in the right direction. Maybe the handling of the Sound TV videola incident had made p.r. history, but it hadn't gotten Mr. Chapman a closed office. Grace was directed to a cluster of cubicles. Chapman's was in the back, against the wall. Perhaps it at least had a window. Before Grace could find out, a woman of her own age stopped her.

This had to be Nancy Ortega, walking toward Chapman's space with a large binder in her arms. She had on a black skirt, a black jacket, and a black mood. Grace said she was the temp, and Ortega said there must be some mistake. In fact, she was going to call the H.R. department but hadn't gotten around to it. She had a million things to do this morning, and now that everyone was away at the convention, maybe she'd catch up.

Sure enough, all the cubicles except hers were empty. Each had its own file cabinet.

"If you're so busy, maybe that's why your boss called for a temp," said Grace, trying not to be too persuasive.

"Impossible. It's not in our budget."

"Don't bother calling," said Grace. "I'll go back and tell them you don't need me."

Nancy Ortega thanked her and proceeded toward Chapman's cubicle. Grace went a few yards in the opposite direction. Then she did an about-face and started walking like Wilma Rudolph, nearly colliding with Ortega, who had deposited the binder and was emerging from Chapman's office.

"Call Security or something," Grace blurted. "Just as I was leaving, I saw a guy run out of here with a handbag." She decided to venture it: "I think it was black." Not very likely that Ortega would have been carrying one in any other color. "Two seconds ago. Maybe he's still waiting for the elevator."

"Oh, my God," said Ortega before she took off.

Grace identified Ortega's desk as the only one with a typewriter. The file drawers were neatly labeled. No Sound TV in "S-V."

She took more time in Chapman's cubicle because it was set far back from the walkway.

Sound TV occupied about an entire third of a drawer. An entire rainbow of colored plastic tabs labeled the file folders: Sound TV–News Clippings; Sound TV–exec bios; Sound TV–promotion announcements; and on and on. Grace scooped it all out and cradled it in her arms. The pile came up to the level of her chest. She got a good grip on it and trudged out.

She waited with three other people in front of the elevators, hoping Ortega wouldn't pop out of one, accompanied by guards.

"You need some help carrying that?" asked a man, and the others seemed to be eyeing her funny.

"Nope. I've got it."

"You ought to call Physical Transfer when you've got that much stuff. You could hurt your back."

Physical Transfer? She recalled the green-uniformed guys wheeling carts filled with file folders. In particular, she remembered the one with his glasses pinned together.

"We were in kind of a hurry." She lowered her voice, confidential. "And those guys don't always get it right."

"Oh, yeah. Some of them don't have all their ducks in a row. They're strange ones."

She looked pretty strange herself; he had let her know that. Too strange to walk unnoticed through the lobby.

The elevator arrived jam-packed. It was lunchtime. Grace got off at twenty-three and followed the signs to the cafeteria. It turned out to be a small room with vending machines, a sink, and refrigerator. Scattered around three tables were a handful of brown baggers, and a few more waited their turn at the pint-sized microwave.

The only real activity was at the fourth table in the far corner. As Grace had expected, the sale of beautiful crocheted sweaters was in full swing.

She dumped her bundle on a chair and joined the ladies picking through the goods. She selected two sweaters, the bulkiest in the bunch, paid a price that nobody in Huddersfield would have *dreamed* of asking for (it wasn't like crocheting took as much material as knitting) and asked if there was anything to carry them in.

The woman who was running the show produced a plastic bag printed with the name of a supermarket.

"I need two," said Grace. "These are big sweaters."

Soon afterward, she was walking past the guards in the lobby with two Red Apple bags, stuffed full. It was still raining, something she hadn't thought about in that windowless cubicle land. Somewhere up there she had forgotten her umbrella.

It was going to strike people on the twenty-third floor as peculiar, the way she had tossed the sweaters on the hallway outside the cafeteria. There was no room for both sweaters and files, and it wasn't like she could get into the ladies' room and stuff them in a trash can. Carson-Heller kept its lavatories locked. Just in case anyone wanted to take something.

Nineteen

Darcy wouldn't have made much of a secretary whether she knew how to work those modern typewriters or not. She was so excited about the files that she was elbow-deep in them before she gave Grace the message.

"Your husband called. He said he wants to know how much you're spending. He also said that something terrible happened last week, and he needs to discuss it pronto."

"Last week? He's dramatizing. Ted saw him Saturday when he went to my house for the Panzer picture. He didn't hear about anything terrible."

There was no longer any need for Ted to mail them the picture. Four other photos of Panzer and other AFV band members were arrayed over the pillows on Darcy's bed.

The area beneath the photos was a tangle of wrinkled coverlet and open file folders. Grace had pulled a chair up, and sat jogging paper into piles and plunking unneeded files down on the floor beside her. Darcy was still on her knees, pawing through copies of press releases and news clippings. Several sheets of onionskin had slid off the bed, and she crushed them with her knees as she moved.

"You're going to be sleeping with paper clips tonight, girl," said Grace, congratulating herself on having steered the mess away from her own bed. There was still plenty to sift through. She'd call Phil later.

They ordered out for pizza and kept going, rereading all the files from the scandal year, giving special attention to the ones in the folders labeled Legal and Image—Carson-Heller's euphemisms for crime and clean-up. They ate the pizza, and they still kept going.

When the last slice lay cold and congealed in its Palm Beach Pizza box, Grace called it quits. There were no more photos of AFV, and the ones they'd found weren't much use. Heywood wasn't in them; neither were any of his friends, according to Darcy.

Grace made her look at them hard, because these weren't exactly passport photos. Looked like everybody had climbed up on a cake of dry ice for the posing session. There was more smoke here than in the back room of The Gavel after a tough day in court, and the lighting was the kind you got when someone went too heavy on the Miser bulbs.

At this point, they couldn't see where Heywood fit in. Darcy had an idea that he managed the band, but the fat bunch of double-spaced typewritten pages in the Legal folder didn't mention any manager.

In fact, almost no one was mentioned specifically. That was the game, the way Carson-Heller convinced Sound TV employees to brief them on the situation. No one had to name names, though there were continual mentions of the band AFV.

At first that looked promising. But now it seemed about as hot as that last slice of pizza, which Darcy was actually cramming into her mouth.

The parts about AFV were done up in question and answer format, interviews between various Sound TV people and Carson-Heller's Bill Chapman—all about bribery and drugs, but as interesting to read as an auto accident claim.

Q: So you're saying that some of the veejays preferred payments of drugs to payments of cash.

A: I'm not saying that I personally did.

Q: And I'm not asking you. I'm not a lawyer. I'm not interested in which individuals did what.

A: Yeah. Well I feel pretty nervous about this. How do I know what you're going to do with what I tell you?

Q: We're on your side, remember? I'm just trying to get the story straight. I'm supposed to be the only one who talks to the press about this, but somebody's bound to spout off, and I don't want any big surprises. Frankly, I'm trying to save everyone's ass. Hey, I watch you all the time. I'm a big Sound TV fan.

All this from Bill Chapman. Which explained to Grace why he hadn't done better than a cubicle with a window. She stole another look at the photos. Maybe Chapman came to work wearing animal heads on his biceps like them.

There wasn't much of a story for him to get straight. The veejays and programming people agreed that someone in AFV had been dangling cash and cocaine in exchange for airplay.

The AFV guy was basically a courier for payments made by a record company called Domination, one of the biggest. It wasn't clear how the arrangements were made. Domination was out in Los Angeles. The band, one of the veejays said, was from "around here." Since Sound TV was headquartered on the west side of Manhattan, presumably that meant the New York area.

When the veejays weren't calling AFV "piss poor" or "pathetic," they described it as "unsigned." According to Darcy, that meant it had no contract with the recording giants. It must have been recording on an independent label.

"So how did it hook up with the big L.A. money?" Grace asked. She had kicked off her shoes and was lying on her bed with her eyes closed. She hoped Darcy would wave the white flag soon and stop crackling those papers.

"The courier and the record execs were old school pals, maybe."

"Where, at Brown? Maybe the record execs and Heywood made up the same lie about going to the same school. That's the best connection we found so far. Looks like I committed a felony for nothing. Proved I could do it, though."

Comforted by this thought, Grace snored softly for a moment, then willed herself awake. She swung her legs over the bed and pushed her feet into slippers.

"I'm about ready to wash up and go nighty-night. I'd advise you to rake that bedspread with a magnet. You get a staple in your back, you risk infection."

Grace had to address these remarks to the thin air, because Darcy was lying down on the carpet next to the far side of her bed. But now her head popped up like the toast was done.

"Heywood's mixed up in this. I'm sure of it."

"Oh, yeah?"

"It says here that the AFV courier got angry with one of the veejays and picked the lock to his apartment and stole things. He let the veejay know it was him."

"I saw that. So?"

"Heywood knows how to pick locks."

"You think so? You thought he went to St. Whatziz and Brown."

"I didn't see him go to school. I saw him pick a lock."

Grace stifled a yawn. "You think it's a rare skill? Like pastry cooking or something? Him and a thousand others can do it." She sat thinking for a minute, then got up.

"Okay," she told Darcy. "Make a list of the people that Chapman interviewed, and go through the Promotion and Position Changes file."

"What for?"

"Look at all those press releases they sent out after the scam about so-and-so joining Sound TV and so-and-so being relieved of his duties. Tomorrow I'm going to talk to one of the clean guys, somebody who was there when it happened and didn't get the shaft."

"How do we locate one of those?"

"I told you. Go through those papers and find somebody Chapman talked to who wasn't relieved of his duties. Now if you'll excuse me, I'm going to relieve myself."

By the time Grace finished with the bathroom, Darcy had compiled a short list of names. The two women were asleep when the phone rang. It was Phil.

Grace moved the hair clip off her hair and listened to the details of last week's car chase and the ordeal in the Whelans' backyard.

She didn't like it. "At least you're in insurance now," she said. "Find out if we're covered for those reindeer."

"The hell with them. Somebody's after you."

"Yeah, and I'm after thirty grand that we can't pay out. It's the cops, Phil. Figure it out."

"No cop with an accent is in Isaacs' camp."

"It's a cop who can put on an accent. Use your head."

"That's the only part of me that wasn't beaten to a pulp. I didn't say anything to Ted, I didn't want him to worry. But didn't he mention how I was moving stiff when he was here? I can hardly get out of a chair."

Go to a masseuse, she was tempted to say, thinking about his dealings with that filthy whore. Instead, she told him to buy Ben-Gay.

"Ben-Gay isn't going to save our necks. Your fugitive is mixed up with big trouble. Who the hell is this guy anyway?"

She tried to find out the next day. At nine sharp, she called Sound TV and asked for the names on Darcy's list. The woman on the other end of the line didn't recognize most of them. Either they had left on their own, or they'd been shown the door without benefit of a press release.

When the woman got huffy, Grace thanked her and hung up. A half hour later, it was Darcy's turn. Two of the names struck oil. One had just left for a vacation. The second, Wayne Finley, would be back at two.

Grace was going to take it from there. None of those Marion Buchsbaum aliases required; she would tell Finley the truth—that she was a law enforcer. He was familiar with legal investigations. She could tell that from a few flips through the Carson-Heller files.

A technician at Sound TV, Finley had been interviewed by Chapman and knew about the payoff schemes. He was one of the people who actually loaded the music videos into machines and played them. But he couldn't have been farther from the selection process.

Apparently, Carson-Heller believed him. Because in the many memos recording the p.r. firm's efforts to assist the prosecution with indictments, Finley's name never came up.

Lucky for him, thought Grace, because Carson-Heller had really done a job on most of those people that talked to them. All the interview transcriptions marked "confidential" had been turned over to the authorities. That was how Carson-Heller made history: it helped clean house. That's what the Sound TV top brass wanted, and they wanted it to seem as if none of them had the slightest inkling of what had been going on.

With that accomplished, the campaigns detailed in the Image file started rolling: the chairman of Sound TV coming on-camera to promise all those fans out there that from now on the station would rock with total integrity; the Have-a-Heart-Beat fund-raisers that flew in kids from

India and Peru for weekends with their favorite musicians; the endless wave of charity events, including one called Let's Party for Jerry's Kids, as if those children didn't have enough problems already.

Soon nobody remembered the videola scandal. But Wayne Finley did. He made that clear when Grace finally reached him. He seemed eager to talk about it. She accepted his invitation to meet him at the studio the following afternoon.

The cab ride from the bus terminal was shorter this time. Sound TV was so far west that Finley was able to show Grace a view of the Hudson River as he led her through the studio. It wasn't raining today. Finley motioned across the water with his coffee cup. "New Jersey."

"I could have swum," said Grace. She liked this guy already, had liked him since he came out to the reception area and rescued her from the dirty looks of the receptionist with earrings the size of embroidery hoops. He was dressed nicely in a long-sleeved plaid shirt and brown pants with a sharp crease. And it cost extra work to press that crease if you were over six feet, like Finley was.

He ushered her into a room where a man and a woman were seated on low-slung chrome and leather swivel chairs, busy pressing buttons. Now here you've got the mark of a decorator who likes gray, thought Grace, until she realized that it was just the color of the machines, and the place was lined with machines. Little red lights gleamed on some of them, and they occasionally made buzzing noises, cutting through the rock music that played softly in the background.

"Here's where I work," Finley told Grace. "Charlene's taking over for me while we talk. She's one of our production assistants. Charlene, Grace Stark."

The woman looked over and waved, then quickly hit a button.

"That's Norm, our director." He nodded briefly before consulting a digital clock.

"And that's the studio." Finley indicated a lone wide window looking out onto a carpeted area where two unmanned television cameras were trained on a small platform. The ceiling was festooned with the kind of lights Grace had seen backstage at Ted's school plays. Only a few were on, but she could make out a tiny slab of imitation wood paneling at the rear of the platform.

"That's all there is to it? That's where these veejay people do the show?"

"They've done it already. Each of them does a whole week's worth in a few hours. It's all here on tape, with the videos, the promo spots, and the commercials." He motioned to a pile of videocassettes in fat gray cases, stacked next to one of the machines. "Charlene's going to load them for me while we go someplace to talk."

If that's all he does for a living, maybe I should apply here myself, thought Grace, who had figured out how to work her VCR months before Phil did. She took another look around. She had to admit, maybe there was more to this pro stuff. Her VCR wasn't something out of *Twenty Thousand Leagues Under the Sea*.

It was nice and neat here. Too bad about those TV sets hung all over the place. They were all showing the same program, just like they did in the electronics section of Sears. Except here you couldn't change the channel. It gave her a headache, the way the picture kept jumping from one thing to another. Girls' legs walking down a street in seamed stockings (and who wore those nowadays?), then a playground blowing up, then a man singing and gnashing his teeth.

Nice station, Sound TV. Grace had signed a petition asking her local cable operator to take it off. Why couldn't her neighborhood get one of those home shopping shows like they had two towns over?

She didn't hold it against Wayne Finley though. He was steering her into a small room with striped carpeting and a bright green molded plastic table surrounded by matching chairs. Not Grace's style—too much like a kid's room that somebody pumped up to full size—but it looked expensive.

Finley jingled some change in his pocket and offered to make a coffee run to the vending machine down the hall. Grace declined. She wanted to get down to basics.

"You were here when the videola thing came down?" she asked him.

"Videola?" A puzzled look passed over his face, where liver lips and a doughy nose kept company with very attractive eyes. The eyes laughed first. "Oh, right. The payoffs. Sure. You've got to excuse me. Videola is the name of some editing equipment I use. The flatbed videola. I got confused for a minute. Yeah, I was here. I'm the old man of Sound TV." He lowered his head and pointed to his thinning hair.

"Bald didn't do bad for Yul Bryner," Grace informed him. "Now what about this band AFV. Do you know them?"

"I did know them. Rather, I knew who they were. I even had to roll their tapes." He laughed hollowly. "That should have tipped off everyone right away that something was screwy. A band like that getting play on a national cable station. They were a lousy two-bit local band, but they caused plenty of trouble around here."

"Was there a guy with them named Heywood?"

Finley pondered this. "Not that I know of. They changed around, though. Panzer was the lead singer and guitarist. I think the backup people came and went. It's like that in these unsuccessful bands."

"Who was the one who ran the payments over here?"

"Summerhays. Scott Summerhays. I wouldn't forget that name. But I had nothing to do with that, you know.

205

There was nothing to indict me on." Finley shot a sudden look at Grace, not suspicious, just wary. He straightened up in his crayon-colored chair and placed his hands on the table. On guard. His voice, however, remained gentle and polite.

"If this questioning has anything to do with me, I'm not going to say anything more until I call my lawyer."

"It's got nothing to do with you. I'm a bondswoman. I'm after one person only."

"Who?"

Grace had been thinking. "Scott Summerhays. I'm pretty sure."

Twenty

What clinched it wasn't the name change, Summerhays to Heywood. That could have been a coincidence. More it was Grace's gut feeling about the break-in at the veejay's apartment. She had a good guess as to what Summerhays stole. If this had been a game show, she would have hammered on her buzzer.

She liked this, putting the puzzle together. In fact, she made herself pause and ask Finley to go down the hall. She said she wanted to try that vending machine coffee after all. Like those diet books always told you, chew slowly for maximum enjoyment.

When they were settled over their paper cups, she asked if Finley recollected the burglary. He sure did.

"Who got hit?"

"One of the veejays. Guy who accepted the cocaine but didn't play the clips. They chose the playlist, the veejays. Tekkies like me just roll them. It's all been changed now. The programming department makes the selections."

"What was this veejay's name?"

Finley sipped his coffee and picked at the clear plastic wrapper around one of the Danishes he'd brought in. "Sure you don't want one?" he said. Grace shook her head. "The name, the name," Finley chanted softly. "Damned if I remember."

Grace wasn't sure herself. "Breslau? Israelow? Landau?"

Finley's hand flew up. "Christ," he yelped. "Booby-trapped by the microwave again. The wrapper's cold as ice, but the icing burned my skin off." He sucked his finger for a while, then said, "Arnie Kaplow."

"Let me have that other Danish," said Grace. Time to celebrate. She hit the nail right on the head. She had a son. There were only a couple of things a young man would own that were worth stealing. Electronic equipment or records. Fine watches came later in life.

Arnie Kaplow. That was the name on the address label stuck to the Sinatra record, the one she'd snagged for Phil over at Heywood's tree house. She bet the same address label was on every record in the front section of the mahogany cabinet.

Finley confirmed that a valuable collection of vintage recordings was taken during the robbery. "Kaplow was pissed as hell. It was pure spite. Summerhays couldn't have cared less about that Big Band junk, being a rocker. He just wanted to do something vile to Kaplow. He let Kaplow know he did it, too. He'd strut around here bragging about his second-story job the same way Kaplow used to brag about his record collection. The two of them deserved each other."

"Why didn't Kaplow tell the cops he knew who did it?"

"Are you joking? That would open the whole can of worms about how cocaine was flowing through here. Anyhow, Summerhays was getting his supplies through some bunch of ugly guys that were tied up with Domination Record. With the Mob, maybe. Nobody wanted to tangle with that. Everyone was looking the other way."

Finley reached for his Danish again, cautiously.

"Somebody investigated it," said Grace. "There were indictments."

"Yeah, but they never went far enough." Finley rose and peeked out into the hallway. When he came back, his voice was lower. "I can't go into this, all right? But it was a cosmetic thing. The veejays got the rap because they were the most visible. Some of the low-level guys at Domination got it, too. Middle-management types."

"How about Summerhays. Was he indicted?"

"Sure. I figured you'd know that since you're his bondsman. Bondsperson."

"Yeah. Well, he's got his past pretty well hidden."

"I see he gave you the slip. Did it the other time, too. He disappeared before his indictment was handed down. Nobody tried too hard to find him, if you ask me."

"What do you know about him?"

"Not much. He played with AFV occasionally, backup guitar. I heard he wasn't much good, did lead vocals on a song or two. Panzer ran the AFV show. I don't get involved in the music side, don't even follow it. The veejays do. They interview big names here in the studio and do emceeing at concerts. That's how one of them met Summerhays. AFV was opening for a hot new group at a concert in some hick town."

"Where was AFV from?"

"Connecticut. Fairfield County. That's really all I know about them. They were strictly basement level. Nobody would have ever heard of them if Domination hadn't used Summerhays to courier the payoffs. They were so bad that Domination didn't sign them, even after they did all that dirty work."

"So why did Domination use them for the payoffs instead of some important band?"

"Big musicians wouldn't work as bagmen. They don't need the money, and they wouldn't stoop so low. Anyhow, AFV was in this area. I guess Domination had drug ties all over the country, sort of like a bank branch in every city."

Grace sensed that Finley wanted to wrap this up. She needed more information about Summerhays. Who could give it? Maybe an enemy.

Kaplow? Finley said he lived in Paris now. He liked the French music scene; people over there were into old American music, Cole Porter and Gershwin, and that's the type of crap Kaplow was into. He never really fit in at Sound TV, he was the kind of guy who spent the weekends at those piano bars in the Village.

Kaplow had escaped indictment by never succumbing to the payoff scheme. The other veejays had served brief prison terms, and Finley was fairly sure that all questions had to go through their lawyers.

Grace slowly drew her finger around the rim of her paper cup.

"Who pulled the plug on videola? One of the other record companies?"

"Are you kidding? They were cooking up schemes of their own. I heard they were willing to up the stakes, top Domination's offers. If it had kept out, this whole station would have floated away on a cloud of white powder."

"Then somebody here blew the whistle."

"Not on your life. This is a cushy place to work. We're all well paid, Mrs. Stark, and I for one plan to stay here as long as possible." Finley licked his fingers and checked the hallway again.

"It was a production company," he said, sitting again. Grace had finished her Danish. Leave it to men to forget napkins. "One of those two-bit operations that put the videos together."

"You mean the record companies don't make them?"

"Nah. They make records. Mostly the clips come from garage operations run by film school grads and Hollywood dropouts. The big labels farm the work out to them."

"Like Domination?"

"All of those big guys. Sometimes unsigned bands hire

them direct. From what I hear through the tech grapevine, that's a nightmare. A bunch of musicians scrape some pennies together. They find a film shop and say, hey, we want something fantastic, maybe like that last Cyndi Lauper thing, but maybe you can pick up the props at a tag sale or something, you know, keep expenses down."

Finley looked at his watch. "Got to go back soon and relieve Charlene. Anyhow, one of these little smoke-and-flashpowder film shops—it starts as film, they transfer it to tape later—one of them didn't like how its clips never got airplay here. It was doing all independent label stuff, and its work wasn't getting any exposure. They had ties to people here, and they knew what was happening, so they sicced the guard dogs on it."

He balled up the plastic wrapper from his Danish and stuck it into his empty cup. "Anything else I can help you with?"

"How would an unsigned band like AFV get its videos made?"

"Photon Films, Sherwood, Connecticut, that's how. I ought to know those buzzards. Used to call them about three times a year. They keep sending us all these clips we can't use, too much skin or slashing, and we keep giving them second chances. Maybe it was better in the old days, when the selection process wasn't so democratic."

"But the videos they made of AFV got shown."

"Yeah, because that was part of the bargain, probably something Summerhays threw into the deal himself. He was on the tapes, and like every other egomaniac musician, he wanted to see his face on TV. Geez, those clips were awful. Photon did a little work for Domination, too. That's probably how everyone made friends."

"You wouldn't happen to have those tapes still."

Finley's liver lips tightened into a wry smile. "Mrs. Stark, you wouldn't want to see them. Anyhow, we don't

have five-year-old clips hanging around here. We probably taped over it to do a station promo."

He stood up and pitched his cup into the wastebasket.
Grace followed suit.

"I got to go now," he said. "One of the things I have to
do today is weed through the new clips that came in,
check them for quality before they go over to Programming. Hope there aren't any from Photon. They offend
even my jaded sensibilities. Come to think of it, Photon
hasn't sent any for a while. Maybe they went out of
business or something."

Grace certainly hoped not. Because her next stop was
going to be Sherwood, Connecticut.

On the bus ride back to Jersey, she thought about the
inscription on the photograph. "You beamed us up,
Scotty." What else did it say? Something like, "Seeing us is
believing us."

Even Ted had thought it was "Star Trek" stuff when he
read it over the phone the other day. But Scotty, that was
Scott Summerhays. Beaming was getting on TV.

She thought about the guy she had looked at through
her gun sight on the cellar steps in Crenshaw. As fugitives
went, he seemed pretty clean-cut. She couldn't imagine
him playing that metal music five years back, dressed like
Panzer and those others. Even now, he looked younger
than Panzer. He must have been the baby of the bunch.

Nice baby, dealing cocaine and ripping off people's
apartments.

It was pretty clever though, using those Kaplow records
to cook up a whole new life. Grace had to admit, when she
was lifting those films from Carson-Heller she got a kick
out of being Marion Buchsbaum. Maybe it would be fun to
do like Heywood did and adopt Marion's identity—talk
about her husband, "the attorney," and lord it over
everyone else.

But Marion had sinus trouble. Who needed that?

Twenty One

No balls would be held in the ballrooms, not in the Sherwood Meadow Plaza. Ballroom A was today the site of a seminar on "Whither Off-Pricing?"; Ballroom B was being readied for a powwow on seafood imports.

Darcy had been here before, on business. Located within commuting distance of New York, Sherwood was bristling with new corporate headquarters. Once a minor Connecticut city, it was lately all the rage with multinationals seeking more living room and big tax abatements.

This time Darcy was on business again, looking for lodgings handy to Photon. Rick Mahon, president of the Photon Companies, as it was now known, might squeeze in an appointment if he happened to be in the squeezing-in mood. That was the opinion of his secretary, reached by phone from New Jersey. Mahon was at a trade show in Dallas, would be back in two days or three, "depending on how boring it gets," said the secretary.

"Leave a local number when you get one," she said, sounding pretty bored herself.

Darcy was waiting for check-out time and an update on

room availability. It looked bad here and everyplace else. Sherwood had plenty of hotels, most of them brand new, but meeting rooms chewed up most of the square footage. What beds existed could be booked up solid by a single convention, and this week there were several.

The county's only other city was Millpoint, once an industrial hub, now grimy and crime-ridden. Most hotel guests in Millpoint had six legs and feelers. Between there and Sherwood were dozens of picturesque Connecticut towns, very wealthy, very historical, and very lacking in accommodations.

Darcy circled the lobby fountain again, preparing for another trek past doorways and easel boards. Grace had been misplaced somehow. They were supposed to be working on the buddy system.

The quest ended in the Lido Lounge, where Grace was spearing jumbo shrimp with the Economic Development Council of the Republic of Ireland. Darcy steered her around the fountain and back to the reservations desk.

"Did you check out the Crystal Court?" Grace asked. "Saltines and cheese. Cheap."

"That's the miniature golf operators. There isn't much money in those courses. Mostly it's land banking."

"Half the time, I don't follow you. But I suppose I'm getting an education."

Next thing Grace learned was that Darcy was going to hunt for a bed-and-breakfast place, a route recommended by the reservations clerk as the only convention-week recourse. Darcy explained it to Grace: something like a boarding house. That didn't go over well. But once the word "exclusive" was tossed in, all was well.

Grace was cheerful today, pointing out sights to Darcy as they drove the streets of Sherwood, happy among all the affluence and construction. They had gotten along well during the entire drive from New Jersey.

There were moments, however, when the faces behind the windshield turned somber. Darcy was still taking it all in, about how she'd shared a bed with a man operating under an alias. Scott, as it happened, was one of her least favorite names.

Grace was proud (smug and unbearable, Darcy would have said) of uncovering the phony background. They were on the route of the drug trail. But the trail was five years old and might be stone cold by now. And now that Grace knew Heywood's past, she knew he would want to run fast.

Unless his supplier was still around here, keeping him on a leash. She had to hope for that, because funds were running dry, and, according to Darcy, these bed-and-breakfasts in private homes were too charming to accept credit cards.

The hotel clerk had jotted down an address in Sherwood's downtown, only about ten blocks square. A Spanish mission post office sat on one corner of the main intersection, looking incongruously hot-blooded as it faced a Greek Revival bank and a white church, complete with steeple. With glass and steel towers rising around it, the area looked quainter than ever.

Their destination was marked with a shingle. "Bed and Breakfast Bureau," Grace read aloud, as they got out of the car. "This isn't the place where you take complaints when some store rips you off, is it?"

It occurred to Darcy that Grace might be purposely trying to annoy her. Before they entered, she wanted something settled.

"You know how you do all the shooting?" she said to Grace, who was busily rooting in her purse. "Here, I do all the talking."

"I've been doing all right on my own so far."

"This is different. We're in snob country. If they don't

like us, they'll claim they're full up. So don't say anything at all during the interview. Period." Darcy thought better of it. "Except, maybe, 'How nice,' something like that."

Now she saw what Grace had been digging for, and warning bells went off. "No LifeSavers, and no offering LifeSavers. Ditto for gum. And you're my aunt, remember that, Auntie."

Carlotta Hughes, bureau manager, ushered them into an office that might have housed a school principal. Fifteen minutes into the interview, Grace hadn't uttered Word One. Yet she looked alert and engaged, meaning that she hadn't decided to take Darcy's advice ultraliterally and act gagged, as Darcy feared she might.

Carlotta asked a few carefully phrased questions, in the manner of Henry James running a credit check. This done, she flipped through a file box, pulling out cards until she'd made a neat little pile, then winnowing them with periodic glances at Grace and Darcy.

A single card was selected at last, and Carlotta excused herself to step into another room. Darcy knew this was for the purpose of making a phone call. Discreetly.

Grace hissed for attention. "I can say, 'How nice.' Right?"

"Control yourself a few more minutes, can't you? We're almost out of the woods."

"I'm going to say it. You said I could say it."

Carlotta appeared again, hands clasped in front of her miniprint wraparound skirt, triumph incarnate. A B&B had been located.

Papers were signed. "I'm so happy you could help us," said Darcy, rising. "It'll be so much more pleasant than a hotel. We couldn't even *get* a hotel room." She could hear herself gushing, but gushing is difficult to stop. "I don't know what my aunt and I would have *done* without your help. Apparently there's a shortage of hotel beds here." Could that be interpreted as a slap against Sherwood and hence Carlotta? As a hedge, she added, "Though I believe new hotels are going up."

A sigh seemed to swell up from the bare hardwood floor. Carlotta walked wearily to the window and pushed the curtains aside. "They're going up all right," she said. "You know the joke around here about Sherwood's official bird, don't you?"

"I don't think I do," Darcy said.

"It's the crane."

No one reacted, though Darcy was braced for someone to do so.

"The *building* crane," said Carlotta, not the type to add, Get it?

Darcy's body tensed as she waited. But again, nothing.

Carlotta explained that she found this joke "particularly humorless," because she herself was "a birder."

There was a pause.

"How nice," said Grace.

Carlotta smiled.

The B&B operators who wanted them were Howard and Mariah Coffin of Darlington. You could get to Darlington from New York on the Metro-North railroad, joining other commuters who spent an hour each weekday hurling stirrers, cups, ashes, and peanut shells to the bar car floor, and the rest of the time trying to keep their town pristine.

Mariah and Howard's house was made of stone, and Mariah and Howard looked a little that way, too. But the news that they had separate rooms for Darcy and Grace warmed up the welcome.

As Grace was led to her room, Darcy used a pretext to come along. The chicken-coop breakfronts, the lowboys, and the Favrile vase had already alerted her that they were on Old Yankee turf. She feared leaving Grace alone with

Mariah. Howard had excused himself to putter around his African violets in something called the Yellow Room, an activity that occupied much of his time, they'd been informed.

"Looks comfy," said Grace, settling herself on the white chenille bedspread.

"This is my daughter Courtney's room. She was up at Yale until last year and used to visit quite often. Now she's overseas with the State Department, and we rarely see her. It's disappointing, but we're happy she has the position she wanted."

"Doing what?" inquired Grace. It looked to Darcy as though she were preparing to kick her shoes off and scratch her legs in their nylons. She hoped not.

"Courtney isn't permitted to discuss it. Not even with us," Mariah said with a satisfied smile. "We're not even sure where she's assigned."

"Maybe she's in on one of those illegal deals that ends up on the eleven o'clock news."

In one of those absurd non sequiturs uttered only by mental patients and New England bluebloods, Mariah invited Darcy and Grace down to tea in twenty minutes. She managed to make it clear that this was not part of the deal, and that breakfast was all that would be served henceforth.

"But we really should get to know each other," she said, mostly in Darcy's direction. "And you must see *your* room. It belongs to my son, Harley. Things are just the opposite with him. When he was up at Dartmouth, we never saw hide nor hair of him. But now he's down at Columbia for graduate work and always dropping in."

Ten minutes later, Darcy barged back into Grace's room with her teeth clenched. "Can't you keep your comments minimal? I just called Mahon's office to leave our number. You want to be out on the street when he tries to reach us?"

Grace stopped scratching to reach behind her. "What's your problem? I kept this out of sight, didn't I?" She flung the pistol onto the dresser, where it landed on a pineapple-crochet doily.

"Don't think you're shocking me. I know you'll put that away as soon as I step outside. I can call your bluff."

It was true, Darcy told herself. Grace set her own limits. So later she barely flinched when Grace rejected her suggestion of bathing and accepted a third cup of tea from Mariah. It would be nice to think that Mariah didn't have to offer it if she didn't want to. But the fact of the matter was, Mariah was probably on automatic pilot. Howard had not appeared at the table, apparently preferring to dine with the African violets.

Grace must have gone on to a fourth cup, because when Darcy emerged from the bathroom, something made her pause in the hallway. Snippets of a conversation below were sliding up the walnut banister.

Mariah's voice was low and controlled. Only the phrases "your niece" and "interesting profession" could be made out. And the intonation, assuming agreement.

Grace did agree, loud and clear. "Marketing, that's the up and coming thing. My sister—that's Darcy's mother—is glad she got into it. It's a good living."

Now Mariah wanted to know something about "took" and "degree."

"UMass," said Grace without missing a beat. "The real campus in Amherst, not one of those two-bit branches. She's got brothers, too. My nephews. Smith, he's up at Harvard, and Wesson's down at Princeton."

In her room Darcy dried her hair, and the blast from the blower was like an ominous, unsettling wind. If Grace was already strewing clues around, how long before Mariah saw through her two guests? Would she find a pistol on the flow-blue plates, a cartridge in the cupboard? From there it would be a non sequitur and a farewell.

Alone, Darcy could have gotten along with these people. She worked with them, and she'd met enough of their type at the college she'd attended—a few steps up the prestige ladder from UMass, but not enough of a brand name for Mariah's taste. Darcy knew enough to keep her leather minis packed, along with any signs of strong emotion.

Grace had done a great job so far, but now she was starting to mess up. Darcy wanted to stay put here, so she could pursue some things on her own. She wasn't convinced that Mahon would know anything more that would help.

She was, however, satisfied that Grace had tracked Heywood's drug source to this area. It made sense. He had mentioned Connecticut several times in an evasive way.

Darcy was going to pursue her own investigation. She knew something about the drug scene here. After all, she'd passed through on business.

Howard, in a rare break from puttering, called Darcy to the upstairs hall phone. It was black and heavy, made of an early plastic, with a straight cord instead of a coil. Howard handed the receiver over and went downstairs in his leather slippers and knockabout cardigan, perhaps to listen to the wireless. He'd said four words in as many days, was Darcy's estimate.

She lifted the receiver, hoping it was Mahon. He was back in town, the secretary had said, but busy meeting some kind of deadline. The secretary also said it served no purpose to keep leaving messages.

Second best. It was Valerie, a friend of Darcy's who lived ten miles from Darlington, but not a good enough friend to put Darcy up. Darcy had called her from New Jersey telling her she'd be vacationing in Valerie's area, and hinting heavily about a need for free lodgings. Valerie had murmured something about cramped conditions in her house. Darcy remembered it as a ten-room Tudor equipped with a Jamaican au pair.

But on one point Valerie could not stand to see a friend in need.

"Okay. About that dealer Jack," was how she answered Darcy's how-are-you. "It isn't true what I said about nobody knowing where he lives. I found out from some girl who went home with him once. Still no last name, though."

"Just the address is fine. Terrific, in fact." Darcy glanced around the telephone table. Nothing to write with. All right, she'd memorize it. It was better not to write things down anyway, considering Grace's propensity for playing scavenger hunt in her handbag.

"It's 151 Shoreline. Right on the water. He moves around a lot, but he's definitely there now."

Darcy chanted it back and told Valerie that she was a doll.

"This way you won't have to wait until next weekend. You know, Darce, I never knew you to be so desperate about scoring blow."

"Well," said Darcy, trying to cut down on syllables. Mariah and Howard were both downstairs, but she knew how well sound traveled in this house.

"Look, this Jack is kind of a creep, I'm warning you. If you can cool out till Friday, just come to the party. Why pay when you can get it from the boys?"

"I'm not much of a party girl." Darcy figured that Howard and Mariah would find nothing to object to in that comment.

"The hell you aren't."

She found the house that evening, an A-frame cottage on a strip of frozen beach that everyone but sea gulls had abandoned for the winter. No one answered the doorbell.

The call from Mahon came the next morning. Darcy

drove Grace over to Photon, which turned out to be a sprawling one-story cinderblock affair in a section of Sherwood still awaiting development. Oddly enough, large letters reading WSHR-TV were affixed to the face of the building.

"Check the address again," Darcy advised.

"No, this is it. Mahon said something about a TV sign. You sure you don't want to come in?"

Once again, Darcy demurred and Grace looked relieved. They had agreed that Grace would call a cab to take her back to Darlington.

Leaving the broken glass and twisted street signs of Photon's neighborhood behind, Darcy swung onto I-95 and headed for the shore. She needed Jack to be in this time, before Grace came back to the B&B with what she'd learned at Photon.

Careening down the left lane, she realized she'd had this kind of feeling before. It was the way she felt when Track-It was about to scoop the Garrison Group.

Darcy was going to use an old marketing strategy to dig information out of this Jack. If he was a dealer who traveled in Valerie's circle, that put him in direct competition with Heywood. There were a thousand dealers who worked the streets for every one in the boutique business, the upscale party trade.

If Grace's information was right, Heywood was around here, cutting into Jack's market. Jack would be the first to be aware of his presence—and the keenest to get rid of him.

The beach cottage had a chimney, and there was smoke curling out of it this time.

"I'm looking for a guy who calls himself either Heywood or Scott Summerhays," she told the man who opened the door. He was Vietnam era, just as Valerie had said. The shoulder-length hair was thin and limp-looking except where wiry gray strands sprang up. Instead of the expected baggy Levis, he wore tight jeans with bleach streaks, an attempt to update that failed completely. His gut sagged over them.

"Nobody here by that name," said the man, his hand still on the door. "I'm Jack."

"Is that right? Well, I heard he's Jack's competitor." That got her ushered into a room with a fireplace, strewn with floor cushions and litter. A television sat in the corner. It was on, playing music videos.

"Sound TV?" asked Darcy.

"Nah, we don't get cable out here. It's some local garbage." He switched it off.

It was cold in this house, obviously intended for summer habitation only. The fireplace might do the trick on some less-than-balmy late August night, but now the logs burning in it lost out to the chill.

Jack followed her eyes up to the high ceiling. "We get bats sometimes," he said with a little giggle. Darcy wasn't going to like him. But she didn't like being cold either, so she accepted his invitation to sit on a cushion near the fire.

She sat cross-legged. Seeing that, so did he, first pulling his own cushion toward her so their knees touched.

"Take off your coat," he said. Not, would you like to take off your coat.

"No thanks. I'd rather keep it on."

"Come on now. Take it off." Soft and insinuating, like he was talking to someone very young or very old. Someone very vulnerable. She slipped the coat off and hung it over her shoulders, defiantly. But she wasn't defiant enough to move her legs away from his.

"What does this pretty girl want from me, huh?" Already—and she couldn't say this surprised her—he was pawing at her hair, pulling a strand through his thumb and forefinger. She could hear his breathing. It wasn't loud, but it was rhythmical and became more so as his hand dropped down to trace the scoop neckline on her cotton sweater.

She wanted to think that she was just watching it, fascinated, the way people at street fairs pay an admission charge to watch snakes eat mice. It would be no use to try to stop him, to push him away and ask questions. The client had set the terms.

Hours later—or so it seemed—she put her clothes on and asked to use the bathroom. Urinating, she felt the irritation. She did not use the mirror.

When she returned he was dressed and poking the fire, studiously ignoring her.

"About Heywood," she said, reaching for her coat. She put it on and remained standing. He kept his back to her. "He's from Huddersfield. You know who he is. Sometimes he calls himself Scott. He's dealing around here now."

"If I knew about him, why would I tell you?" He turned now and looked into her face, something he hadn't done when he was inside her. She looked back. "You could be D.E.A. for all I know."

"I'm not. Heywood is."

He was paying attention now. She had the papers from Heywood's file with her. She pulled them out of her purse and showed them to him, along with a copy of Heywood's arrest warrant and the bond papers.

"Okay. You've convinced me. I hear things are heating up there in Mass. Somebody gave his name to the feds, and now he's a vampire. We don't want him around here. You live around here? No? You're from up there. There wouldn't be anyone else with you, would there? This lady who posted the bond, maybe?"

Darcy had wanted to tell him about Grace. It was odd how he read her mind. So odd, that all she said was, "Possibly."

"Tell me where you're staying, and I'll ask around and call you."

That's what she had come for, but now she couldn't bring herself to give this man her number. "I'll be back," she lied.

He stretched out on the floor with his eyes closed and his hands on his stomach. "Anytime you want, doll. You didn't want to like it, but you did."

It was late when she got back to Darlington, but Grace was still out. Darcy opened the "hot" faucet on the bathtub all the way, but tepid was what she got. The Coffins kept the water heater turned down. They saw no reason why one would want to boil one's skin off.

Twenty Two

Nobody seemed to close doors at Photon, so Grace got quite a tour as Rick Mahon's secretary searched for her boss.

"He wouldn't be in any of these," said the secretary, jerking her thumb toward two pint-sized offices that faced each other across the corridor. "That's all WSHR."

"You share the building with a TV station?" Grace paused for a moment. A large glass window allowed a view from the hallway into something that resembled the Sound TV control room. Or anyway it looked like Sound TV might look after a tornado.

After talking to herself for a few dozen feet, the secretary realized Grace was missing and walked back to her.

"WSHR is ours," said the secretary, bending over to tie the shoelace on her jogging shoes. This secretary definitely would not fit in at Carson-Heller. Her jeans didn't even look designer. "It's a UHF station. Photon bought it a couple of years ago and moved it over here."

"How come nobody's in there?" said Grace, taking another disdainful look at the equipment. It looked like that Heathkit hi-fi set Phil had tried to build when they first got married. Part of it was still out in the garage.

"It kind of runs itself. We get this home shopping show sent in by satellite. That's what's on now." The secretary pointed to a monitor hanging over a counter cluttered with empty soda bottles. Grace peered at a close-up of a necklace being poked by a knitting needle. She couldn't make out the price.

"Can you pick up this station in Darlington?"

"Sure."

As they continued on, Grace considered asking Mariah Coffin if she could tune in. The Coffins did have a television set, even if they tried to hide it in a console cabinet with doors. Grace wasn't certain what a UHF station was, but if it wasn't educational, the Coffins might not have it. Every time they watched TV you could hear those public television trumpets.

Grace kind of hoped Mahon would be in the makeup room. She would have liked a closer look at the jars and cases littered over vanities topped by bulb-rimmed mirrors. Just like in the movies, if some of the bulbs hadn't been missing.

But Mahon hadn't been around, according to the young man who was lifting plastic bag liners out of the wastebaskets. He advised the secretary to try props.

They found him there, a gray-bearded man wearing squarish brown eyeglasses in a distant corner of an enormous room with a ceiling so high that it looked like an airplane hangar. Grace figured that it must stretch up to the building's second story. The secretary led her past clumps of men and women working with electric tools and airbrushes. The noise was deafening, and the dust made her fear for her coat.

"Your basic Road Warrior rip-off," said Rick Mahon, motioning to the structures at his back as he stepped forward to greet them. Grace could make neither head nor tail of them. Some looked like rocks, huge and colorless. Mahon suggested they move to his office, so he wouldn't need to yell. He did need to clean, however. Everything was coated with grime, including the lone window. Grace was invited to sit in a creaky wooden swivel chair once its seat was cleared of papers. Mahon made himself comfortable across from her, parking his feet on the desktop mess and collapsing a Styrofoam cup in the process.

"You need me for anything?" said the secretary, who was leaning in the doorway.

"Nope. We're fine," said Mahon, patting the pocket on his T-shirt and withdrawing a roll of Tums. "Want one?" he asked Grace.

"How's the burn coming along?" asked the secretary.

"Wicked." Mahon displayed the long bandage on the inside of his arm. "It was hurting like hell the whole time I was in Dallas."

The secretary started toward him. "Maybe you should see the doctor again. You could get an infec—"

The feet came down from the desk with a thud. "Okay, Irene. Enough. We're two days behind on the Ill Wind clip, and you're talking doctors." He popped some Tums into his mouth. Three, Grace estimated. Phil was also a three-Tums man. "Get Bobby on the phone, okay? See if he can look at those motorized spots."

The secretary fled. "Sorry about that," said Mahon, chewing.

"What's with the burn?" asked Grace.

"Nothing. It's from the hot glue we use on the props."

"You're the president, and you're using glue."

"I'm the president, and I'm doing everything." He reached into his pants pocket to send a Tic-Tac chaser after the Tums. "I'm even talking to you when I've got six projects backed up and a TV station to run. Irene said you're from the Law? Looking for Scott Summerhays?"

228

"Right. He's a fugitive. He was arrested in Huddersfield. I'm his bondswoman."

Mahon stretched out clasped hands and cracked the knuckles. He smoothed his hair behind the earpieces of his glasses. He wore it longish and blunt-edged, television bandleader style. Unlike the monochrome gray beard, it was heavily laced with orange.

"Unbelievable," he said.

"Why unbelievable?"

"Nobody's seen Scotty for five, six years. Huddersfield." Mahon shook his head. "I thought they hid him better than that. I thought he was maybe in the Bolivian jungles."

"Close. He's been dealing cocaine."

"Naturally. That was Scotty's talent. He wasn't much on guitar. Didn't deserve that nice maple-neck Rickenbacker of his. Couldn't sing much either. Well, he could, but he had a fruity sound. Didn't go with that wee-wee-wee-wee stuff he blasted out of his big stack of Marshalls."

"You know who supplied him with drugs? That would help."

"Same people who supplied Panzer, another guy I'd like to see swinging from a long rope."

"Panzer also dealt?"

"He didn't then. He took up where Scotty left off. When the megascandal broke, his hands were clean, so he's still crawling around these parts, probably pushing dope in schoolyards. They didn't have to disappear him."

"Who's 'they'?"

Mahon wiped his glasses on a corner of his shirt and blinked at her. "Who told you to come here?"

"I found out about this place through Sound TV."

"Yeah, well, I don't know who you talked to at Sound TV, but you obviously don't know the whole story."

"I know it. I know about the videola payoffs. I know that Scott Summerhays was making the deliveries."

"Then you shouldn't be asking about his suppliers. You should know that they're people who are very tight with Domination Records. They still are, you know."

"So?"

"So nobody's going to go after them. Not even that new hotshot in the U.S. Attorney's office, the Eliot Ness type. I hear where he wants to reopen the whole videola thing, push harder this time. He'll learn better."

"I'm not interested in any of that. I just want to find Summerhays. I posted bond for him in Massachusetts. I want to know where his suppliers are because I think he's sticking close to them."

Mahon lowered his feet to the floor and tugged violently on his desk drawer. "I quit smoking, but I need to smoke. You mind? I've got to do it whether you mind or not."

He thrashed through the contents of the drawer and came up with a cigarette and matches. "I'd like to find the bastard, too," he said after a deep inhale. "He almost ruined this business. The suppliers are around here, somewhere in the county. They're big bad boys, call themselves the Organization. That's all I know. That's all anybody knows."

Now Mahon was opening the window at the side of his desk. Grace's chair squeaked in protest as the blast of cold air hit her.

"I know. Nobody can stand smoke anymore. I'll exhale out the window."

He pulled his chair over and sat talking to the frozen lawn outside. "I was the head prop guy when it happened, up to my ears in gaffer's tape and hot glue." Mahon looked at the bandage on his arm. "Guess things haven't changed so much. But this company was jumping back then. Sound TV was hot and hungry for clips."

"They said you haven't been sending them much lately."

230

Mahon blew smoke out the window. "We're going to be sending them less. I took control of the company about two years ago, and I'm trying to pull out of music videos altogether. I don't have the stamina for it anymore, dealing with these moron musicians. They can't relate to a camera, they won't take direction, they don't want to spend anything. All the good directors and tech people are ditching it, going back to commercials, cable, whatever."

"But you're still doing some of it?"

"It's money, and my partners and I borrowed plenty to buy this place out."

"So you weren't in charge in the videola days."

"Hell, no." Mahon gazed at a spot on the lawn. "We were doing the sickest of the sick music videos then. Now I run it clean. We do your basic sci-fi thing, cycle the footage to make it look like the musicians are emoting even if they can't act their way out of paper bags. We stage some concerts. It'd be cheaper to shoot actual performances, but these rockers with double-digit I.Q.'s won't allow us to fool with the lighting."

He finished his cigarette, tossed it outside, and crossed back to the desk. He dug into a pile of papers and pulled out a packaged videocassette.

"This is what I want to do more of. I'm proud of this."

He handed it to Grace. "Gardening on Your Terrace," she read aloud.

"It's fast, it's easy, it's cheap, it's marketable. We're talking to one of the big discount chains about supplying all their stores with it. You saw our UHF station?"

"Mind closing the window?" said Grace from the depths of her coat.

"Sure." It went down with a slam. "We picked up that station for a song. Bought one in your neck of the woods, too. WPNV, serving Massachusetts' Pioneer Valley. No one wants to invest in UHF these days."

"I'm not sure what that is."

"That's the problem. It stands for ultra high frequency, the channels past thirteen. The ones you probably think you can't receive on your TV set."

"What channel do you use?" said Grace, who wanted to check the price on that necklace.

"Forty-six down here, fifty-eight up your way. The people I bought them from were going broke. They were paying for syndicated programs, old sit-coms, and all that. You wouldn't believe how much that costs. I worked a deal where we show the clips we produced, costing us zip. The rest of the time we get this teleshopping show out of Texas. The programming is free, plus they give us five percent of the sales they ring up out of our areas."

"Very inventive."

"You bet I am. I have to be. Because Scotty Summerhays and his Domination Record pals pretty near sank this ship. Once the thing hit the papers, Domination pulled all its contracts out of here. As if we were to blame."

"You weren't?"

"Good question. We were—not me personally, you understand—because this place was a party scene for every cokehead in town."

"And you object to that?" Grace was still trying to size Mahon up. She had a hunch. Finley said a production company had blown the whistle on videola. It might have been Photon.

"You bet I do. Do you know some of the technicians say they can't work the long shifts here without snorting? I hear that, and they're out on the street." Mahon pounded his chest. "*I* work the hours without drugs. *I* want everybody else to do it."

Grace believed it.

"The old owners let everyone run wild, and look what happened. AFV was a bunch of zeros playing the local club circuit. Thought it was cool to hang out here with the big names who recorded for Domination. The creative

execs from Domination flew in to oversee the shoots.
That's how they hooked up with Scotty."

"Photon made some videos of AFV?"

"Sure, probably on short ends of film that some director
scraped off the reel after shooting a commercial. They had
pals here. I wasn't one. Scotty broke in here one night and
ripped off an old Bolex I used to keep in the office.
Worthless, but sentimental value and all that. Picked the
lock. He did that to people he didn't like. I see you're
nodding. They must have told you at Sound TV."

"Would you have them around, these old AFV tapes?"

Mahon waved toward his desk. "Do I look like the type
of person who throws things out? It would just take a
while to dredge them up. Why do you want them?"

"I didn't see Summerhays when I bailed him out. I want
to take a look at him."

"Sure. Give me some time. And let me know if I can do
anything else. I would love to see that s.o.b. served up to
justice. I come from law-abiding people. In fact, my
brother-in-law is a cop."

"You don't say," said Grace, unsurprised. "I'd like to
bring someone else over to see these tapes. And I need to
see them tomorrow."

"Tomorrow? Are you joking? How do you think I'm
going to do that with everything else that's going on?"

She knew he loved it.

It took a half hour for a cab to come and drive Grace
back to Darlington. It wasn't worth it. Channel 46 didn't
come in on the Coffins' lousy TV set, and Darcy was in a
foul mood.

It took some prodding to get Darcy over to Photon the
next day. Grace had plenty of other questions to ask
Mahon, but the crucial thing was the I.D. Once Darcy saw
the tape, Grace would know if she was shadowing the
right person.

The secretary took a look at Darcy's mink coat, expressed her feelings on animal rights, and showed them into a room furnished mostly with technical equipment.

"This is where we do video editing," she said, staring at Darcy's coat one more time before leaving.

Mahon came in carrying four black plastic cases, his hair and skin coated with oil.

"The Mole Fogger," he said, pointing to his hair. "Gets mineral oil over everything. Smoke effects. Every idiot rocker wants it."

He loaded one of the tapes.

"Oops. Somebody forgot to rewind. He pressed a button and crossed his arms, waiting. "You want to see one with Summerhays on it, right?"

"Right," said Grace. "But we might be interested in questioning some of the other band members. They may know where he is."

Mahon shook his head. "They're all out in California. All except Panzer."

"Too bad," said Grace. "Panzer's the one who can't know I'm looking for Summerhays."

"How come?" Darcy was stroking her fur as if to smooth its injured feelings.

"He's a dealer, working through the same Organization Summerhays is in. If we talked to him, the Organization would know we were in town."

"That would be n.g.," said Mahon. "They are not nice fellows." He pressed another button and a picture appeared.

"I remember this garbage. Ten gallons of mineral oil."

But through the fog, Darcy was able to make her I.D. She nodded to Grace, indicating that the lead singer was indeed Heywood, big as life and five years younger.

It was difficult for her to believe that she'd known this person intimately. The body she had unwrapped so many times from striped shirts and pleated pants was tightly encased in studded leather. For all the exposed areas, he looked more clothed than ever before.

The real shock was elsewhere on the big screen. Panzer showed up more clearly on the video than he had in the photographs. She could see that he was the man who had battered her flesh the day before. Panzer wasn't anybody's real name. The real name was Jack.

Twenty Three

The way Alejandro saw it, Heywood had crossed him again, and Alejandro didn't like it. He was one pissed-off Colombian, but he argued his case with rapid rounds of logic. To act emotional, Alejandro often reflected, was to be foreign.

Heywood was staying at Alejandro's home in an unincorporated area bordering the North End of Millpoint. Alejandro had lived in the U.S. for several years; his official status was resident alien. But he had not yet finished with his living room, attacking and removing traces of alienage the way other people go after dust. It was a ceaseless task, and a thankless one. And it could not be done by a cleaning woman.

Alejandro was angry because Heywood was not cooperating about the television viewing diary. One red-letter day, the A.C. Nielsen Company had called him to ask if he'd fill it out. An opportunity like this, a giant step to assimilation, was not to be missed. It might help make up for the setbacks, which were numerous. He would enroll in a health club, for instance, only to find that everyone else was building home gyms.

The Organization's leadership watched for that kind of

thing. They were Colombians, Venezuelans, Cubans, and Mexicans, on guard for the slightest whiff of Colombia, Venezuela, Cuba, or Mexico on their middle managers. Several years ago they found this house for Alejandro and flew him up. They gave him a booklet entitled "Blending in with the Neighbors." It told him to shovel his walk, mow his lawn, wash his car. He was also advised to keep an airline ticket handy and a full tank of gas in the car.

Alejandro no longer made mistakes like he did the first year, pouring a lip of cement on the roof and sprinkling it with broken bottles. That wasn't Middle Class U.S.A., it was Bourgeois Bogota. Too bad, though. As a kid in Medellin he had always coveted those rich people's homes in the capital, sparkling with glass shards.

There was one South American item that the higher-ups had allowed him to keep: his Browning BDA Super. They were a craze in Colombia but rare up here. Americans didn't seem to like them because they weren't all-steel. Another complaint was that they lacked a safety.

That didn't bother Alejandro. His .38 Super lay on the kitchen table. It jumped from time to time, as he punctuated his defense of the TV viewing diary with chops of the side of his hand. This was what the Organization called a safe house. That's what he was trying to impress upon Heywood.

"You're *not* a Nielsen family, you're a control group," Heywood told him, not for the first time. "Nielsen families get gizmos, not these stinking little diaries. They wire their TVs up to computers or something."

"Maybe," said Alejandro, opening a can of Sprite. Sprite and Slice were his favorite soft drinks. If he couldn't pronounce them, they had to be the most American.

Scott, that was hard to say, too. That used to be this guy's name. Now he was fatter, and his name was Heywood. He was dangerous like a grenade or a mine, and he wouldn't write in the Nielsen book.

"Make a note anyway. Make a note of what you watching."

Alejandro congratulated himself on his remarkable self-control. Okay, when he put down the soda can, he did nudge the Super a little toward Heywood's side. That caught Heywood's eye, he could tell; the diary opened, and a pencil started scratching. But he hadn't yelled. That was the important thing.

Now that the argument was over, Heywood moved back to the couch in front of the TV to finish watching his show. Alejandro noticed with satisfaction that he'd placed the diary and pencil on top of the set. He didn't like what Heywood was watching, though. Some kind of variety show with singers, and one of them looked old. That's the kind of thing you watched in Colombia, picking it up from a Mexican broadcast. It was the afternoon. A Nielsen family should have been watching a game show. Or sports, maybe.

There was no place to note this in the viewing diary, but Heywood and he were not a close family. There was nowhere to write this either, but what Alejandro mostly watched these days was Heywood.

Alejandro used to have a real family, a wife and three kids. One day last year, his wife took the airline ticket he was told to keep around the house. Then she packed the kids in the car with its full tank of gas. That got her to the airport, where they all boarded a plane back to Colombia.

The Organization didn't like it. It looked peculiar to live in this district as a bachelor. Bicycles, kites, neighbors' kids coming over to see the hamsters—that made everything seem normal. Alejandro still walked out to the car at eight every weekday morning to scrape it off and start it up. He and the guys in the two next-door driveways always waved to each other with their free hands, the ones that weren't holding briefcases.

But ever since his wife left, Alejandro felt people spying on him when he came home at noon or so. He could see the miniblinds moving.

Miniblinds, that's what he needed himself. The decorator had said so. Miniblinds in the study to keep the glare off his personal computer, and new drapes for the living room. Once the decorator was through with the first floor, he was going to throw a party for the whole neighborhood. He'd serve white wine and Evian, with a small selection of hard stuff. Maybe they would even play a board game about U.S. pop culture. "The Honeymooners"? "Leave It to Beaver"? Alejandro had all the answers. He knew what the Organization wanted. He had studied up.

He would show the guests his home office and talk about his marketing consulting job. Self-employment is a mixed bag, he'd say. Just try to collect from your clients. And the hours are endless. But arranging your own schedule, that's the good part. A few morning meetings and, boom, you go home.

A change in volume told him that Heywood had changed the channel. "Make a note," Alejandro called out before lumbering to the fridge for another soda. He paused in front of the door to listen for the rustling of pages. Content, he popped open a can.

Settled back in the living room, he saw Heywood begin reaching for the remote control device then change his mind. Too lazy to write it in the diary and too restless to sit still. A moment later, he was up and heading for the stairs.

"Write it," said Alejandro.

"Write what? I wrote it already."

Alejandro put his soda down and strolled to the set. "You make a line here. See? 'Set on, nobody viewing.'" He looked at his watch. "Five-fifteen. You draw the lines here until anybody start viewing."

"So start viewing." Heywood tossed this over his shoulder as he ran up the stairs, probably for a snort. Alejandro knew he was dying for it. A bad practice, getting involved with the merchandise.

When the neighbors came for the party, Alejandro would be lying to them. He wasn't really in marketing, he was in distribution and inventory, making sure that the goods stayed in stock and that new shipments arrived safely.

Jack did the sales and marketing. He had worked out pretty well, even if Alejandro hated his hair and clothes. Jack had a whole fleet of dealers working under him these days, all of them doing club and party business on the Connecticut Gold Coast. Most of them were well dressed, professional looking. Like this Heywood. But Heywood wasn't any use anymore.

Alejandro had a nice operation, none of that Millpoint street pushing. Oh, yes, the Organization had started him out that way, down in the East End. It was bad business, lots of collection problems and shooting. Alejandro banged the Super against his Sprite can. It made him mad just to think of it.

Of course, there still were problems. All the supply snags. No, the station wagons from Alabama weren't pulling up to Alejandro's house as often as they used to. Still, he should explain those visits to his party guests. Mention something about relatives in Florida. The wagons all had Florida plates.

Meanwhile, Heywood was bothering him about wanting a territory. He said he wanted to work off some debts to the Organization.

He hadn't said anything about his arrest. That was like lying, and the Organization didn't like liars. Naturally, they found out. Naturally, Jack went up to Huddersfield the next day. He found out that Heywood had run, which was smart. He also saw that a woman was looking for him, the one who paid his bail.

Even a woman could track down a fool like Heywood. Jack saw him dealing out in the open in New Jersey. The Organization's people in Huddersfield were trying to find the woman, but maybe she would find Heywood first. Then the court might discover all kinds of things about Heywood and the Domination Records deal. That would be of great interest to that young man in the U.S. Attorney's office who was looking into the recording industry.

Alejandro believed Heywood would talk if he were caught. It was simple for Americans to exchange names for freedom. Resident aliens had to trade a lot more than that.

Alejandro wished the Organization would make up its mind about what to do with Heywood. In Colombia it would have been solved long ago, thought Alejandro.

At least the guy could cook a little. Alejandro batted the Super .38 idly around the table, musing on what he wanted for dinner. When he looked up, Heywood was frozen on the stairs.

Alejandro stopped handling the Super, and Heywood came down.

"You got to pick up food at the supermarket," Alejandro told him. "You know the Japanese thing you make the other time. Make it for dinner. Classy." One more try and he was sure he'd start liking it.

"Okay, but I can't run out there all the time. I'm a fugitive, remember? Got to find that one-armed man who killed—" Heywood interrupted himself. "See, there was this American TV show—"

"David Janssen," said Alejandro, very annoyed. Except for the "j" sound, that wasn't even a hard one. "You going to be okay in the supermarket, don't worry."

But Alejandro worried later. Heywood was still at the
A&P when the doorbell rang. Just one steady buzz; it used
to be some bars from the *Dr. Zhivago* movie theme until
Alejandro wised up.

It was Jack. He sprawled on the couch in the living
room, noticed the Super on the coffee table, and moved to
an armchair.

"Where's Scotty?"

"Heywood," corrected Alejandro, careful to control the
aspiration on the initial consonant. "Shopping. You stay
for dinner? He going to make teriyaki."

"Japanese shit again," yawned Jack. "When are you
going to get into Thai food?"

Alejandro made a mental note to record this in a
looseleaf organizer notebook he kept upstairs.

"Let's hope he comes back. I found out where that
woman is, the bondsman." Jack gave an account of Darcy's
visit, with many explicit sexual details. Alejandro was not
impressed. His tastes were different, and he thought Jack
should have found out where she was staying, or at least a
last name.

"Names can be changed," countered Jack. "We've got a
description of the bondsman babe from the Huddersfield
people, and I can describe Scotty's girlfriend pretty pre-
cisely. We've been asking around the hotels. The Organization has contacts with the help."

Jack was running his hands through his slick hair.
Alejandro had always considered Jack hopelessly without
style, but now he wondered if Jack was onto something.
The men's magazines talked about longer hair lengths
and the "wet-look." Could that mean hair like Jack's,
Alejandro wondered. He suppressed a wish to go check
his own hair in the bathroom mirror and concentrated on
this matter of the two women.

"They could be staying with family, friends," he suggested.

"Nobody stays with family, man. That's a Latin thing."
Jack watched anxiety wash over Alejandro's face, relishing
it as usual.

"Maybe I'll stay for dinner after all." Jack reached for the
remote, and the television screen lit up with a crackle of
static electricity. Jack flicked through the channels, stopping when he came to the image of a faucet-type water
filter. The camera stayed on it so long that it might have
been mistaken for a still picture, had there not been a
woman's hand stroking it. Beneath it were the words,
"Retail $39.99, Our Price $19.99." Following that was a
toll-free order number.

"Watch the education channel," said Alejandro.

"Are you kidding? They have good bargains on this
channel sometimes."

This was going to look very bad in the Nielsen diary.

By the time Alejandro made his second request about the
educational channel, it and almost every other station had
signed off. Heywood was in bed, Alejandro was testing the
antacid effects of various types of soft drinks on Japanese
food, and Jack was considering the porcelain doll shown
on channel 46.

During dinner Jack was tempted to compare notes with
Heywood concerning Darcy's physical attributes. He
couldn't do that, however, because he and Alejandro had
agreed that Heywood was not going to know about the
proximity of his pursuers. If Heywood knew, he might
think it wise to move on. They didn't want Heywood to
do any thinking.

A woman was on the TV screen now, chatting sprightly
with disembodied voices. Viewers were phoning in to talk
about the porcelain doll and what a great buy it was and
how it was going to be worth thousands in a couple of
years.

"Idiots," said Alejandro, who had bought a necklace for his wife from this program shortly after its debut. He was glad she had left him before the TV shopping jokes began making the rounds.

It was time to get down to business. The television went off, and the phone books were hauled out of a cabinet.

Alejandro made one call to the Huddersfield people, telling them they could lay off the lady bondsman's husband. Her approximate whereabouts were known.

It was Jack's job to fine-tune the whereabouts. Alejandro didn't like vagueness, and the idea of the Organization checking around with the hotel staff sounded pretty vague to him. He wanted to go direct.

Jack worked through the entire Yellow Pages section in the Sherwood directory. No Grace Stark had checked in at any of the hotels. The Huddersfield people had spelled out the name, so Jack knew he had it right.

It wasn't good to appear too inquisitive, so Jack made the whole series of calls again, trying Darcy as a last name. You never knew, the girl might go by her last name. Nothing turned up.

"Change the voice this time," said Alejandro, when they were ready to start round three. He was still guzzling soda, but it didn't help.

"You've got to be joking, man. I can't use some phony voice. Why don't you do it?"

"Nobody likes Spanish accents. French, that's okay. Spanish is trash." Alejandro had made some private attempts to mold his own English pronunciation to the Maurice Chevalier model. He was not yet ready to go public with it.

The Sherwood Meadow Plaza clerk recognized that Jack was calling for the third time. He asked if it was some sort of emergency.

"It's urgent," said Jack, quite honestly.

"A young woman and an older one?" said the clerk. "I doubt it. That doesn't sound like people on business, which is about all we have here. I think you'll find that's the case all over the area. It's a very heavy convention time."

Jack rested the phone receiver on his chest and told Alejandro.

"Very, very nice," said Alejandro. "They stay with friends, then. Now we never find them."

Jack put the receiver to his ear again. "Let's suppose someone comes to your hotel when you're all booked up. What do you tell them? I mean, they've got to stay someplace, right?"

The clerk informed him of the hotel's referral policy.

"They do that on the day shift, too?" asked Jack.

"Absolutely. I work days myself part of the week. In fact, I think I remember referring a mother-daughter pair about a week ago. The young one was quite striking. She looked a little like Elizabeth Taylor."

Jack hung up. "They got sent to a bed and breakfast bureau."

Alejandro nodded. It sounded familiar. Perhaps he had already recorded this phrase in his organizer notebook, along with other strange names for furniture.

At 8:55 A.M., Jack was in front of the door of the Sherwood Bed and Breakfast Bureau. At 8:59, Carlotta appeared with her key at the ready.

Jack stood between her and the lock. "Did two ladies come by here last week by any chance? A young one and an old one? You find a place for them to stay?"

"That's confidential," said Carlotta. She asked him to step aside.

"The young one looked something like Liz Taylor? Look, it's an emergency. We've got to reach them. There's been a death in the family."

"You are welcome to leave a message with me, and I will notify them."

"Oh, I couldn't tell them that way. That's so impersonal."

"Just leave your number, and I'll have them call you."

"If they hear I'm looking for them, they'll know it's bad news. That would be the same as some stranger telling them it happened."

"Then I'm afraid I can't help you," said Carlotta, opening the door and slipping inside.

When the door was locked behind her, she considered calling the Coffins. But it would only upset them, and they had such nice large rooms.

In the end, she did nothing. She disapproved heartily of family emergencies. For that matter, she didn't think much of Elizabeth Taylor.

Twenty Four

Grace and Darcy did the hard things. Darcy had to rent a car, because Heywood might have recognized the BMW. She searched the county for the cheapest rental place, then held her breath while they shuffled her deck of credit cards. The credit line was blown on every one except a VISA issued by a Delaware bank. The car rental people slapped their machine down on virgin plastic. The interest rate on that card approached usury.

Grace shopped for the Wash'n Dri and the thermoses. Damned if she was going to sit in a car night after night without soup and coffee, and damned if she wasn't going to wipe her hands once in a while.

As for Mahon, all he had to do was make a few phone calls. He had an ad agency on tap, and they worked up a nice spread. Darcy went out early for the Sunday paper to see how it looked.

They'd put it in the right place, under the Friday listings in the television supplement. The photo of Jack bawling into a microphone came right out of Grace's Carson-Heller file. It was topped by a message in fat script: "Payola: The Dark Days of Radio and Television."

The small picture of Alan Freed in the corner lent a nice documentary look. Darcy liked the way they had framed it in a circle. Grace liked Freed's old radio microphone.

Words under the graphics advised viewers to tune in to Channel 46, WSHR-TV, on Friday at 9 P.M. Or, in western Massachusetts, Channel 58, WPNV-TV.

Connecticut ad copy didn't usually list the Massachusetts station, Mahon said. But it would seem perfectly normal if it did. His ad agency might have supplied one piece of artwork for the two areas.

It was important for everyone to know that the show would be seen in two federal judicial districts, including the one where Heywood was arrested. Not many people tuned in to UHF channels, but advertising pumped the number up. Anyway, the Organization would figure out that even a handful of viewers who recognized Heywood might be a handful too many. A lot of people in western Massachusetts knew him, and they knew he'd been arrested. If word got around that he was connected to the videola crimes, the feds might have to do something about it this time.

Okay, Mahon had done a little more than make phone calls. He had actually put together a show. It was a matter of stringing the AFV clips together with some documentary voice-over. He dug up a college broadcasting major who needed a few extra bucks. The kid found some newspaper clippings and hobbled a script together.

Photon even borrowed some footage about radio payola from the local public television station. The rights to use it would cost quite a bit.

The fee came due when the program aired. It might not air at all, because the tape might be missing. The Photon technicians left it out every night, clearly visible on a counter, with its label showing. Mahon made sure they did.

Heywood wasn't familiar with the new interior layout of the building. But he was a bright boy. He could figure it out. It was the job of Grace and Darcy to stop him before he got that far.

It was freezing in the rented car, but Grace didn't want to start it up and throw on the heater. Every half hour, that was the maximum, she said. A stakeout was supposed to be quiet.

"We haven't checked out the east wing for two hours." Darcy protested. "While you drive over there you can turn a little heat on."

They were paying attention to the doors. Someone with the locksmithing talents of Heywood didn't need to bust windows. He'd enter by a door and disarm the alarm system.

There were three doors, not counting the front one. The one on the west side seemed a likely candidate: it was the way Heywood had entered the time he stole Mahon's camera. But that was in the wing that housed the video production area. The WSHR studio was on the other side. A burglar looking for a tape scheduled for this week's broadcast might enter through there. It would be quick in and quick out, just like drive-in fast food.

A narrow driveway surrounded the building. Grace drove half its length, rolling her window down when she reached the eastern door.

"Are you out of your mind?" asked Darcy, shivering in her bulletproof raincoat.

"Just listening for the alarm."

It had occurred to them both that the Organization might send someone over to do it the crude way, tossing a rock through a window. But they didn't think so. The alarm system was described on little yellow signs posted all over the building. It was the kind that was connected directly to the local police station.

The cops weren't going to answer any alarms this time.

Grace had made it very clear to Mahon that she'd lose the bond if she didn't do this solo. They went around and around arguing about it, but it looked like Mahon had gotten it straight. Two nights here in this burnt-out neighborhood, and not a single cruiser had come by.

Cars were scarce, period. Actually, that spared Grace and Darcy from a lot of wear and tear. Each time a vehicle approached, they had to duck down. They had a wide view of the street from where they sat. That gave them time to make the car look empty.

The rear of the building with the third service door was a problem. The structure rubbed backsides with three ramshackle houses. The driveway reached back there and continued circling around to the front: there was no paved access between the rear door and the street that fronted the houses. However, someone could approach by foot through one of the yards. Grace drove back there occasionally to keep an eye on it.

She rolled the window up and settled for the wait at the east wing.

"You lowered the temperature about twenty degrees," complained Darcy. "The alarm isn't going to go off. They won't send an amateur."

"Maybe. Maybe they can't spare Heywood. Or maybe they're sending a different pro."

Silence. They had thought of this before.

Grace changed position. This waiting was murder on the lower back. "I bet they send him, though."

"How can you be sure?"

"They wouldn't mind if he got shot. They're probably pissing their pants about that Friday TV show. You heard what Mahon said. Some gung-ho federal prosecutor wants to reopen the videola case. It would be handy for him to question someone who's already arrested."

There was no doubt that the Organization knew about the television program. In a stroke of genuis, Mahon had phoned some selected Domination executives, asking them to tape some reminiscences about videola for the show. Naturally, they had declined. It was a safe bet they had spread the word.

It was a smart move not to rely on the television listings, Darcy said. Being Colombian, those drug king-pins probably didn't watch American TV.

Grace yawned. It would be light soon, and they'd have to throw in the towel. Mariah didn't like it how they were sleeping during the day. Even Howard seemed miffed, as if they were some kind of sick species of African violet.

Darcy shifted in her seat. "Grace?"

"Not again."

"My bladder isn't as tough as yours."

"Hold it in five more minutes. We're almost out of here."

It felt good to be doing it again, almost as good as singing. The grass was wet and cold against Heywood's arms and belly. He hoped there was no dog. It looked like a house that might have a dog, a large, angry one. They often went along with busted tires in the yard.

He crept on his elbows past a large piece of rusted machinery. Now that dawn had broken, he recognized it as a car axle. This was the kind of neighborhood that woke up early. Still, he chose this time because he hated to work in the dark, it seemed so sneaky. First light was lovely and artistic, and he thought of what he did as artistry.

Alejandro hadn't liked it, of course. He'd been in a foul mood since Sunday morning when he saw that ad. Saturday night, actually. He always got the Sunday paper the night before, so he could get a jump on charting out his Nielsen viewing for the week.

But Heywood was free of that now, making his way

toward the back door of Photon on his elbows and belly. His down jacket would be ruined. He would like to think the Organization would replace it, but he doubted that. They only wanted him replaced.

Though this might persuade them of his use. He was at the door now. This was the important part. He extracted the tools from his pocket and stood, working quickly. It all came back to him.

In moments he was inside. Disarming the alarm system took somewhat longer, but he worked cheerfully. It was light enough so that he didn't need a flashlight. He disliked flashlights, with their tight little funnels of illumination. They were so limiting, and his possibilities seemed so endless right now. He was doing a good job, and the Organization would notice.

He wished they had given him a gun. The wish became more fervent than ever when he found the tape in the television studio, left out in the open. He was supposed to leave quickly, but instead he paused to fiddle with buttons and play the tape. He turned up the volume and listened to his singing, or rather Scott Summerhays' singing. He thought of himself as Heywood most of the time now.

He had learned so much from the Big Band vocalists that he could hardly stand to listen to his old voice. The tightness of the lower register bothered him. It also bothered him that he had obviously been led into a trap.

Most bothersome of all was the fact that he didn't know if he cared anymore.

He pocketed the tape and hurried down the hall. Instinct told him to leave by a different door than the one through which he'd entered, but that wasn't the plan. Anyway, he had dawdled too long playing the tape, and there was no time to disarm the other alarms.

Crouching, he applied slow pressure to the door, ready to throw himself to the ground. When it was open a crack, he saw another crouching figure directly across from him, about fifty feet away.

"Darcy!" he called out.

She straightened, embarrassed, pulling her skirt down.

He heard a car door open nearby, followed by footsteps on the driveway. He stood and kicked the door wide open before him.

He was on the asphalt now, hands thrust high.

"You guessed it. It's me," said the bondswoman from behind her semiautomatic.

"It is I," corrected Alejandro, who had been crossing the lawn as Grace approached Heywood. The Browning Super .38 was extended before him.

Darcy was the first to look up. There were four cops on the roof, each with a gun trained on Alejandro.

Later, she was told that one of them was Mahon's brother-in-law. And later she realized they'd all seen her peeing in the grass.

Twenty Five

Pancakes, waffles, it didn't matter what she made, Phil brought his paperwork to the kitchen table anyway. For all the thanks Grace got, you'd think he'd been living on hotel room service instead of on those terrible marshmallow cookies. He claimed he had them only once or twice, but the red cellophane pull-strings from their packages were all over the house.

"Watch where you put the coffee," Phil said. "Those forms are the same as money."

That was another thing that was all over the house: completed applications for homeowner's insurance, life insurance, auto insurance. Phil Stark may have been slow off the block, but now he was the Ray-Mar Insurance Company's star agent. He had gotten a pin of some kind.

Grace heard more about that than Phil heard about the ceremony in Sherwood where the police commissioner was going to commend her. She's been given total credit for Heywood's capture; she didn't have to give up the bond.

Well, anyone could crack a drug trafficking ring, she supposed. Selling insurance was a lot harder, to hear Phil tell it. She had to hand it to him, actually. Who would have thought that people who used clotheslines had so much to spend on insurance? That was Phil's genius, according to the letter they gave him along with the pin. He had "opened untapped business in the downmarket."

She wished he had also watered the plants.

The phone rang. Grace made a move for it, but Phil stopped her with a look. He put down his pen and got it. It didn't take long.

"Again?" she asked.

He resumed his scribbling and said nothing.

"When are they going to let up?"

"I changed the number again, but they got it. Goddamn cops walk all over the phone company."

"Where are you going tonight? One of those towns with all the satellite dishes? Telford?"

Phil scribbled.

"It's Telford. You told me last night. They don't have streetlights. No money for streetlights, but they've got satellite dishes and insurance."

"They better have insurance. That's what pays the bills around here."

"You better have it, too. Driving in the dark over there with maniacs after you."

"At least it's just cops now. The Latins stopped."

That's as close as he got to acknowledging what she did in Connecticut. But she didn't care if he praised her. She cared if he lived. She had found that out on her trip, after her dinner with the man with the stiff upper lip and the Rolex.

The phone rang again, and Phil got it again. It was for her this time, the *Courier-Inquirer*.

"You'll have to read all about it in the *Crusader*," she said, not very nicely. She had been nice the first time.

"We both get our creep calls," she told Phil when she hung up.

He gave her a letter to mail as she headed out the door,

the third payment against the forfeited bonds. A dhurrie rug was still many months away, but Phil was catching up on the forfeits.

The *Crusader's* reception area didn't look bad at all. A Haitian cotton-covered couch, cut flowers on a glass end table. Darcy's touch.

"Nah, she's never around," Eric told Grace in answer to her question. "Too busy whipping the ad reps into shape. She checks up on almost every call report they file. You wouldn't believe how they used to lie. Darcy is fucking unbelievable. Two days after she got here, she brought in three new ad accounts. In January, which is usually a complete loss for us. Three accounts."

"Tapping the downmarket?" asked Grace.

Eric looked offended. "Are you joking? We're upscale all the way. Who do you think wants to read about drug arrests and Sound TV? Fucking blue-collar workers?"

Grace looked over the proofs of the story about her tristate adventure. She still had a problem.

"You can call it a 'portrait' all you want. I say it's the world's lousiest picture of me."

Eric said something about airbrushing and asked her about some names and dates. Then he leaned back, took a drag of his cigarette, and allowed himself a coughing spasm. Eric was as close as he got to relaxed.

"It's dynamite, you've got to admit," he said. "To tell you the truth, we're up ten ad pages over last year, first, because Darcy is a fantastic ad manager, and second, because some key accounts know this story is coming down." He pointed to the plaque hanging over his head. "American Society of Weekly Newspapers. Last year, we were runner-up. This time it's going to be Numero Uno. We got a scoop."

"You know what my husband says? He says some papers pay for exclusives."

Eric coughed, more tightly this time. "Not legit papers.

Not even the *Courier-Inquirer,* rich as they are. Just the supermarket garbage."

"This could be good for supermarket garbage."

"Yeah, but who reads that shit?"

"I do."

Eric busied himself flicking ash.

"This is the last of the drug stories, isn't it?" said Grace.

"Hell, no. We follow up on everything."

"But after Heywood there weren't any other arrests, were there?"

"It calmed down quite a bit."

"Because everyone stopped dealing. Because they were afraid their friends would inform on them."

"You got to hand it to the feds, it worked," said Eric.

"You know all those things I told you about my husband getting threats from the police. Remember how I explained to you how the dry cleaner died?"

"Yeah, but the dry cleaner stuff is old. And the threats—to be frank, who's interested?"

"The cops are going to be, when you report that some of their co-workers are telling a grand jury about the Barkan murder. Seems there's evidence on them, so they're giving evidence about their buddies to get off. You're going to say that some of them are talking about the telephone harassment, too."

"We can't print any of that. It isn't happening."

"I say it is. But you're not going to say I said so."

"We'd have to confirm it with another source."

Grace got up and looked at her watch. "Just enough time to drop by the *Courier-Inquirer* office before the editor goes out for lunch. That'll give them enough time to run my drug story tomorrow. When is it your paper comes out? Tuesday?"

Eric twisted around in his desk chair, following her glance to the plaque above him.

"Have a seat, Mrs. Stark."

* * *

The sidewalks were strewn with discarded Christmas trees and slippery with ice. Twice, Grace nearly fell and broke the contents of her paper bags, but she made it. Unwrapping her muffler in the overheated courthouse, she made her rounds.

"Vodka, my favorite," said Inez, the court clerk. The public defender hustled by. He said nothing about the whiskey Grace had left on his desk, but his briefcase was bulging.

Grace headed toward arraignment court, where, according to Inez's tip, a Bad Paper and a Family Dispute were due in.

In the corridor, two cops gave her black looks. That was going to change.

The insurance thing was going to work out well. Phil was selling so many individual policies that Marty was going to let him graduate to commercial. And who was first on the scene after an arson? The insurance man got called before the cops. Grace would get over the minute the arrest was made and post bond.

Should amount to plenty of business. An entire town near Huddersfield was going up in flames.

Grace searched in her pockets for the business cards:

Grace Stark, Bondswoman
Anytime—Anywhere

She'd had them done on ivory stock this time, ten times better than those first cheesy ones she got from Minit Print. This was for keeps.

Grace crossed the lobby, passing the cardboard display filled with *Crusader*s. Next week, it was going to be her story. She couldn't wait. The headline was going to be great: The Videola Connection.

And the week after that, Cop Wars.